Eric Arthur Blair (George Orwell) was born in 1903 in India, where his father worked for the Civil Service. The family moved to England in 1907 and in 1917 Orwell entered Eton, where he contributed regularly to the various college magazines. He left in 1921 and joined the Indian Imperial Police in Burma the following year. He resigned in 1928 having come to hate imperialism, as *Burmese Days* (1934), his first novel, shows.

After this he lived for several years in poverty, at times among tramps, experiences which he relates in *Down and Out in Paris and London* (1933). For a time he worked as a schoolteacher but due to poor health he gave this up and worked as a part-time assistant in a Hampstead bookshop; later he was able to earn his living reviewing novels for the *New English Weekly*, a post he kept until 1940. In 1936 he visited areas of mass unemployment in Lancashire and Yorkshire and *The Road to Wigan Pier* (1937) is a powerful description of the poverty he saw there.

At the end of 1936 Orwell went to Spain to fight for the Republicans and was wounded; his account of the civil war, *Homage to Catalonia*, is considered by many to be his greatest achievement. During the Second World War he was a member of the Home Guard and worked for the BBC Eastern Service from 1940 to 1943. As literary editor of *Tribune* he contributed a regular page of political and literary commentary. From 1945 Orwell was the *Observer*'s war correspondent and later became a regular contributor to the *Manchester Evening News*. His unique political allegory *Animal Farm* was published in 1945, and it was this novel, together with *Nineteen Eighty-Four* (1949), which brought Orwell world-wide fame.

Orwell suffered from tuberculosis and was in and out of hospital from 1947 until his death in 1950 at the age of forty-six.

All Orwell's works have been published in Penguins.

GEORGE ORWELL

INSIDE THE WHALE

AND OTHER ESSAYS

PENGUIN BOOKS

IN ASSOCIATION WITH
MARTIN SECKER & WARBURG

Penguin Books Ltd, Harmondsworth, Middlesex, England
Viking Penguin Inc., 40 West 23rd Street, New York, New York 10010, U.S.A.
Penguin Books Australia Ltd, Ringwood, Victoria, Australia
Penguin Books Canada Ltd, 2801 John Street, Markham, Ontario, Canada L3R 1B4
Penguin Books (N.Z.) Ltd, 182–190 Wairau Road, Auckland 10, New Zealand

—

This selection first published in Penguin Books as *Selected Essays* 1957
Reprinted 1960
Reprinted as *Inside the Whale and Other Essays* 1962
Reprinted 1964, 1966, 1967, 1968, 1969, 1970, 1971, 1972, 1974, 1976 (twice),
1977, 1978, 1979, 1980, 1981, 1982, 1983, 1984

—

—

Made and printed in Great Britain by
Hazell Watson & Viney Limited,
Member of the BPCC Group,
Aylesbury, Bucks
Set in Monotype Baskerville

CONTENTS

BIBLIOGRAPHICAL NOTE

'Inside the Whale' first appeared in the book *Inside the Whale* (1940), 'Down the Mine' in *The Road to Wigan Pier* (1937), 'England Your England' in *The Lion and the Unicorn* (1941). All three essays were included in the selection *England Your England* (1953).

'Shooting an Elephant' first appeared in *New Writing* First Series No. 2 (Autumn 1936), 'Lear, Tolstoy and the Fool' in *Polemic* No. 7 (March 1947), 'Politics *vs* Literature: An Examination of *Gulliver's Travels*' in *Polemic* No. 5 (September 1946), 'Politics and the English Language' in *Horizon* No. 76 (April 1946), 'The Prevention of Literature' in *Polemic* No. 2 (1945/6); these five essays were included in the selection *Shooting an Elephant* (1950).

'Boys' Weeklies' first appeared in *Horizon* No. 3 (March 1940), and was included in *Inside the Whale* (1940) and *Critical Essays* (1946).

INSIDE THE WHALE

WHEN Henry Miller's novel, *Tropic of Cancer*, appeared in 1935, it was greeted with rather cautious praise, obviously conditioned in some cases by a fear of seeming to enjoy pornography. Among the people who praised it were T. S. Eliot, Herbert Read, Aldous Huxley, John dos Passos, Ezra Pound – on the whole, not the writers who are in fashion at this moment. And in fact the subject matter of the book, and to a certain extent its mental atmosphere, belong to the twenties rather than to the thirties.

Tropic of Cancer is a novel in the first person, or autobiography in the form of a novel, whichever way you like to look at it. Miller himself insists that it is straight autobiography, but the tempo and method of telling the story are those of a novel. It is a story of the American Paris, but not along quite the usual lines, because the Americans who figure in it happen to be people without money. During the boom years, when dollars were plentiful and the exchange-value of the franc was low, Paris was invaded by such a swarm of artists, writers, students, dilettanti, sight-seers, debauchees, and plain idlers as the world has probably never seen. In some quarters of the town the so-called artists must actually have outnumbered the working population – indeed, it has been reckoned that in the late twenties there were as many as 30,000 painters in Paris, most of them impostors. The populace had grown so hardened to artists that gruff-voiced lesbians in corduroy breeches and young men in Grecian or medieval costume could walk the streets without attracting a glance, and along the Seine banks by Notre Dame it was almost impossible to pick one's way between the sketching-stools. It was the age of dark horses and neglected genii; the phrase on everybody's lips was

'*Quand je serai lancé*'. As it turned out, nobody was '*lancé*', the slump descended like another Ice Age, the cosmopolitan mob of artists vanished, and the huge Montparnasse cafés which only ten years ago were filled till the small hours by hordes of shrieking poseurs have turned into darkened tombs in which there are not even any ghosts. It is this world – described in, among other novels, Wyndham Lewis's *Tarr* – that Miller is writing about, but he is dealing only with the under side of it, the lumpen-proletarian fringe which has been able to survive the slump because it is composed partly of genuine artists and partly of genuine scoundrels. The neglected genii, the paranoiacs who are always 'going to' write the novel that will knock Proust into a cocked hat, are there, but they are only genii in the rather rare moments when they are not scouting about for the next meal. For the most part it is a story of bug-ridden rooms in working-men's hotels, of fights, drinking bouts, cheap brothels, Russian refugees, cadging, swindling, and temporary jobs. And the whole atmosphere of the poor quarters of Paris as a foreigner sees them – the cobbled alleys, the sour reek of refuse, the bistros with their greasy zinc counters and worn brick floors, the green waters of the Seine, the blue cloaks of the Republican Guard, the crumbling iron urinals, the peculiar sweetish smell of the Metro stations, the cigarettes that come to pieces, the pigeons in the Luxembourg Gardens – it is all there, or at any rate the feeling of it is there.

On the face of it no material could be less promising. When *Tropic of Cancer* was published the Italians were marching into Abyssinia and Hitler's concentration camps were already bulging. The intellectual foci of the world were Rome, Moscow, and Berlin. It did not seem to be a moment at which a novel of outstanding value was likely to be written about American dead-beats cadging drinks in the Latin Quarter. Of course a novelist is not obliged to write directly about contemporary history, but a novelist who simply disregards the major public events of the moment is generally either a footler or a plain idiot. From a mere account of the subject matter of *Tropic of Cancer* most people would probably assume it to be no more than a bit of naughty-naughty left over from the twenties. Actually, nearly everyone who read it saw at once that it was nothing of the kind, but a very remarkable book. How or why remarkable? That question is never easy to answer. It is better to begin by describing the impression that *Tropic of Cancer* has left on my own mind.

When I first opened *Tropic of Cancer* and saw that it was full of unprintable words, my immediate reaction was a refusal to be impressed. Most people's would be the same, I believe. Nevertheless, after a lapse of time the atmosphere of the book, besides innumerable details, seemed to linger in my memory in a peculiar way. A year later Miller's second book, *Black Spring*, was published. By this time *Tropic of Cancer* was much more vividly present in my mind than it had been when I first read it. My first feeling about *Black Spring* was that it showed a falling-off, and it is a fact that it has not the same unity as the other book. Yet after another year there were many passages in *Black Spring* that had also rooted themselves in my memory. Evidently these books are of the sort to leave a flavour behind them – books that 'create a world of their own', as the saying goes. The books that do this are not necessarily good books, they may be good bad books like *Raffles* or the *Sherlock Holmes* stories, or perverse and morbid books like *Wuthering Heights* or *The House with the Green Shutters*. But now and again there appears a novel which opens up a new world not by revealing what is strange, but by revealing what is familiar. The truly remarkable thing about *Ulysses*, for instance, is the commonplaceness of its material. Of course there is much more in *Ulysses* than this, because Joyce is a kind of poet and also an elephantine pedant, but his real achievement has been to get the familiar on to paper. He dared – for it is a matter of *daring* just as much as of technique – to expose the imbecilities of the inner mind, and in doing so he discovered an America which was under everybody's nose. Here is a whole world of stuff which you supposed to be of its nature incommunicable, and somebody has managed to communicate it. The effect is to break down, at any rate momentarily, the solitude in which the human being lives. When you read certain passages in *Ulysses* you feel that Joyce's mind and your mind are one, that he knows all about you though he has never heard your name, that there exists some world outside time and space in which you and he are together. And though he does not resemble Joyce in other ways, there is a touch of this quality in Henry Miller. Not everywhere, because his work is very uneven, and sometimes, especially in *Black Spring*, tends to slide away into mere verbiage or into the squashy universe of the surrealists. But read him for five pages, ten pages, and you feel the peculiar relief that comes not so much from understanding as from *being understood*. 'He knows all about me,' you feel; 'he wrote this specially for me'. It is as though you could hear a voice speaking to you, a friendly American voice, with no humbug in it, no moral purpose, merely an implicit assumption that we are all alike. For the moment you have got away from the lies and simplifications, the stylized, marionette-like quality of ordinary fiction, even quite good fiction, and are dealing with the recognizable experiences of human beings.

But what kind of experience? What kind of human beings? Miller is writing about the man in the street, and it is incidentally rather a pity that it should be a street full of brothels. That is the penalty of leaving your native land. It means transferring your roots into shallower soil. Exile is probably more damaging to a novelist than to a painter or even a poet, because its effect is to take him out of contact with working life and narrow down his range to the street, the café, the church, the brothel and the studio. On the whole, in Miller's books you are reading about people living the expatriate life, people drinking, talking, meditating, and fornicating, not about people working, marrying, and bringing up children; a pity, because he would have described the one set of activities as well as the other. In *Black Spring* there is a wonderful flashback of New York, the swarming Irish-infested New York of the O. Henry period, but the Paris scenes are the best, and, granted their utter worthlessness as social types, the drunks and dead-beats of the cafés are handled with a feeling for character and a mastery of technique that are unapproached in any at all recent novel. All of them are not only credible but completely familiar; you have the feeling that all their adventures have happened to yourself. Not that they are anything very startling in the way of adventures. Henry gets a job with a melancholy Indian student, gets another job at a dreadful French school during a cold snap when the lavatories are frozen solid, goes on drinking bouts in Le Havre with his friend Collins, the sea captain, goes to brothels where there are wonderful Negresses, talks with his friend Van Norden, the novelist, who has got the great novel of the world in his head but can never bring himself to begin writing it. His friend Karl, on the verge of starva-tion, is picked up by a wealthy widow who wishes to marry him. There are interminable Hamlet-like conversations in which Karl tries to decide which is worse, being hungry or sleeping with an old woman. In great detail he describes his visits to the widow, how he went to the hotel dressed in his best, how before going in he neglected to urinate, so that the whole evening was one long crescendo of torment, etc., etc. And after all, none of it is true, the widow doesn't even exist – Karl has simply invented her in order to make himself seem important. The whole book is in this vein, more or less. Why is it that these monstrous trivialities are so engrossing? Simply because the whole atmosphere is deeply familiar, because you have all the while the feeling that these things are happening to *you*. And you have this feeling because somebody has chosen to drop the Geneva language of the ordinary novel and drag the *real-politik* of the inner mind into the open. In Miller's case it is not so much a question of exploring the mechanisms of the mind as of owning up to everyday facts and everyday emotions. For the truth is that many ordinary people, perhaps an actual majority, do speak and behave in just the way that is recorded here. The callous coarseness with which the characters in *Tropic of Cancer* talk is very rare in fiction, but it is extremely common in real life; again and again I have heard just such conversations from people who were not even aware that they were talking coarsely. It is worth noticing that *Tropic of Cancer* is not a young man's book. Miller was in his forties when it was published, and though since then he has produced three or four others, it is obvious that this first book had been lived with for years. It is one of those books that are slowly matured in poverty and obscurity, by people who know what they have got to do and therefore are able to wait. The prose is astonishing, and in parts of *Black Spring* is even better. Unfortunately I cannot quote; unprintable words occur almost everywhere. But get hold of *Tropic of Cancer*, get hold of *Black Spring* and read especially the first hundred pages. They give you an idea of what can still be done, even at this late date, with English prose. In them, English is treated as a spoken language, but spoken *without fear*, i.e. without fear of rhetoric or of the unusual or poetical word. The adjective has come back, after its ten years' exile. It is a flowing, swelling prose, a prose with rhythms in it, something quite different from the flat cautious statements and snack-bar dialects that are now in fashion.

When a book like *Tropic of Cancer* appears, it is only natural that the first thing people notice should be its obscenity. Given our current notions of literary decency, it is not at all easy to approach an unprintable book with detachment. Either one is shocked and disgusted, or one is morbidly thrilled, or one is determined above all else not to be impressed. The last is probably the commonest reaction, with the result that unprintable books often get less attention than they deserve. It is rather the fashion to say that nothing is easier than to write an obscene book, that people only do it in order to get themselves talked about and make money, etc., etc. What makes it obvious that this is *not* the case is that books which are obscene in the police-court sense are distinctly uncommon. If there were easy money to be made out of dirty words, a lot more people would be making it. But, because 'obscene' books do not appear very frequently, there is a tendency to lump them together, as a rule quite unjustifiably. *Tropic of Cancer* has been vaguely associated with two other books, *Ulysses* and *Voyage au bout de la nuit*, but in neither case is there much resemblance. What Miller has in common with Joyce is a willingness to mention the inane, squalid facts of everyday life. Putting aside differences of technique, the funeral scene in *Ulysses*, for instance, would fit into *Tropic of Cancer*; the whole chapter is a sort of confession, an *exposé* of the frightful inner callousness of the human being. But there the resemblance ends. As a novel, *Tropic of Cancer* is far inferior to *Ulysses*. Joyce is an artist, in a sense in which Miller is not and probably would not wish to be, and in any case he is attempting much more. He is exploring different states of consciousness, dream, reverie (the 'bronze-by-gold' chapter), drunkenness, etc., and dovetailing them all into a huge complex pattern, almost like a Victorian ' plot'. Miller is simply a hard-boiled person talking about life, an ordinary American businessman with intellectual courage and a gift for words. It is perhaps significant that he *looks* exactly like everyone's idea of an American business-man. As for the comparison with *Voyage au bout de la nuit*, it is even further from the point. Both books use unprintable words, both are in some sense autobiographical, but that is all. *Voyage au bout de la nuit* is a book-with-a-purpose, and its purpose is to protest against the horror and meaningless-ness of modern life – actually, indeed, of *life*. It is a cry of unbearable disgust, a voice from the cesspool. *Tropic of Cancer* is almost exactly the opposite. The thing has become so unusual as to seem almost anomalous, but it is the book of a man who is happy. So is *Black Spring*, though slightly less so, because tinged in places with nostalgia. With years of lumpen-proletarian life behind him, hunger, vagabond-age, dirt, failure, nights in the open, battles with immigra-tion officers, endless struggles for a bit of cash, Miller finds that he is enjoying himself. Exactly the aspects of life that fill Céline with horror are the ones that appeal to him. So far from protesting, he is *accepting*. And the very word 'acceptance' calls up his real affinity, another American, Walt Whitman.

But there is something rather curious in being Whitman in the nineteen-thirties. It is not certain that if Whitman himself were alive at the moment he would write anything in the least degree resembling *Leaves of Grass*. For what he is saying, after all, is 'I accept', and there is a radical difference between acceptance now and acceptance then. Whitman was writing in a time of unexampled prosperity, but more than that, he was writing in a country where freedom was something more than a word. The democracy, equality, and comradeship that he is always talking about are not remote ideals, but something that existed in front of his eyes. In mid-nineteenth-century America men felt themselves free and equal, *were* free and equal, so far as that is possible outside a society of pure communism. There was poverty and there were even class distinctions, but except for the Negroes there was no permanently submerged class. Everyone had inside him, like a kind of core, the knowledge that he could earn a decent living, and earn it without bootlicking. When you read about Mark Twain's Mississippi raftsmen and pilots, or Bret Harte's Western gold-miners, they seem more remote than the cannibals of the Stone Age. The reason is simply that they are free human beings. But it is the same even with the peaceful domesticated America of the Eastern states, the America of *Little Women*, *Helen's Babies*, and *Riding Down from Bangor*. Life has a buoyant, carefree quality that you can feel as you read, like a physical sensation in your belly. It is this that Whitman is celebrating, though actually he does it very badly, because he is one of those writers who tell you what you ought to feel instead of making you feel it. Luckily for his beliefs, perhaps, he died too early to see the deterioration in American life that came with the rise of large-scale industry and the exploiting of cheap immigrant labour.

Miller's outlook is deeply akin to that of Whitman, and

nearly everyone who has read him has remarked on this. *Tropic of Cancer* ends with an especially Whitmanesque passage, in which, after the lecheries, the swindles, the fights, the drinking bouts, and the imbecilities, he simply sits down and watches the Seine flowing past, in a sort of mystical acceptance of thing-as-it-is. Only, what is he accepting? In the first place, not America, but the ancient bone-heap of Europe, where every grain of soil has passed through innumerable human bodies. Secondly, not an epoch of expansion and liberty, but an epoch of fear, tyranny, and regimentation. To say 'I accept' in an age like our own is to say that you accept concentration camps, rubber truncheons, Hitler, Stalin, bombs, aeroplanes, tinned food, machine guns, putsches, purges, slogans, Bedaux belts, gas masks, submarines, spies, provocateurs, press censorship, secret prisons, aspirins, Hollywood films, and political murders. Not *only* those things, of course, but those things among others. And on the whole this is Henry Miller's attitude. Not quite always, because at moments he shows signs of a fairly ordinary kind of literary nostalgia. There is a long passage in the earlier part of *Black Spring*, in praise of the Middle Ages, which as prose must be one of the most remarkable pieces of writing in recent years, but which displays an attitude not very different from that of Chesterton. In *Max and the White Phagocytes* there is an attack on modern American civilization (breakfast cereals, cellophane, etc.) from the usual angle of the literary man who hates industrialism. But in general the attitude is 'Let's swallow it whole'. And hence the seeming preoccupation with indecency and with the dirty-handkerchief side of life. It is only seeming, for the truth is that ordinary everyday life consists far more largely of horrors than writers of fiction usually care to admit. Whitman himself 'accepted' a great deal that his contemporaries found unmentionable. For he is not only writing of the prairie, he also wanders through the city and notes the shattered skull of the suicide, the 'grey sick faces of onanists', etc., etc. But unquestionably our own age, at any rate in Western

Europe, is less healthy and less hopeful than the age in which Whitman was writing. Unlike Whitman, we live in a *shrinking* world. The 'democratic vistas' have ended in barbed wire. There is less feeling of creation and growth, less and less emphasis on the cradle, endlessly rocking, more and more emphasis on the teapot, endlessly stewing. To accept civilization *as it is* practically means accepting decay. It has ceased to be a strenuous attitude and become a passive attitude – even 'decadent', if that word means anything.

But precisely because, in one sense, he is passive to experience, Miller is able to get nearer to the ordinary man than is possible to more purposive writers. For the ordinary man is also passive. Within a narrow circle (home life, and perhaps the trade union or local politics) he feels himself master of his fate, but against major events he is as helpless as against the elements. So far from endeavouring to influence the future, he simply lies down and lets things happen to him. During the past ten years literature has involved itself more and more deeply in politics, with the result that there is now less room in it for the ordinary man than at any time during the past two centuries. One can see the change in the prevailing literary attitude by comparing the books written about the Spanish civil war with those written about the war of 1914–18. The immediately striking thing about the Spanish war books, at any rate those written in English, is their shocking dullness and badness. But what is more significant is that almost all of them, right-wing or left-wing, are written from a political angle, by cocksure partisans telling you what to think, whereas the books about the Great War were written by common soldiers or junior officers who did not even pretend to understand what the whole thing was about. Books like *All Quiet on the Western Front*, *Le Feu*, *A Farewell to Arms*, *Death of a Hero*, *Good-bye to All That*, *Memoirs of an Infantry Officer*, and *A Subaltern on the Somme* were written not by propagandists but by *victims*. They are saying in effect, 'What the hell is all this about? God knows. All we can do is to endure.' And though he is not writing about war, nor, on the whole, about un-happiness, this is nearer to Miller's attitude than the omniscience which is now fashionable. The *Booster*, a short-lived periodical of which he was part-editor, used to describe itself in its advertisements as 'non-political, non-educational, non-progressive, non-co-operative, non-ethical, non-literary, non-consistent, non-contemporary', and Miller's own work could be described in nearly the same terms. It is a voice from the crowd, from the underling, from the third-class carriage, from the ordinary, non-political, non-moral, passive man.

I have been using the phrase 'ordinary man' rather loosely, and I have taken it for granted that the 'ordinary man' exists, a thing now denied by some people. I do not mean that the people Miller is writing about constitute a majority, still less that he is writing about proletarians. No English or American novelist has as yet seriously attempted that. And again, the people in *Tropic of Cancer* fall short of being ordinary to the extent that they are idle, disreputable, and more or less 'artistic'. As I have said already, this a pity, but it is the necessary result of expatriation. Miller's 'ordinary man' is neither the manual worker nor the suburban householder, but the derelict, the *déclassé*, the adventurer, the American intellectual without roots and without money. Still, the experiences even of this type over-lap fairly widely with those of more normal people. Miller has been able to get the most out of his rather limited material because he has had the courage to identify with it. The ordinary man, the 'average sensual man', has been given the power of speech, like Balaam's ass.

It will be seen that this is something out of date, or at any rate out of fashion. The average sensual man is out of fashion. Preoccupation with sex and truthfulness about the inner life are out of fashion. American Paris is out of fashion. A book like *Tropic of Cancer*, published at such a time, must be either a tedious preciosity or something unusual, and I think a majority of the people who have read it would agree that it is not the first. It is worth trying to discover just what this escape from the current literary fashion means. But to do that one has got to see it against its background – that is, against the general development of English literature in the twenty years since the Great War.

II

When one says that a writer is fashionable one practically always means that he is admired by people under thirty. At the beginning of the period I am speaking of, the years during and immediately after the war, the writer who had the deepest hold upon the thinking young was almost certainly Housman. Among people who were adolescent in the years 1910–25, Housman had an influence which was enormous and is now not at all easy to understand. In 1920, when I was about seventeen, I probably knew the whole of the *Shropshire Lad* by heart. I wonder how much impression the *Shropshire Lad* makes at this moment on a boy of the same age and more or less the same cast of mind? No doubt he has heard of it and even glanced into it; it might strike him as cheaply clever – probably that would be about all. Yet these are the poems that I and my contemporaries used to recite to ourselves, over and over, in a kind of ecstasy, just as earlier generations had recited Meredith's 'Love in a Valley', Swinburne's 'Garden of Proserpine', etc., etc.

> With rue my heart is laden
>   For golden friends I had,
> For many a roselipt maiden
>   And many a lightfoot lad.
>
> By brooks too broad for leaping
>   The lightfoot boys are laid;
> The roselipt girls are sleeping
>   In fields where roses fade.

It just tinkles. But it did not seem to tinkle in 1920. Why does the bubble always burst? To answer that question one has to take account of the *external* conditions that make certain writers popular at certain times. Housman's poems had not attracted much notice when they were first published. What was there in them that appealed so deeply to a single generation, the generation born round about 1900?

In the first place, Housman is a 'country' poet. His poems are full of the charm of buried villages, the nostalgia of place-names, Clunton and Clunbury, Knighton, Ludlow, 'on Wenlock Edge', 'in summer time on Bredon', thatched roofs and the jingle of smithies, the wild jonquils in the pastures, the 'blue, remembered hills'. War poems apart, English verse of the 1910–25 period is mostly 'country'. The reason no doubt was that the *rentier*-professional class was ceasing once and for all to have any real relationship with the soil; but at any rate there prevailed then, far more than now, a kind of snobbism of belonging to the country and despising the town. England at that time was hardly more an agricultural country than it is now, but before the light industries began to spread themselves it was easier to think of it as one. Most middle-class boys grew up within sight of a farm, and naturally it was the picturesque side of farm life that appealed to them – the ploughing, harvesting, stack-thrashing and so forth. Unless he has to do it himself a boy is not likely to notice the horrible drudgery of hoeing turnips, milking cows with chapped teats at four o'clock in the morning, etc., etc. Just before, just after, and for that matter, during the war was the great age of the 'Nature poet', the heyday of Richard Jefferies and W. H. Hudson. Rupert Brooke's 'Grantchester', the star poem of 1913, is nothing but an enormous gush of 'country' sentiment, a sort of accumulated vomit from a stomach stuffed with place-names. Considered as a poem 'Grantchester' is something worse than worthless, but as an illustration of what the thinking middle-class young of that period *felt* it is a valuable document.

Housman, however, did not enthuse over the rambler roses in the week-ending spirit of Brooke and the others. The 'country' motif is there all the time, but mainly as a background. Most of the poems have a quasi-human subject, a kind of idealized rustic, in reality Strephon or Corydon brought up to date. This in itself had a deep appeal. Experience shows that overcivilized people enjoy reading about rustics (key-phrase, 'close to the soil') because they imagine them to be more primitive and passionate than themselves. Hence the 'dark earth' novel of Sheila Kaye-Smith, etc. And at that time a middle-class boy, with his 'country' bias, would identify with an agricultural worker as he would never have done with a town worker. Most boys had in their minds a vision of an idealized ploughman, gipsy, poacher, or gamekeeper. always pictured as a wild, free, roving blade, living a life of rabbit-snaring, cockfighting, horses, beer, and women. Masefield's 'Everlasting Mercy', another valuable period-piece, immensely popular with boys round about the war years, gives you this vision in a very crude form. But Housman's Maurices and Terences could be taken seriously where Masefield's Saul Kane could not; on this side of him, Housman was Masefield with a dash of Theocritus. Moreover all his themes are adolescent – murder, suicide, unhappy love, early death. They deal with the simple, intelligible disasters that give you the feeling of being up against the 'bedrock facts' of life:

> The sun burns on the half-mown hill,
> By now the blood has dried;
> And Maurice among the hay lies still
> And my knife is in his side.

And again:

> They hand us now in Shrewsbury jail
> And whistles blow forlorn,
> And trains all night groan on the rail
> To men who die at morn.

It is all more or less in the same tune. Everything comes unstuck. 'Ned lies long in the churchyard and Tom lies long in jail'. And notice also the exquisite self-pity – the 'nobody loves me' feeling:

The diamond drops adorning
The low mound on the lea,
These are the tears of morning,
That weeps, but not for thee.

Hard cheese, old chap! Such poems might have been written expressly for adolescents. And the unvarying sexual pessimism (the girl always dies or marries somebody else) seemed like wisdom to boys who were herded together in public schools and were half-inclined to think of women as something unattainable. Whether Housman ever had the same appeal for girls I doubt. In his poems the woman's point of view is not considered, she is merely the nymph, the siren, the treacherous half-human creature who leads you a little distance and then gives you the slip.

But Housman would not have appealed so deeply to the people who were young in 1920 if it had not been for another strain in him, and that was his blasphemous, antinomian, 'cynical' strain. The fight that always occurs between the generations was exceptionally bitter at the end of the Great War; this was partly due to the war itself, and partly it was an indirect result of the Russian Revolution, but an intellectual struggle was in any case due at about that date. Owing probably to the ease and security of life in England, which even the war hardly disturbed, many people whose ideas were formed in the eighties or earlier had carried them quite unmodified into the nineteen-twenties. Meanwhile, so far as the younger generation was concerned, the official beliefs were dissolving like sand-castles. The slump in religious belief, for instance, was spectacular. For several years the old-young antagonism took on a quality of real hatred. What was left of the war generation had crept out of the massacre to find their elders still bellowing the slogans of 1914, and a slightly younger generation of boys were writhing under dirty-minded celibate schoolmasters. It was to these that Housman appealed, with his implied sexual revolt and his personal grievance against God. He was patriotic, it was true, but in a harmless old-fashioned way, to the tune of

23

red coats and 'God save the Queen' rather than steel helmets and 'Hang the Kaiser'. And he was satisfyingly anti-Christian – he stood for a kind of bitter, defiant paganism, a conviction that life is short and the gods are against you, which exactly fitted the prevailing mood of the young; and all in charming fragile verse that was composed almost entirely of words of one syllable.

It will be seen that I have discussed Housman as though he were merely a propagandist, an utterer of maxims and quotable 'bits'. Obviously he was more than that. There is no need to under-rate him now because he was over-rated a few years ago. Although one gets into trouble nowadays for saying so, there are a number of his poems ('Into my heart an air that kills', for instance, and 'Is my team plough-ing?') that are not likely to remain long out of favour. But at bottom it is always a writer's tendency, his 'purpose', his 'message', that makes him liked or disliked. The proof of this is the extreme difficulty of seeing any literary merit in a book that seriously damages your deepest beliefs. And no book is ever truly neutral. Some or other tendency is always discernible, in verse as much as in prose, even if it does no more than determine the form and the choice of imagery. But poets who attain wide popularity, like Housman, are as a rule definitely gnomic writers.

After the war, after Housman and the Nature poets, there appears a group of writers of completely different tendency – Joyce, Eliot, Pound, Lawrence, Wyndham Lewis, Aldous Huxley, Lytton Strachey. So far as the middle and late twenties go, these are 'the movement', as surely as the Auden-Spender group have been 'the move-ment' during the past few years. It is true that not all of the gifted writers of the period can be fitted into the pattern. E. M. Forster, for instance, though he wrote his best book in 1923 or thereabouts, was essentially pre-war, and Yeats does not seem in either of his phases to belong to the twenties. Others who were still living, Moore, Conrad, Bennett, Wells, Norman Douglas, had shot their bolt before the war ever happened. On the other hand, a writer who should be added to the group, though in the narrowly literary sense he hardly 'belongs', is Somerset Maugham. Of course the dates do not fit exactly; most of these writers had already published books before the war, but they can be classified as post-war in the same sense that the younger men now writing are post-slump. Equally, of course, you could read through most of the literary papers of the time without grasping that these people *are* 'the movement'. Even more then than at most times the big shots of literary journalism were busy pretending that the age-before-last had not come to an end. Squire ruled the *London Mercury*, Gibbs and Walpole were the gods of the lending libraries, there was a cult of cheeriness and manliness, beer and cricket, briar pipes and monogamy, and it was at all times possible to earn a few guineas by writing an article denouncing 'high-brows'. But all the same it was the despised highbrows who had captured the young. The wind was blowing from Europe, and long before 1930 it had blown the beer-and-cricket school naked, except for their knighthoods.

But the first thing one would notice about the group of writers I have named above is that they do not look like a group. Moreover several of them would strongly object to being coupled with several of the others. Lawrence and Eliot were in reality antipathetic, Huxley worshipped Lawrence but was repelled by Joyce, most of the others would have looked down on Huxley, Strachey, and Maugham, and Lewis attacked everyone in turn; indeed, his reputation as a writer rests largely on these attacks. And yet there is a certain temperamental similarity, evident enough now, though it would not have been so a dozen years ago. What it amounts to is *pessimism of outlook*. But it is necessary to make clear what is meant by pessimism.

If the keynote of the Georgian poets was 'beauty of Nature', the keynote of the post-war writers would be 'tragic sense of life'. The spirit behind Housman's poems, for instance, is not tragic, merely querulous; it is hedonism disappointed. The same is true of Hardy, though one ought to make an exception of *The Dynasts*. But the Joyce-Eliot group come later in time, puritanism is not their main adversary, they are able from the start to 'see through' most of the things that their predecessors had fought for. All of them are temperamentally hostile to the notion of 'progress'; it is felt that progress not only doesn't happen, but *ought not* to happen. Given this general similarity, there are, of course, differences of approach between the writers I have named as well as different degrees of talent. Eliot's pessimism is partly the Christian pessimism, which implies a certain indifference to human misery, partly a lament over the decadence of Western civilization ('We are the hollow men, we are the stuffed men', etc., etc.), a sort of twilight-of-the-gods feeling, which finally leads him, in *Sweeney Agonistes* for instance, to achieve the difficult feat of making modern life out to be worse than it is. With Strachey it is merely a polite eighteenth-century scepticism mixed up with a taste for debunking. With Maugham it is a kind of stoical resignation, the stiff upper lip of the pukka sahib somewhere east of Suez, carrying on with his job without believing in it, like an Antonine Emperor. Lawrence at first sight does not seem to be a pessimistic writer, because, like Dickens, he is a 'change-of-heart' man and constantly insisting that life here and now would be all right if only you looked at it a little differently. But what he is demanding is a movement away from our mechanized civilization, which is not going to happen. Therefore his exasperation with the present turns once more into idealization of the past, this time a safely mythical past, the Bronze Age. When Lawrence prefers the Etruscans (*his* Etruscans) to ourselves it is difficult not to agree with him, and yet, after all, it is a species of defeatism, because that is not the direction in which the world is moving. The kind of life that he is always pointing to, a life centring round the simple mysteries – sex, earth, fire, water, blood – is merely a lost cause. All he has been able to produce, therefore, is a wish that things would happen in a way in which they are manifestly not going to happen. 'A wave of generosity or a wave of death', he says, but it is obvious that there are no waves of generosity this side of the horizon. So he flees to Mexico, and then dies at forty-five, a few years before the wave of death gets going. It will be seen that once again I am speaking of these people as though they were not artists, as though they were merely propagandists putting a 'message' across. And once again it is obvious that all of them are more than that. It would be absurd, for instance, to look on *Ulysses* as *merely* a show-up of the horror of modern life, the 'dirty *Daily Mail* era', as Pound put it. Joyce actually is more of a 'pure artist' than most writers. But *Ulysses* could not have been written by someone who was merely dabbling with word-patterns; it is the product of a special vision of life, the vision of a Catholic who has lost his faith. What Joyce is saying is 'Here is life without God. Just look at it!' and his technical innovations, important though they are, are primarily to serve this purpose.

But what is noticeable about all these writers is that what 'purpose' they have is very much up in the air. There is no attention to the urgent problems of the moment, above all no politics in the narrower sense. Our eyes are directed to Rome, to Byzantium, to Montparnasse, to Mexico, to the Etruscans, to the Subconscious, to the solar plexus – to everywhere except the places where things are actually happening. When one looks back at the twenties, nothing is queerer than the way in which every important event in Europe escaped the notice of the English intelligentsia. The Russian Revolution, for instance, all but vanishes from the English consciousness between the death of Lenin and the Ukraine famine – about ten years. Throughout those years Russia means Tolstoy, Dostoievsky, and exiled counts driving taxi-cabs. Italy means picture-galleries, ruins, churches, and museums – but not Black-shirts. Germany means films, nudism, and psychoanalysis – but not Hitler, of whom hardly anyone had heard till 1931. In 'cultured' circles art-for-art's-saking extended practically to a worship of the meaningless. Literature was supposed to consist solely in the manipulation of words. To judge a book by its subject matter was the unforgivable sin, and even to be aware of its subject matter was looked on as a lapse of taste. About 1928, in one of the three genuinely funny jokes that *Punch* has produced since the Great War, an intolerable youth is pictured informing his aunt that he intends to 'write'. 'And what are you going to write about, dear?' asks the aunt. 'My dear aunt,' says the youth crushingly, 'one doesn't write *about* anything, one just *writes*.' The best writers of the twenties did not subscribe to this doctrine, their 'purpose' is in most cases fairly overt, but it is usually a 'purpose' along moral-religious-cultural lines. Also, when translatable into political terms, it is in no case 'left'. In one way or another the tendency of all the writers in this group is conservative. Lewis, for instance, spent years in frenzied witch-smellings after 'Bolshevism', which he was able to detect in very unlikely places. Recently he has changed some of his views, perhaps influenced by Hitler's treatment of artists, but it is safe to bet that he will not go very far leftward. Pound seems to have plumped definitely for Fascism, at any rate the Italian variety. Eliot has remained aloof, but if forced at the pistol's point to choose between Fascism and some more democratic form of socialism, would probably choose Fascism. Huxley starts off with the usual despair-of-life, then, under the influence of Lawrence's 'dark abdomen', tries something called Life-Worship, and finally arrives at pacifism – a tenable position, and at this moment an honourable one, but probably in the long run involving rejection of socialism. It is also noticeable that most of the writers in this group have a certain tenderness for the Catholic Church, though not usually of a kind that an orthodox Catholic would accept.

The mental connexion between pessimism and a re-actionary outlook is no doubt obvious enough. What is perhaps less obvious is just *why* the leading writers of the twenties were predominantly pessimistic. Why always the sense of decadence, the skulls and cactuses, the yearning after lost faith and impossible civilizations? Was it not, after all, *because* these people were writing in an exceptionally comfortable epoch? It is just in such times that 'cosmic despair' can flourish. People with empty bellies never despair of the universe, nor even think about the universe, for that matter. The whole period 1910–30 was a prosperous one, and even the war years were physically tolerable if one happened to be a non-combatant in one of the Allied countries. As for the twenties, they were the golden age of the *rentier*-intellectual, a period of irresponsibility such as the world had never before seen. The war was over, the new totalitarian states had not arisen, moral and religious tabus of all descriptions had vanished, and the cash was rolling in. 'Disillusionment' was all the fashion. Everyone with a safe £500 a year turned highbrow and began training himself in *taedium vitae*. It was an age of eagles and of crumpets, facile despairs, backyard Hamlets, cheap return tickets to the end of the night. In some of the minor characteristic novels of the period, books like *Told by an Idiot*, the despair-of-life reaches a Turkish-bath atmosphere of self-pity. And even the best writers of the time can be convicted of a too Olympian attitude, a too great readiness to wash their hands of the immediate practical problem. They see life very comprehensively, much more so than those who come immediately before or after them, but they see it through the wrong end of the telescope. Not that that invalidates their books, as books. The first test of any work of art is survival, and it is a fact that a great deal that was written in the period 1910–30 has survived and looks like continuing to survive. One has only to think of *Ulysses*, *Of Human Bondage*, most of Lawrence's early work, especially his short stories, and virtually the whole of Eliot's poems up to about 1930, to wonder what is now being written that will wear so well.

But quite suddenly, in the years 1930–5, something happens. The literary climate changes. A new group of writers, Auden and Spender and the rest of them, has made its appearance, and although technically these writers owe something to their predecessors, their 'tendency' is entirely different. Suddenly we have got out of the twilight of the gods into a sort of Boy Scout atmosphere of bare knees and community singing. The typical literary man ceases to be a cultured expatriate with a leaning towards the Church, and becomes an eager-minded schoolboy with a leaning towards Communism. If the keynote of the writers of the twenties is 'tragic sense of life', the keynote of the new writers is 'serious purpose'.

The differences between the two schools are discussed at some length in Mr Louis MacNeice's book *Modern Poetry*. This book is, of course, written entirely from the angle of the younger group and takes the superiority of their standards for granted. According to Mr MacNeice:

> The poets of *New Signatures*,* unlike Yeats and Eliot, are emotionally partisan. Yeats proposed to turn his back on desire and hatred; Eliot sat back and watched other people's emotions with ennui and an ironical self-pity. . . . The whole poetry, on the other hand, of Auden, Spender, and Day Lewis implies that they have desires and hatreds of their own and, further, that they think some things *ought* to be desired and others hated.

And again:

> The poets of *New Signatures* have swung back . . . to the Greek preference for information or statement. The first requirement is to have something to say, and after that you must say it as well as you can.

In other words, 'purpose' has come back, the younger writers have 'gone into politics'. As I have pointed out already, Eliot & Co. are not really so non-partisan as Mr MacNeice seems to suggest. Still, it is broadly true that in the twenties the literary emphasis was more on technique and less on subject matter than it is now.

The leading figures in this group are Auden, Spender, Day Lewis, MacNeice, and there is a long string of writers of more or less the same tendency, Isherwood, John Lehmann, Arthur Calder-Marshall, Edward Upward, Alec Brown, Philip Henderson, and many others. As before, I

* Published in 1932.

am lumping them together simply according to tendency. Obviously there are very great variations in talent. But when one compares these writers with the Joyce-Eliot generation, the immediately striking thing is how much easier it is to form them into a group. Technically they are closer together, politically they are almost indistinguishable, and their criticisms of one another's work have always been (to put it mildly) good-natured. The outstanding writers of the twenties were of very varied origins, few of them had passed through the ordinary English educational mill (incidentally, the best of them, barring Lawrence, were not Englishmen), and most of them had had at some time to struggle against poverty, neglect, and even downright persecution. On the other hand, nearly all the younger writers fit easily into the public-school-university-Bloomsbury pattern. The few who are of proletarian origin are of the kind that is declassed early in life, first by means of scholarships and then by the bleaching-tub of London 'culture'. It is significant that several of the writers in this group have been not only boys but, subsequently, masters at public schools. Some years ago I described Auden as 'a sort of gutless Kipling'. As criticism this was quite unworthy, indeed it was merely a spiteful remark, but it is a fact that in Auden's work, especially his earlier work, an atmosphere of uplift – something rather like Kipling's *If* or Newbolt's *Play up, Play up, and Play the Game!* – never seems to be very far away. Take, for instance, a poem like 'You're leaving now, and it's up to you boys'. It is pure scoutmaster, the exact note of the ten-minutes' straight talk on the dangers of self-abuse. No doubt there is an element of parody that he intends, but there is also a deeper resemblance that he does not intend. And of course the rather priggish note that is common to most of these writers is a symptom of release. By throwing 'pure art' overboard they have freed themselves from the fear of being laughed at and vastly enlarged their scope. The prophetic side of Marxism, for example, is new material for poetry and has great possibilities.

We are nothing
We have fallen
Into the dark and shall be destroyed.
Think though, that in this darkness
We hold the secret hub of an idea
Whose living sunlit wheel revolves in future years outside.
                              (Spender, *Trial of a Judge*)

But at the same time, by being Marxized literature has moved no nearer to the masses. Even allowing for the time-lag, Auden and Spender are somewhat farther from being popular writers than Joyce and Eliot, let alone Lawrence. As before, there are many contemporary writers who are outside the current, but there is not much doubt about what *is* the current. For the middle and late thirties, Auden, Spender & Co. *are* 'the movement', just as Joyce, Eliot & Co. were for the twenties. And the movement is in the direction of some rather ill-defined thing called Communism. As early as 1934 or 1935 it was considered eccentric in literary circles not to be more or less 'left'. Between 1935 and 1939 the Communist Party had an almost irresistible fascination for any writer under forty. It became as normal to hear that so-and-so had 'joined' as it had been a few years earlier, when Roman Catholicism was fashionable, to hear that So-and-so had 'been received'. For about three years, in fact, the central stream of English literature was more or less directly under Communist control. How was it possible for such a thing to happen? And at the same time, what is meant by 'Communism'? It is better to answer the second question first.

The Communist movement in Western Europe began as a movement for the violent overthrow of capitalism, and degenerated within a few years into an instrument of Russian foreign policy. This was probably inevitable when the revolutionary ferment that followed the Great War had died down. So far as I know, the only comprehensive history of this subject in English is Franz Borkenau's book, *The Communist International*. What Borkenau's facts even more than his deductions make clear is that Communism could never have developed along its present lines if any real revolutionary feeling had existed in the industrialized countries. In England, for instance, it is obvious that no such feeling has existed for years past. The pathetic membership figures of all extremist parties show this clearly. It is only natural, therefore, that the English Communist movement should be controlled by people who are mentally subservient to Russia and have no real aim except to manipulate British foreign policy in the Russian interest. Of course such an aim cannot be openly admitted, and it is this fact that gives the Communist Party its very peculiar character. The more vocal kind of Communist is in effect a Russian publicity agent posing as an international socialist. It is a pose that is easily kept up at normal times, but becomes difficult in moments of crisis, because of the fact that the U.S.S.R. is no more scrupulous in its foreign policy than the rest of the Great Powers. Alliances, changes of front, etc., which only make sense as part of the game of power politics have to be explained and justified in terms of international socialism. Every time Stalin swaps partners, 'Marxism' has to be hammered into a new shape. This entails sudden and violent changes of 'line', purges, denunciations, systematic destruction of party literature, etc., etc. Every Communist is in fact liable at any moment to have to alter his most fundamental convictions, or leave the party. The unquestionable dogma of Monday may become the damnable heresy of Tuesday, and so on. This has happened at least three times during the past ten years. It follows that in any Western country a Communist Party is always unstable and usually very small. Its long-term membership really consists of an inner ring of intellectuals who have identified with the Russian bureaucracy, and a slightly larger body of working-class people who feel a loyalty towards Soviet Russia without necessarily understanding its policies. Otherwise there is only a shifting membership, one lot coming and another going with each change of 'line'.

In 1930 the English Communist Party was a tiny, barely

legal organization whose main activity was libelling the Labour Party. But by 1935 the face of Europe had changed, and left-wing politics changed with it. Hitler had risen to power and begun to rearm, the Russian five-year plans had succeeded, Russia had reappeared as a great military power. As Hitler's three targets of attack were, to all appearances, Great Britain, France, and the U.S.S.R., the three countries were forced into a sort of uneasy *rapprochement*. This meant that the English or French Communist was obliged to become a good patriot and imperialist – that is, to defend the very things he had been attacking for the past fifteen years. The Comintern slogans suddenly faded from red to pink. 'World revolution' and 'Social-Fascism' gave way to 'Defence of democracy' and 'Stop Hitler'. The years 1935–9 were the period of anti-Fascism and the Popular Front, the heyday of the Left Book Club, when red Duchesses and 'broadminded' deans toured the battlefields of the Spanish war and Winston Churchill was the blue-eyed boy of the *Daily Worker*. Since then, of course, there has been yet another change of 'line'. But what is important for my purpose is that it was during the 'anti-Fascist' phase that the younger English writers gravitated towards Communism.

The Fascism-democracy dogfight was no doubt an attraction in itself, but in any case their conversion was due at about that date. It was obvious that *laissez-faire* capitalism was finished and that there had got to be some kind of reconstruction; in the world of 1935 it was hardly possible to remain politically indifferent. But why did these young men turn towards anything so alien as Russian Communism? Why should *writers* be attracted by a form of socialism that makes mental honesty impossible? The explanation really lies in something that had already made itself felt before the slump and before Hitler: middle-class unemployment.

Unemployment is not merely a matter of not having a job. Most people can *get* a job of sorts, even at the worst of times. The trouble was that by about 1930 there was no activity, except perhaps scientific research, the arts, and left-wing politics, that a thinking person could believe in. The debunking of Western civilization had reached its climax and 'disillusionment' was immensely widespread. Who now could take it for granted to go through life in the ordinary middle-class way, as a soldier, a clergyman, a stockbroker, an Indian Civil Servant, or what-not? And how many of the values by which our grandfathers lived could not be taken seriously? Patriotism, religion, the Empire, the family, the sanctity of marriage, the Old School Tie, birth, breeding, honour, discipline – anyone of ordinary education could turn the whole lot of them inside out in three minutes. But what do you achieve, after all, by getting rid of such primal things as patriotism and religion? You have not necessarily got rid of the need for *something to believe in*. There had been a sort of false dawn a few years earlier when numbers of young intellectuals, including several quite gifted writers (Evelyn Waugh, Christopher Hollis, and others), had fled into the Catholic Church. It is significant that these people went almost invariably to the Roman Church and not, for instance, to the C. of E., the Greek Church, or the Protestants sects. They went, that is, to the Church with a world-wide organization, the one with a rigid discipline, the one with power and prestige behind it. Perhaps it is even worth noticing that the only latter-day convert of really first-rate gifts, Eliot, has embraced not Romanism but Anglo-Catholicism, the ecclesiastical equivalent of Trotskyism. But I do not think one need look farther than this for the reason why the young writers of the thirties flocked into or towards the Communist Party. It was simply something to believe in. Here was a Church, an army, an orthodoxy, a discipline. Here was a Fatherland and – at any rate since 1935 or thereabouts – a Fuehrer. All the loyalties and superstitions that the intellect had seemingly banished could come rushing back under the thinnest of disguises. Patriotism, religion, empire, military glory – all in one word, Russia. Father, king, leader, hero, saviour – all in one word, Stalin. God – Stalin. The devil –

Hitler. Heaven – Moscow. Hell – Berlin. All the gaps were filled up. So, after all, the 'Communism' of the English intellectual is something explicable enough. It is the patriotism of the deracinated.

But there is one other thing that undoubtedly contributed to the cult of Russia among the English intelligentsia during these years, and that is the softness and security of life in England itself. With all its injustices, England is still the land of habeas corpus, and the overwhelming majority of English people have no experience of violence or illegality. If you have grown up in that sort of atmosphere it is not at all easy to imagine what a despotic régime is like. Nearly all the dominant writers of the thirties belonged to the soft-boiled emancipated middle class and were too young to have effective memories of the Great War. To people of that kind such things as purges, secret police, summary executions, imprisonment without trial, etc., etc., are too remote to be terrifying. They can swallow totalitarianism *because* they have no experience of anything except liberalism. Look, for instance, at this extract from Mr Auden's poem ' Spain ' (incidentally this poem is one of the few decent things that have been written about the Spanish war) :

To-morrow for the young, the poets exploding like bombs,
The walks by the lake, the weeks of perfect communion;
    To-morrow the bicycle races
Through the suburbs on summer evenings. But to-day the struggle.

To-day the deliberate increase in the chances of death,
The conscious acceptance of guilt in the necessary murder:
    To-day the expending of powers
On the flat ephemeral pamphlet and the boring meeting.

The second stanza is intended as a sort of thumb-nail sketch of a day in the life of a 'good party man'. In the morning a couple of political murders, a ten-minutes' interlude to stifle 'bourgeois' remorse, and then a hurried luncheon and a busy afternoon and evening chalking walls and distributing leaflets. All very edifying. But notice the phrase 'necessary murder'. It could only be written by a person to whom murder is at most a *word*. Personally I would not speak so lightly of murder. It so happens that I have seen the bodies of numbers of murdered men – I don't mean killed in battle, I mean murdered. Therefore I have some conception of what murder means – the terror, the hatred, the howling relatives, the post-mortems, the blood, the smells. To me, murder is something to be avoided. So it is to any ordinary person. The Hitlers and Stalins find murder necessary, but they don't advertise their callousness, and they don't speak of it as murder; it is 'liquidation', 'elimination', or some other soothing phrase. Mr Auden's brand of amoralism is only possible if you are the kind of person who is always somewhere else when the trigger is pulled. So much of left-wing thought is a kind of playing with fire by people who don't even know that fire is hot. The warmongering to which the English intelligentsia gave themselves up in the period 1935–9 was largely based on a sense of personal immunity. The attitude was very different in France, where the military service is hard to dodge and even literary men know the weight of a pack.

Towards the end of Mr Cyril Connolly's recent book, *Enemies of Promise*, there occurs an interesting and revealing passage. The first part of the book is, more or less, an evaluation of present-day literature. Mr Connolly belongs exactly to the generation of the writers of 'the movement', and with not many reservations their values are his values. It is interesting to notice that among prose-writers he admires chiefly those specialising in violence – the would-be tough American school, Hemingway, etc. The latter part of the book, however, is autobiographical and consists of an account, fascinatingly accurate, of life at a preparatory school and Eton in the years 1910–20. Mr Connolly ends by remarking:

Were I to deduce anything from my feelings on leaving Eton, it might be called *The Theory of Permanent Adolescence*. It is the theory that the experiences undergone by boys at the great public schools are so intense as to dominate their lives and to arrest their development.

When you read the second sentence in this passage, your natural impulse is to look for the misprint. Presumably there is a 'not' left out, or something. But no, not a bit of it! He means it! And what is more, he is merely speaking the truth, in an inverted fashion. 'Cultured' middle-class life has reached a depth of softness at which a public-school education – five years in a lukewarm bath of snobbery – can actually be looked back upon as an eventful period. To nearly all the writers who have counted during the thirties, what more has ever happened than Mr Connolly records in *Enemies of Promise*? It is the same pattern all the time; public school, university, a few trips abroad, then London. Hunger, hardship, solitude, exile, war, prison, persecution, manual labour – hardly even words. No wonder that the huge tribe known as 'the right left people' found it so easy to condone the purge-and-Ogpu side of the Russian régime and the horrors of the first Five-Year Plan. They were so gloriously incapable of understanding what it all meant.

By 1937 the whole of the intelligentsia was mentally at war. Left-wing thought had narrowed down to 'anti-Fascism', i.e. to a negative, and a torrent of hate-literature directed against Germany and the politicians supposedly friendly to Germany was pouring from the Press. The thing that, to me, was truly frightening about the war in Spain was not such violence as I witnessed, nor even the party feuds behind the lines, but the immediate reappearance in left-wing circles of the mental atmosphere of the Great War. The very people who for twenty years had sniggered over their own superiority to war hysteria were the ones who rushed straight back into the mental slum of 1915. All the familiar wartime idiocies, spy-hunting, orthodoxy-sniffing (Sniff, sniff. Are you a good anti-Fascist?), the retailing of atrocity stories, came back into vogue as though the intervening years had never happened.

Before the end of the Spanish war, and even before Munich, some of the better of the left-wing writers were beginning to squirm. Neither Auden nor, on the whole, Spender wrote about the Spanish war in quite the vein that was expected of them. Since then there has been a change of feeling and much dismay and confusion, because the actual course of events has made nonsense of the left-wing orthodoxy of the last few years. But then it did not need very great acuteness to see that much of it was nonsense from the start. There is no certainty, therefore, that the next orthodoxy to emerge will be any better than the last.

On the whole the literary history of the thirties seems to justify the opinion that a writer does well to keep out of politics. For any writer who accepts or partially accepts the discipline of a political party is sooner or later faced with the alternative: toe the line, or shut up. It is, of course, possible to toe the line and go on writing – after a fashion. Any Marxist can demonstrate with the greatest of ease that 'bourgeois' liberty of thought is an illusion. But when he has finished his demonstration there remains the psychological *fact* that without this 'bourgeois' liberty the creative powers wither away. In the future a totalitarian literature may arise, but it will be quite different from anything we can now imagine. Literature as we know it is an individual thing, demanding mental honesty and a minimum of censorship. And this is even truer of prose than of verse. It is probably not a coincidence that the best writers of the thirties have been poets. The atmosphere of orthodoxy is always damaging to prose, and above all it is completely ruinous to the novel, the most anarchical of all forms of literature. How many Roman Catholics have been good novelists? Even the handful one could name have usually been bad Catholics. The novel is practically a Protestant form of art; it is a product of the free mind, of the autonomous individual. No decade in the past hundred and fifty years has been so barren of imaginative prose as the nineteen-thirties. There have been good poems, good sociological works, brilliant pamphlets, but practically no fiction of any value at all. From 1933 onwards the mental climate was increasingly against it. Anyone sensitive enough to be touched by the *zeitgeist* was also involved in politics. Not everyone, of course, was definitely *in* the political racket, but practically everyone was on its periphery and more or less mixed up in propaganda campaigns and squalid controversies. Communists and near-Communists had a disproportionately large influence in the literary reviews. It was a time of labels, slogans, and evasions. At the worst moments you were expected to lock yourself up in a constipating little cage of lies; at the best a sort of voluntary censorship ('Ought I to say this? Is it pro-Fascist?') was at work in nearly everyone's mind. It is almost inconceivable that good novels should be written in such an atmosphere. Good novels are not written by orthodoxy-sniffers, nor by people who are conscience-stricken about their own unorthodoxy. Good novels are written by people who are *not frightened*. This brings me back to Henry Miller.

III

If this were a likely moment for the launching of 'schools' of literature, Henry Miller might be the starting-point of a new 'school'. He does at any rate mark an unexpected swing of the pendulum. In his books one gets right away from the 'political animal' and back to a viewpoint not only individualistic but completely passive – the view-point of a man who believes the world-process to be outside his control and who in any case hardly wishes to control it.

I first met Miller at the end of 1936, when I was passing through Paris on my way to Spain. What most intrigued me about him was to find that he felt no interest in the Spanish war whatever. He merely told me in forcible terms that to go to Spain at that moment was the act of an idiot. He could understand anyone going there from purely selfish motives, out of curiosity, for instance, but to mix oneself up in such things *from a sense of obligation* was sheer stupidity.

In any case my ideas about combating Fascism, defending democracy, etc., etc., were all baloney. Our civilization was destined to be swept away and replaced by something so different that we should scarcely regard it as human – a prospect that did not bother him, he said. And some such outlook is implicit throughout his work. Everywhere there is the sense of the approaching cataclysm, and almost everywhere the implied belief that it doesn't matter. The only political declaration which, so far as I know, he has ever made in print is a purely negative one. A year or so ago an American magazine, the *Marxist Quarterly*, sent out a questionnaire to various American writers asking them to define their attitude on the subject of war. Miller replied in terms of extreme pacifism, an individual refusal to fight, with no apparent wish to convert others to the same opinion – practically, in fact, a declaration of irresponsibility.

However, there is more than one kind of irresponsibility. As a rule, writers who do not wish to identify themselves with the historical process at the moment either ignore it or fight against it. If they can ignore it, they are probably fools. If they can understand it well enough to want to fight against it, they probably have enough vision to realize that they cannot win. Look, for instance, at a poem like 'The Scholar Gipsy', with its railing against the 'strange disease of modern life' and its magnificent defeatist simile in the final stanza. It expresses one of the normal literary attitudes, perhaps actually the prevailing attitude during the last hundred years. And on the other hand there are the 'progressives', the yea-sayers, the Shaw-Wells type, always leaping forward to embrace the ego-projections which they mistake for the future. On the whole the writers of the twenties took the first line and the writers of the thirties the second. And at any given moment, of course, there is a huge tribe of Barries and Deepings and Dells who simply don't notice what is happening. Where Miller's work is symptomatically important is in its avoidance of any of these attitudes. He is neither pushing the world-process forward nor trying to drag it back, but on the other hand he is by no means ignoring it. I should say that he believes in the impending ruin of Western Civilization much more firmly than the majority of 'revolutionary' writers; only he does not feel called upon to do anything about it. He is fiddling while Rome is burning, and, unlike the enormous majority of people who do this, fiddling with his face towards the flames.

In *Max and the White Phagocytes* there is one of those revealing passages in which a writer tells you a great deal about himself while talking about somebody else. The book includes a long essay on the diaries of Anais Nin, which I have never read, except for a few fragments, and which I believe have not been published. Miller claims that they are the only true feminine writing that has ever appeared, whatever that may mean. But the interesting passage is one in which he compares Anais Nin – evidently a completely subjective, introverted writer – to Jonah in the whale's belly. In passing he refers to an essay that Aldous Huxley wrote some years ago about El Greco's picture, *The Dream of Philip the Second*. Huxley remarks that the people in El Greco's pictures always look as though they were in the bellies of whales, and professes to find something peculiarly horrible in the idea of being in a 'visceral prison'. Miller retorts that, on the contrary, there are many worse things than being swallowed by whales, and the passage makes it clear that he himself finds the idea rather attractive. Here he is touching upon what is probably a very widespread fantasy. It is perhaps worth noticing that everyone, at least every English-speaking person, invariably speaks of Jonah and the *whale*. Of course the creature that swallowed Jonah was a fish, and was so described in the Bible (Jonah i. 17), but children naturally confuse it with a whale, and this fragment of baby-talk is habitually carried into later life – a sign, perhaps, of the hold that the Jonah myth has upon our imaginations. For the fact is that being inside a whale is a very comfortable, cosy, homelike thought. The historical Jonah, if he can be so called, was glad enough to escape, but in imagination, in day-dream, countless people have envied him. It is, of course, quite obvious why. The whale's belly is simply a womb big enough for an adult. There you are, in the dark, cushioned space that exactly fits you, with yards of blubber between yourself and reality, able to keep up an attitude of the completest indifference, no matter what happens. A storm that would sink all the battleships in the world would hardly reach you as an echo. Even the whale's own movements would probably be imperceptible to you. He might be wallowing among the surface waves or shooting down into the blackness of the middle seas (a mile deep, according to Herman Melville), but you would never notice the difference. Short of being dead, it is the final, unsurpassable stage of irresponsibility. And however it may be with Anais Nin, there is no question that Miller himself is inside the whale. All his best and most characteristic passages are written from the angle of Jonah, a willing Jonah. Not that he is especially introverted – quite the contrary. In his case the whale happens to be transparent. Only he feels no impulse to alter or control the process that he is undergoing. He has performed the essential Jonah act of allowing himself to be swallowed, remaining passive, accepting.

It will be seen what this amounts to. It is a species of quietism, implying either complete unbelief or else a degree of belief amounting to mysticism. The attitude is '*Je m'en fous*' or 'Though He slay me, yet will I trust in Him', whichever way you like to look at it; for practical purposes both are identical, the moral in either case being 'Sit on your bum'. But in a time like ours, is this a defensible attitude? Notice that it is almost impossible to refrain from asking this question. At the moment of writing we are still in a period in which it is taken for granted that books ought always to be positive, serious, and 'constructive'. A dozen years ago this idea would have been greeted with titters. ('My dear aunt, one doesn't write *about* anything, one just *writes*.') Then the pendulum swung away from the frivolous notion that art is merely technique, but it swung a very long distance, to the point of asserting that a book can only be 'good' if it is founded on a 'true' vision of life. Naturally the people who believe this also believe that they are in possession of the truth themselves. Catholic critics, for instance, tend to claim that books are only 'good' when they are of Catholic tendency. Marxist critics make the same claim more boldy for Marxist books. For instance, Mr Edward Upward ('A Marxist Interpretation of Literature,' in *The Mind in Chains*):

> Literary criticism which aims at being Marxist must ... proclaim that no book written *at the present time* can be 'good' unless it is written from a Marxist or near-Marxist viewpoint.

Various other writers have made similar or comparable statements. Mr Upward italicizes 'at the present time' because he realizes that you cannot, for instance, dismiss *Hamlet* on the ground that Shakespeare was not a Marxist. Nevertheless his interesting essay only glances very shortly at this difficulty. Much of the literature that comes to us out of the past is permeated by and in fact founded on beliefs (the belief in the immortality of the soul, for example) which now seem to us false and in some cases contemptibly silly. Yet it is 'good' literature, if survival is any test. Mr Upward would no doubt answer that a belief which was appropriate several centuries ago might be inappropriate and therefore stultifying now. But this does not get one much farther, because it assumes that in any age there will be *one* body of belief which is the current approximation to truth, and that the best literature of the time will be more or less in harmony with it. Actually no such uniformity has ever existed. In seventeenth-century England, for instance, there was a religious and political cleavage which distinctly resembled the left-right antagonism of to-day. Looking back, most modern people would feel that the bourgeois-Puritan viewpoint was a better approximation to truth than the Catholic-feudal one. But it is certainly not the case that all or even a majority of the best writers of the time were puritans. And more than this, there exist 'good' writers whose world-view would in *any* age be recognized as false and silly. Edgar Allan Poe is an example. Poe's outlook is at best a wild romanticism and at worst is not far from being insane in the literal clinical sense. Why is it, then, that stories like *The Black Cat*, *The Tell-tale Heart*, *The Fall of the House of Usher* and so forth, which might very nearly have been written by a lunatic, do not convey a feeling of falsity? Because they are true within a certain framework, they keep the rules of their own peculiar world, like a Japanese picture. But it appears that to write successfully about such a world you have got to believe in it. One sees the difference immediately if one compares Poe's *Tales* with what is, in my opinion, an insincere attempt to work up a similar atmosphere, Julian Green's *Minuit*. The thing that immediately strikes one about *Minuit* is that there is no reason why any of the events in it should happen. Everything is completely arbitrary; there is no emotional sequence. But this is exactly what one does *not* feel with Poe's stories. Their maniacal logic, in its own setting, is quite convincing. When, for instance, the drunkard seizes the black cat and cuts its eye out with his penknife, one knows exactly *why* he did it, even to the point of feeling that one would have done the same oneself. It seems therefore that for a creative writer possession of the 'truth' is less important than emotional sincerity. Even Mr Upward would not claim that a writer needs nothing beyond a Marxist training. He also needs talent. But talent, apparently, is a matter of being able to *care*, of really *believing* in your beliefs, whether they are true or false. The difference between, for instance, Céline and Evelyn Waugh is a difference of emotional intensity. It is the difference between genuine despair and a despair that is at least partly a pretence. And with this there goes another consideration which is perhaps less obvious: that there are occasions when an 'untrue' belief is more likely to be sincerely held than a 'true' one.

If one looks at the books of personal reminiscence written about the war of 1914–18, one notices that nearly all that have remained readable after a lapse of time are written from a passive, negative angle. They are the records of something completely meaningless, a nightmare happening in a void. That was not actually the truth about the war, but it was the truth about the individual reaction. The soldier advancing into a machine-gun barrage or standing waist-deep in a flooded trench knew only that here was an appalling experience in which he was all but helpless. He was likelier to make a good book out of his helplessness and his ignorance than out of a pretended power to see the whole thing in perspective. As for the books that were written during the war itself, the best of them were nearly all the work of people who simply turned their backs and tried not to notice that the war was happening. Mr E. M. Forster has described how in 1917 he read *Prufrock* and other of Eliot's early poems, and how it heartened him at such a time to get hold of poems that were 'innocent of public-spiritedness':

> They sang of private disgust and diffidence, and of people who seemed genuine because they were unattractive or weak. ... Here was a protest, and a feeble one, and the more congenial for being feeble. ... He who could turn aside to complain of ladies and drawing rooms preserved a tiny drop of our self-respect, he carried on the human heritage.

That is very well said. Mr MacNeice, in the book I have referred to already, quotes this passage and somewhat smugly adds:

> Ten years later less feeble protests were to be made by poets and the human heritage carried on rather differently. ... The contemplation of a world of fragments becomes boring and Eliot's successors are more interested in tidying it up.

Similar remarks are scattered throughout Mr MacNeice's book. What he wishes us to believe is that Eliot's 'successors' (meaning Mr MacNeice and his friends) have in some way 'protested' more effectively than Eliot did by publishing *Prufrock* at the moment when the Allied armies were assaulting the Hindenburg Line. Just where these 'protests' are to be found I do not know. But in the contrast between

Mr Forster's comment and Mr MacNeice's lies all the difference between a man who knows what the 1914–18 war was like and a man who barely remembers it. The truth is that in 1917 there was nothing that a thinking and a sensitive person could do, except to remain human, if possible. And a gesture of helplessness, even of frivolity, might be the best way of doing that. If I had been a soldier fighting in the Great War, I would sooner have got hold of *Prufrock* than *The First Hundred Thousand* or Horatio Bottomley's *Letters to the Boys in the Trenches*. I should have felt, like Mr Forster, that by simply standing aloof and keeping touch with pre-war emotions, Eliot was carrying on the human heritage. What a relief it would have been at such a time, to read about the hesitations of a middle-aged highbrow with a bald spot! So different from bayonet-drill! After the bombs and the food-queues and the recruiting-posters, a human voice! What a relief!

But, after all, the war of 1914–18 was only a heightened moment in an almost continuous crisis. At this date it hardly even needs a war to bring home to us the disintegration of our society and the increasing helplessness of all decent people. It is for this reason that I think that the passive, non-co-operative attitude implied in Henry Miller's work is justified. Whether or not it is an expression of what people *ought* to feel, it probably comes somewhere near to expressing what they *do* feel. Once again it is the human voice among the bomb-explosions, a friendly American voice, 'innocent of public-spiritedness'. No sermons, merely the subjective truth. And along those lines, apparently, it is still possible for a good novel to be written. Not necessarily an edifying novel, but a novel worth reading and likely to be remembered after it is read.

While I have been writing this essay another European war has broken out. It will either last several years and tear Western civilization to pieces, or it will end inconclusively and prepare the way for yet another war which will do the job once and for all. But war is only 'peace intensified'. What is quite obviously happening, war or no war, is the break-up of *laissez-faire* capitalism and of the liberal-Christian culture. Until recently the full implications of this were not foreseen, because it was generally imagined that socialism could preserve and even enlarge the atmosphere of liberalism. It is now beginning to be realized how false this idea was. Almost certainly we are moving into an age of totalitarian dictatorships – an age in which freedom of thought will be at first a deadly sin and later on a meaningless abstraction. The autonomous individual is going to be stamped out of existence. But this means that literature, in the form in which we know it, must suffer at least a temporary death. The literature of liberalism is coming to an end and the literature of totalitarianism has not yet appeared and is barely imaginable. As for the writer, he is sitting on a melting iceberg; he is merely an anachronism, a hangover from the bourgeois age, as surely doomed as the hippopotamus. Miller seems to me a man out of the common because he saw and proclaimed this fact a long while before most of his contemporaries – at a time, indeed, when many of them were actually burbling about a renaissance of literature. Wyndham Lewis had said years earlier that the major history of the English language was finished, but he was basing this on different and rather trivial reasons. But from now onwards the all-important fact for the creative writer is going to be that this is not a writer's world. That does not mean that he cannot help to bring the new society into being, but he can take no part in the process *as a writer*. For *as a writer* he is a liberal, and what is happening is the destruction of liberalism. It seems likely, therefore, that in the remaining years of free speech any novel worth reading will follow more or less along the lines that Miller has followed – I do not mean in technique or subject matter, but in implied outlook. The passive attitude will come back, and it will be more consciously passive than before. Progress and reaction have both turned out to be swindles. Seemingly there is nothing left but quietism – robbing reality of its terrors by simply submitting to it. Get inside the whale – or rather, admit you are inside the whale (for you *are*, of course). Give yourself over to the world-process, stop fighting against it or pretending that you control it; simply accept it, endure it, record it. That seems to be the formula that any sensitive novelist is now likely to adopt. A novel on more positive, 'constructive' lines, and not emotionally spurious, is at present very difficult to imagine.

But do I mean by this that Miller is a 'great author', a new hope for English prose? Nothing of the kind. Miller himself would be the last to claim or want any such thing. No doubt he will go on writing – anybody who has once started always goes on writing – and associated with him there are a number of writers of approximately the same tendency, Lawrence Durrell, Michael Fraenkel and others, almost amounting to a 'school'. But he himself seems to me essentially a man of one book. Sooner or later I should expect him to descend into unintelligibility, or into charlatanism: there are signs of both in his later work. His last book, *Tropic of Capricorn*, I have not even read. This was not because I did not want to read it, but because the police and Customs authorities have so far managed to prevent me from getting hold of it. But it would surprise me if it came anywhere near *Tropic of Cancer* or the opening chapters of *Black Spring*. Like certain other autobiographical novelists, he had it in him to do just one thing perfectly, and he did it. Considering what the fiction of the nineteen-thirties has been like, that is something.

Miller's books are published by the Obelisk Press in Paris. What will happen to the Obelisk Press, now that war has broken out and Jack Kathane, the publisher, is dead, I do not know, but at any rate the books are still procurable. I earnestly counsel anyone who has not done so to read at least *Tropic of Cancer*. With a little ingenuity, or by paying a little over the published price, you can get hold of it, and even if parts of it disgust you, it will stick in your memory. It is also an 'important' book, in a sense different from the sense in which that word is generally used. As a rule novels are spoken of as 'important' when they are either a 'terrible indictment' of something or other or when they introduce some technical innovation. Neither of these applies to *Tropic of Cancer*. Its importance is merely symptomatic. Here in my opinion is the only imaginative prose-writer of the slightest value who has appeared among the English-speaking races for some years past. Even if that is objected to as an overstatement, it will probably be admitted that Miller is a writer out of the ordinary, worth more than a single glance; and after all, he is a completely negative, unconstructive, amoral writer, a mere Jonah, a passive acceptor of evil, a sort of Whitman among the corpses. Symptomatically, that is more significant than the mere fact that five thousand novels are published in England every year and four thousand nine hundred of them are tripe. It is a demonstration of the *impossibility* of any major literature until the world has shaken itself into its new shape.

1940

DOWN THE MINE

OUR civilization, *pace* Chesterton, is founded on coal, more completely than one realizes until one stops to think about it. The machines that keep us alive, and the machines that make machines, are all directly or indirectly dependent upon coal. In the metabolism of the Western world the coal-miner is second in importance only to the man who ploughs the soil. He is a sort of caryatid upon whose shoulders nearly everything that is not grimy is supported. For this reason the actual process by which coal is extracted is well worth watching, if you get the chance and are willing to take the trouble.

When you go down a coal-mine it is important to try and get to the coal face when the 'fillers' are at work. This is not easy, because when the mine is working visitors are a nuisance and are not encouraged, but if you go at any other time, it is possible to come away with a totally wrong impression. On a Sunday, for instance, a mine seems almost peaceful. The time to go there is when the machines are roaring and the air is black with coal dust, and when you can actually see what the miners have to do. At those times the place is like hell, or at any rate like my own mental picture of hell. Most of the things one imagines in hell are there – heat, noise, confusion, darkness, foul air, and, above all, unbearably cramped space. Everything except the fire, for there is no fire down there except the feeble beams of Davy lamps and electric torches which scarcely penetrate the clouds of coal dust.

When you have finally got there – and getting there is a job in itself: I will explain that in a moment – you crawl through the last line of pit props and see opposite you a shiny black wall three or four feet high. This is the coal face. Overhead is the smooth ceiling made by the rock from which the coal has been cut; underneath is the rock again, so that the gallery you are in is only as high as the ledge of coal itself, probably not much more than a yard. The first impression of all, overmastering everything else for a while, is the frightful, deafening din from the conveyor belt which carries the coal away. You cannot see very far, because the fog of coal dust throws back the beam of your lamp, but you can see on either side of you the line of half-naked kneeling men, one to every four or five yards, driving their shovels under the fallen coal and flinging it swiftly over their left shoulders. They are feeding it on to the conveyor belt, a moving rubber belt a couple of feet wide which runs a yard or two behind them. Down this belt a glittering river of coal races constantly. In a big mine it is carrying away several tons of coal every minute. It bears it off to some place in the main roads where it is shot into tubs holding half a ton, and thence dragged to the cages and hoisted to the outer air.

It is impossible to watch the 'fillers' at work without feeling a pang of envy for their toughness. It is a dreadful job that they do, an almost superhuman job by the standard of an ordinary person. For they are not only shifting monstrous quantities of coal, they are also doing it in a position that doubles or trebles the work. They have got to remain kneeling all the while – they could hardly rise from their knees without hitting the ceiling – and you can easily see by trying it what a tremendous effort this means. Shovelling is comparatively easy when you are standing up, because you can use your knee and thigh to drive the shovel along; kneeling down, the whole of the strain is thrown upon your arm and belly muscles. And the other conditions do not exactly make things easier. There is the heat – it varies, but in some mines it is suffocating – and the coal dust that stuffs up your throat and nostrils and collects along your eyelids, and the unending rattle of the conveyor belt, which in that confined space is rather like the rattle of a machine gun. But the fillers look and work as though they were made of iron. They really do look like iron – hammered iron statues – under the smooth coat of coal dust which clings to them from head to foot. It is only when you see miners down the mine and naked that you realize what splendid men they are. Most of them are small (big men are at a disadvantage in that job) but nearly all of them have the most noble bodies; wide shoulders tapering to slender supple waists, and small pronounced buttocks and sinewy thighs, with not an ounce of waste flesh anywhere. In the hotter mines they wear only a pair of thin drawers, clogs and knee-pads; in the hottest mines of all, only the clogs and knee-pads. You can hardly tell by the look of them whether they are young or old. They may be any age up to sixty or even sixty-five, but when they are black and naked they all look alike. No one could do their work who had not a young man's body, and a figure fit for a guardsman at that; just a few pounds of extra flesh on the waist-line, and the constant bending would be impossible. You can never forget that spectacle once you have seen it – the line of bowed, kneeling figures, sooty black all over, driving their huge shovels under the coal with stupendous force and speed. They are on the job for seven and a half hours, theoretically without a break, for there is no time 'off'. Actually they snatch a quarter of an hour or so at some time during the shift to eat the food they have brought with them, usually a hunk of bread and dripping and a bottle of cold tea. The first time I was watching the 'fillers' at work I put my hand upon some dreadful slimy thing among the coal dust. It was a chewed quid of tobacco. Nearly all the miners chew tobacco, which is said to be good against thirst.

Probably you have to go down several coal-mines before you can get much grasp of the processes that are going on round you. This is chiefly because the mere effort of getting from place to place makes it difficult to notice anything else. In some ways it is even disappointing, or at least is unlike what you have expected. You get into the cage, which is a steel box about as wide as a telephone box and two or three times as long. It holds ten men, but they pack it like pilchards in a tin, and a tall man cannot stand upright in it. The steel door shuts upon you, and somebody working the winding gear above drops you into the void. You have the usual momentary qualm in your belly and a bursting sensation in the ears, but not much sensation of movement till you get near the bottom, when the cage slows down so abruptly that you could swear it is going upwards again. In the middle of the run the cage probably touches sixty miles an hour; in some of the deeper mines it touches even more. When you crawl out at the bottom you are perhaps four hundred yards underground. That is to say you have a tolerable-sized mountain on top of you; hundreds of yards of solid rock, bones of extinct beasts, subsoil, flints, roots of growing things, green grass and cows grazing on it – all this suspended over your head and held back only by wooden props as thick as the calf of your leg. But because of the speed at which the cage has brought you down, and the complete blackness through which you have travelled, you hardly feel yourself deeper down than you would at the bottom of the Piccadilly tube.

What *is* surprising, on the other hand, is the immense horizontal distances that have to be travelled underground. Before I had been down a mine I had vaguely imagined the miner stepping out of the cage and getting to work on a ledge of coal a few yards away. I had not realized that before he even gets to work he may have had to creep along passages as long as from London Bridge to Oxford Circus. In the beginning, of course, a mine shaft is sunk somewhere near a seam of coal. But as that seam is worked out and fresh seams are followed up, the workings get further and further from the pit bottom. If it is a mile from the pit bottom to the coal face, that is probably an average distance; three miles is a fairly normal one; there are even said to be a few mines where it is as much as five miles. But these distances bear no relation to distances above ground. For in all that mile or three miles as it may be, there is hardly anywhere outside the main road, and not many places even there, where a man can stand upright.

You do not notice the effect of this till you have gone a few hundred yards. You start off, stooping slightly, down the dim-lit gallery, eight or ten feet wide and about five high, with the walls built up with slabs of shale, like the stone walls in Derbyshire. Every yard or two there are wooden props holding up the beams and girders; some of the girders have buckled into fantastic curves under which you have to duck. Usually it is bad going underfoot – thick dust or jagged chunks of shale, and in some mines where there is water it is as mucky as a farm-yard. Also there is the track for the coal tubs, like a miniature railway track with sleepers a foot or two apart, which is tiresome to walk on. Everything is grey with shale dust; there is a dusty fiery smell which seems to be the same in all mines. You see mysterious machines of which you never learn the purpose, and bundles of tools slung together on wires, and sometimes mice darting away from the beam of the lamps. They are surprisingly common, especially in mines where there are or have been horses. It would be interesting to know how they got there in the first place; possibly by falling down the shaft – for they say a mouse can fall any distance uninjured, owing to its surface area being so large relative to its weight. You press yourself against the wall to make way for lines of tubs jolting slowly towards the shaft, drawn by an endless steel cable operated from the surface. You creep through sacking curtains and thick wooden doors which, when they are opened, let out fierce blasts of air. These doors are an important part of the ventilation system. The exhausted air is sucked out of one shaft by means of fans, and the fresh air enters the other of its own accord. But if left to itself the air will take the shortest way round, leaving the deeper workings unventilated; so all the short cuts have to be partitioned off.

At the start to walk stooping is rather a joke, but it is a joke that soon wears off. I am handicapped by being exceptionally tall, but when the roof falls to four feet or less it is a tough job for anybody except a dwarf or a child. You not only have to bend double, you have also got to

55

keep your head up all the while so as to see the beams and
girders and dodge them when they come. You have, therefore, a constant crick in the neck, but this is nothing to the
pain in your knees and thighs. After half a mile it becomes
(I am not exaggerating) an unbearable agony. You begin to
wonder whether you will ever get to the end – still more,
how on earth you are going to get back. Your pace grows
slower and slower. You come to a stretch of a couple of
hundred yards where it is all exceptionally low and you
have to work yourself along in a squatting position. Then
suddenly the roof opens out to a mysterious height – scene
of an old fall of rock, probably – and for twenty whole yards
you can stand upright. The relief is overwhelming. But
after this there is another low stretch of a hundred yards
and then a succession of beams which you have to crawl
under. You go down on all fours; even this is a relief after
the squatting business. But when you come to the end of the
beams and try to get up again, you find that your knees have
temporarily struck work and refuse to lift you. You call
a halt, ignominiously, and say that you would like to rest
for a minute or two. Your guide (a miner) is sympathetic. He
knows that your muscles are not the same as his. 'Only another four hundred yards,' he says encouragingly; you feel
that he might as well say another four hundred miles. But
finally you do somehow creep as far as the coal face. You
have gone a mile and taken the best part of an hour; a miner
would do it in not much more than twenty minutes. Having got there, you have to sprawl in the coal dust and get
your strength back for several minutes before you can even
watch the work in progress with any kind of intelligence.

Coming back is worse than going, not only because you
are already tired out but because the journey back to the
shaft is slightly uphill. You get through the low places at the
speed of a tortoise, and you have no shame now about
calling a halt when your knees give way. Even the lamp you
are carrying becomes a nuisance and probably when you
stumble you drop it; whereupon, if it is a Davy lamp, it
goes out. Ducking the beams becomes more and more of an

effort, and sometimes you forget to duck. You try walking head down as the miners do, and then you bang your back-bone. Even the miners bang their backbones fairly often. This is the reason why in very hot mines, where it is neces-sary to go about half naked, most of the miners have what they call 'buttons down the back' – that is, a permanent scab on each vertebra. When the track is down hill the miners sometimes fit their clogs, which are hollow under-neath, on to the trolley rails and slide down. In mines where the 'travelling' is very bad all the miners carry sticks about two and a half feet long, hollowed out below the handle. In normal places you keep your hand on top of the stick and in the low places you slide your hand down into the hollow. These sticks are a great help, and the wooden crash-helmets – a comparatively recent invention – are a godsend. They look like a French or Italian steel helmet, but they are made of some kind of pith and very light, and so strong that you can take a violent blow on the head without feeling it. When finally you get back to the surface you have been perhaps three hours underground and travelled two miles, and you are more exhausted than you would be by a twenty-five-mile walk above ground. For a week afterwards your thighs are so stiff that coming down-stairs is quite a difficult feat; you have to work your way down in a peculiar sidelong manner, without bending the knees. Your miner friends notice the stiffness of your walk and chaff you about it. ('How'd ta like to work down pit, eh?' etc.) Yet even a miner who has been long away from work – from illness, for instance – when he comes back to the pit, suffers badly for the first few days.

It may seem that I am exaggerating, though no one who has been down an old-fashioned pit (most of the pits in England are old-fashioned) and actually gone as far as the coal face, is likely to say so. But what I want to emphasize is this. Here is this frightful business of crawling to and fro, which to any normal person is a hard day's work in itself; and it is not part of the miner's work at all, it is merely an extra, like the City man's daily ride in the Tube. The miner does that journey to and fro, and sandwiched in between there are seven and a half hours of savage work. I have never travelled much more than a mile to the coal face; but often it is three miles, in which case I and most people other than coal-miners would never get there at all. This is the kind of point that one is always liable to miss. When you think of the coal-mine you think of depth, heat, darkness, blackened figures hacking at walls of coal; you don't think, necessarily, of those miles of creeping to and fro. There is the question of time, also. A miner's working shift of seven and a half hours does not sound very long, but one has got to add on to it at least an hour a day for 'travelling', more often two hours and sometimes three. Of course, the 'travelling' is not technically work and the miner is not paid for it; but it is as like work as makes no difference. It is easy to say that miners don't mind all this. Certainly, it is not the same for them as it would be for you or me. They have done it since childhood, they have the right muscles hardened, and they can move to and fro underground with a startling and rather horrible agility. A miner puts his head down and runs, with a long swinging stride, through places where I can only stagger. At the workings you see them on all fours, skipping round the pit props almost like dogs. But it is quite a mistake to think that they enjoy it. I have talked about this to scores of miners and they all admit that the 'travelling' is hard work; in any case when you hear them discussing a pit among themselves the 'travelling' is always one of the things they discuss. It is said that a shift always returns from work faster than it goes; nevertheless the miners all say that it is the coming away after a hard day's work, that is especially irksome. It is part of their work and they are equal to it, but certainly it is an effort. It is comparable, perhaps, to climbing a smallish mountain before and after your day's work.

When you have been down in two or three pits you begin to get some grasp of the processes that are going on underground. (I ought to say, by the way, that I know nothing whatever about the technical side of mining: I am merely describing what I have seen.) Coal lies in thin seams between enormous layers of rock, so that essentially the process of getting it out is like scooping the central layer from a Neapolitan ice. In the old days the miners used to cut straight into the coal with pick and crowbar – a very slow job because coal, when lying in its virgin state, is almost as hard as rock. Nowadays the preliminary work is done by an electrically-driven coal-cutter, which in principle is an immensely tough and powerful band-saw, running horizontally instead of vertically, with teeth a couple of inches long and half an inch or an inch thick. It can move backwards or forwards on its own power, and the men operating it can rotate it this way or that. Incidentally it makes one of the most awful noises I have ever heard, and sends forth clouds of coal dust which make it impossible to see more than two to three feet and almost impossible to breathe. The machine travels along the coal face cutting into the base of the coal and undermining it to the depth of five feet or five feet and a half; after this it is comparatively easy to extract the coal to the depth to which it has been undermined. Where it is 'difficult getting', however, it has also to be loosened with explosives. A man with an electric drill, like a rather small version of the drills used in street-mending, bores holes at intervals in the coal, inserts blasting powder, plugs it with clay, goes round the corner if there is one handy (he is supposed to retire to twenty-five yards distance) and touches off the charge with an electric current. This is not intended to bring the coal out, only to loosen it. Occasionally, of course, the charge is too powerful, and then it not only brings the coal out but brings the roof down as well.

After the blasting has been done the 'fillers' can tumble the coal out, break it up and shovel it on to the conveyor belt. It comes out first in monstrous boulders which may weigh anything up to twenty tons. The conveyor belt shoots it on to tubs, and the tubs are shoved into the main road and hitched on to an endlessly revolving steel cable which drags them to the cage. Then they are hoisted, and at the surface the coal is sorted by being run over screens, and if necessary is washed as well. As far as possible the 'dirt' – the shale, that is – is used for making the roads below. All that cannot be used is sent to the surface and dumped; hence the monstrous 'dirt-heaps', like hideous grey mountains, which are the characteristic scenery of the coal areas. When the coal has been extracted to the depth to which the machine has cut, the coal face has advanced by five feet. Fresh props are put in to hold up the newly exposed roof, and during the next shift the conveyor belt is taken to pieces, moved five feet forward and re-assembled. As far as possible the three operations of cutting, blasting and extraction are done in three separate shifts, the cutting in the afternoon, the blasting at night (there is a law, not always kept, that forbids its being done when other men are working near by), and the 'filling' in the morning shift, which lasts from six in the morning until half past one.

Even when you watch the process of coal-extraction you probably only watch it for a short time, and it is not until you begin making a few calculations that you realize what a stupendous task the 'fillers' are performing. Normally each man has to clear a space four or five yards wide. The cutter has undermined the coal to the depth of five feet, so that if the seam of coal is three or four feet high, each man has to cut out, break up and load on to the belt something between seven and twelve cubic yards of coal. This is to say, taking a cubic yard as weighing twenty-seven hundred-weight, that each man is shifting coal at a speed approaching two tons an hour. I have just enough experience of pick and shovel work to be able to grasp what this means. When I am digging trenches in my garden, if I shift two tons of earth during the afternoon, I feel that I have earned my tea. But earth is tractable stuff compared with coal, and I don't have to work kneeling down, a thousand feet underground, in suffocating heat and swallowing coal dust with every breath I take; nor do I have to walk a mile bent double before I begin. The miner's job would be as much beyond my power as it would be to perform on a flying trapeze or to win the Grand National. I am not a manual labourer and please God I never shall be one, but there are some kinds of manual work that I could do if I had to. At a pitch I could be a tolerable road-sweeper or an inefficient gardener or even a tenth-rate farm hand. But by no conceivable amount of effort or training could I become a coal-miner; the work would kill me in a few weeks.

Watching coal-miners at work, you realize momentarily what different universes people inhabit. Down there where coal is dug is a sort of world apart which one can quite easily go through life without ever hearing about. Probably a majority of people would even prefer not to hear about it. Yet it is the absolutely necessary counterpart of our world above. Practically everything we do, from eating an ice to crossing the Atlantic, and from baking a loaf to writing a novel, involves the use of coal, directly or indirectly. For all the arts of peace coal is needed; if war breaks out it is needed all the more. In time of revolution the miner must go on working or the revolution must stop, for revolution as much as reaction needs coal. Whatever may be happening on the surface, the hacking and shovelling have got to continue without a pause, or at any rate without pausing for more than a few weeks at the most. In order that Hitler may march the goose-step, that the Pope may denounce Bolshevism, that the cricket crowds may assemble at Lords, that the poets may scratch one another's backs, coal has got to be forthcoming. But on the whole we are not aware of it; we all know that we 'must have coal', but we seldom or never remember what coal-getting involves. Here am I sitting writing in front of my comfortable coal fire. It is April but I still need a fire. Once a fortnight the coal cart drives up to the door and men in leather jerkins carry the coal indoors in stout sacks smelling of tar and shoot it clanking into the coal-hole under the stairs. It is only very rarely, when I make a definite mental effort, that I connect this coal with that far-off labour in the mines. It is just 'coal' – something that I have got to have; black stuff that arrives mysteriously from nowhere in particular, like manna except that you have to pay for it. You could quite easily drive a car right across the north of England and never once remember that hundreds of feet below the road you are on the miners are hacking at the coal. Yet in a sense it is the miners who are driving your car forward. Their lamp-lit world down there is as necessary to the daylight world above as the root is to the flower.

It is not long since conditions in the mines were worse than they are now. There are still living a few very old women who in their youth have worked underground, with the harness round their waists, and a chain that passed between their legs, crawling on all fours and dragging tubs of coal. They used to go on doing this even when they were pregnant. And even now, if coal could not be produced without pregnant women dragging it to and fro, I fancy we should let them do it rather than deprive ourselves of coal. But most of the time, of course, we should prefer to forget that they were doing it. It is so with all types of manual work; it keeps us alive, and we are oblivious of its existence. More than anyone else, perhaps, the miner can stand as the type of the manual worker, not only because his work is so exaggeratedly awful, but also because it is so vitally necessary and yet so remote from our experience, so invisible, as it were, that we are capable of forgetting it as we forget the blood in our veins. In a way it is even humiliating to watch coal-miners working. It raises in you a momentary doubt about your own status as an 'intellectual' and a superior person generally. For it is brought home to you, at least while you are watching, that it is only because miners sweat their guts out that superior persons can remain superior. You and I and the editor of the *Times Lit. Supp.*, and the poets and the Archbishop of Canterbury and Comrade X, author of *Marxism for Infants* – all of us *really* owe the comparative decency of our lives to poor drudges underground, blackened to the eyes, with their throats full of coal dust, driving their shovels forward with arms and belly muscles of steel.

1937

ENGLAND YOUR ENGLAND

As I write, highly civilized human beings are flying overhead, trying to kill me.

They do not feel any enmity against me as an individual, nor I against them. They are 'only doing their duty', as the saying goes. Most of them, I have no doubt, are kind-hearted law-abiding men who would never dream of committing murder in private life. On the other hand, if one of them succeeds in blowing me to pieces with a well-placed bomb, he will never sleep any the worse for it. He is serving his country, which has the power to absolve him from evil.

One cannot see the modern world as it is unless one recognizes the overwhelming strength of patriotism, national loyalty. In certain circumstances it can break down, at certain levels of civilization it does not exist, but as a *positive* force there is nothing to set beside it. Christianity and international Socialism are as weak as straw in comparison with it. Hitler and Mussolini rose to power in their own countries very largely because they could grasp this fact and their opponents could not.

Also, one must admit that the divisions between nation and nation are founded on real differences of outlook. Till recently it was thought proper to pretend that all human beings are very much alike, but in fact anyone able to use his eyes knows that the average of human behaviour differs enormously from country to country. Things that could happen in one country could not happen in another. Hitler's June Purge, for instance, could not have happened in England. And, as western peoples go, the English are very highly differentiated. There is a sort of backhanded admission of this in the dislike which nearly all foreigners feel for our national way of life. Few Europeans can endure living in England, and even Americans often feel more at home in Europe.

When you come back to England from any foreign country, you have immediately the sensation of breathing a different air. Even in the first few minutes dozens of small things conspire to give you this feeling. The beer is bitterer, the coins are heavier, the grass is greener, the advertisements are more blatant. The crowds in the big towns, with their mild knobbly faces, their bad teeth and gentle manners, are different from a European crowd. Then the vastness of England swallows you up, and you lose for a while your feeling that the whole nation has a single identifiable character. Are there really such things as nations? Are we not 46 million individuals, all different? And the diversity of it, the chaos! The clatter of clogs in the Lancashire mill towns, the to-and-fro of the lorries on the Great North Road, the queues outside the Labour Exchanges, the rattle of pin-tables in the Soho pubs, the old maids biking to Holy Communion through the mists of the autumn mornings – all these are not only fragments, but *characteristic* fragments, of the English scene. How can one make a pattern out of this muddle?

But talk to foreigners, read foreign books or newspapers, and you are brought back to the same thought. Yes, there *is* something distinctive and recognizable in English civilization. It is a culture as individual as that of Spain. It is somehow bound up with solid breakfasts and gloomy Sundays, smoky towns and winding roads, green fields and red pillar-boxes. It has a flavour of its own. Moreover it is continuous, it stretches into the future and the past, there is something in it that persists, as in a living creature. What can the England of 1940 have in common with the England of 1840? But then, what have you in common with the child of five whose photograph your mother keeps on the mantelpiece? Nothing, except that you happen to be the same person.

And above all, it is *your* civilization, it is *you*. However much you hate it or laugh at it, you will never be happy away from it for any length of time. The suet puddings and the red pillar-boxes have entered into your soul. Good or evil, it is yours, you belong to it, and this side the grave you will never get away from the marks that it has given you.

Meanwhile England, together with the rest of the world, is changing. And like everything else it can change only in certain directions, which up to a point can be foreseen. That is not to say that the future is fixed, merely that certain alternatives are possible and others not. A seed may grow or not grow, but at any rate a turnip seed never grows into a parsnip. It is therefore of the deepest importance to try and determine what England *is*, before guessing what part England *can play* in the huge events that are happening.

II

National characteristics are not easy to pin down, and when pinned down they often turn out to be trivialities or seem to have no connexion with one another. Spaniards are cruel to animals, Italians can do nothing without making a deafening noise, the Chinese are addicted to gambling. Obviously such things don't matter in themselves. Nevertheless, nothing is causeless, and even the fact that Englishmen have bad teeth can tell one something about the realities of English life.

Here are a couple of generalizations about England that would be accepted by almost all observers. One is that the English are not gifted artistically. They are not as musical as the Germans or Italians, painting and sculpture have never flourished in England as they have in France. Another is that, as Europeans go, the English are not intellectual. They have a horror of abstract thought, they feel no need for any philosophy or systematic 'world-view'. Nor is this because they are 'practical', as they are so fond of claiming for themselves. One has only to look at their methods of town-planning and water-supply, their obstinate clinging to everything that is out of date and a nuisance, a spelling system that defies analysis and a system of weights and

measures that is intelligible only to the compilers of arith-
metic books, to see how little they care about mere
efficiency. But they have a certain power of acting without
taking thought. Their world-famed hypocrisy – their
double-faced attitude towards the Empire, for instance – is
bound up with this. Also, in moments of supreme crisis the
whole nation can suddenly draw together and act upon a
species of instinct, really a code of conduct which is understood by almost everyone, though never formulated. The
phrase that Hitler coined for the Germans, 'a sleep-walking
people', would have been better applied to the English.
Not that there is anything to be proud of in being a sleep-
walker.

But here it is worth noticing a minor English trait which
is extremely well marked though not often commented on,
and that is a love of flowers. This is one of the first things
that one notices when one reaches England from abroad,
especially if one is coming from southern Europe. Does it
not contradict the English indifference to the arts? Not
really, because it is found in people who have no aesthetic
feelings whatever. What it does link up with, however, is
another English characteristic which is so much a part of us
that we barely notice it, and that is the addiction to hobbies
and spare-time occupations, the *privateness* of English life.
We are a nation of flower-lovers, but also a nation of
stamp-collectors, pigeon-fanciers, amateur carpenters,
coupon-snippers, darts-players, crossword-puzzle fans. All
the culture that is most truly native centres round things
which even when they are communal are not official – the
pub, the football match, the back garden, the fireside and
the 'nice cup of tea'. The liberty of the individual is still
believed in, almost as in the nineteenth century. But this
has nothing to do with economic liberty, the right to
exploit others for profit. It is the liberty to have a home of
your own, to do what you like in your spare time, to choose
your own amusements instead of having them chosen for
you from above. The most hateful of all names in an
English ear is Nosey Parker. It is obvious, of course, that

even this purely private liberty is a lost cause. Like all other modern peoples, the English are in process of being numbered, labelled, conscripted, 'co-ordinated'. But the pull of their impulses is in the other direction, and the kind of regimentation that can be imposed on them will be modified in consequence. No party rallies, no Youth Movements, no coloured shirts, no Jew-baiting or 'spontaneous' demonstrations. No Gestapo either, in all probability.

But in all societies the common people must live to some extent *against* the existing order. The genuinely popular culture of England is something that goes on beneath the surface, unofficially and more or less frowned on by the authorities. One thing one notices if one looks directly at the common people, especially in the big towns, is that they are not puritanical. They are inveterate gamblers, drink as much beer as their wages will permit, are devoted to bawdy jokes, and use probably the foulest language in the world. They have to satisfy these tastes in the face of astonishing, hypocritical laws (licensing laws, lottery acts, etc., etc.) which are designed to interfere with everybody but in practice allow everything to happen. Also, the common people are without definite religious belief, and have been so for centuries. The Anglican Church never had a real hold on them, it was simply a preserve of the landed gentry, and the Nonconformist sects only influenced minorities. And yet they have retained a deep tinge of Christian feeling, while almost forgetting the name of Christ. The power-worship which is the new religion of Europe, and which has infected the English intelligentsia, has never touched the common people. They have never caught up with power politics. The 'realism' which is preached in Japanese and Italian newspapers would horrify them. One can learn a good deal about the spirit of England from the comic coloured postcards that you see in the windows of cheap stationers' shops. These things are a sort of diary upon which the English people have unconsciously recorded themselves. Their old-fashioned outlook, their graded snobberies, their mixture of bawdiness and hypocrisy, their extreme gentleness, their deeply moral attitude to life, are all mirrored there.

The gentleness of the English civilization is perhaps its most marked characteristic. You notice it the instant you set foot on English soil. It is a land where the bus conductors are good-tempered and the policemen carry no revolvers. In no country inhabited by white men is it easier to shove people off the pavement. And with this goes something that is always written off by European observers as 'decadence' or hypocrisy, the English hatred of war and militarism. It is rooted deep in history, and it is strong in the lower-middle class as well as the working class. Successive wars have shaken it but not destroyed it. Well within living memory it was common for 'the redcoats' to be booed at in the street and for the landlords of respectable public-houses to refuse to allow soldiers on the premises. In peace-time, even when there are two million unemployed, it is difficult to fill the ranks of the tiny standing Army, which is officered by the county gentry and a specialized stratum of the middle class, and manned by farm labourers and slum proletarians. The mass of the people are without military knowledge or tradition, and their attitude towards war is invariably defensive. No politician could rise to power by promising them conquests or military 'glory', no Hymn of Hate has ever made any appeal to them. In the last war the songs which the soldiers made up and sang of their own accord were not vengeful but humorous and mock-defeatist.* The only enemy they ever named was the sergeant-major.

In England all the boasting and flag-wagging, the 'Rule Britannia' stuff, is done by small minorities. The patriotism of the common people is not vocal or even conscious. They do not retain among their historical memories the name of a

---

* For example:

> I don't want to join the bloody Army,
> I don't want to go unto the war;
> I want no more to roam,
> I'd rather stay at home
> Living on the earnings of a whore.

But it was not in that spirit that they fought.

single military victory. English literature, like other literatures, is full of battle-poems, but it is worth noticing that the ones that have won for themselves a kind of popularity are always a tale of disasters and retreats. There is no popular poem about Trafalgar or Waterloo, for instance. Sir John Moore's army at Corunna, fighting a desperate rearguard action before escaping overseas (just like Dunkirk!) has more appeal than a brilliant victory. The most stirring battle-poem in English is about a brigade of cavalry which charged in the wrong direction. And of the last war, the four names which have really engraved themselves on the popular memory are Mons, Ypres, Gallipoli and Passchendaele, every time a disaster. The names of the great battles that finally broke the German armies are simply unknown to the general public.

The reason why the English anti-militarism disgusts foreign observers is that it ignores the existence of the British Empire. It looks like sheer hypocrisy. After all, the English have absorbed a quarter of the earth and held on to it by means of a huge navy. How dare they then turn round and say that war is wicked?

It is quite true that the English are hypocritical about their Empire. In the working class this hypocrisy takes the form of not knowing that the Empire exists. But their dislike of standing armies is a perfectly sound instinct. A navy employs comparatively few people, and it is an external weapon which cannot affect home politics directly. Military dictatorships exist everywhere, but there is no such thing as a naval dictatorship. What English people of nearly all classes loathe from the bottom of their hearts is the swaggering officer type, the jingle of spurs and the crash of boots. Decades before Hitler was ever heard of, the word 'Prussian' had much the same significance in England as 'Nazi' has to-day. So deep does this feeling go that for a hundred years past the officers of the British Army, in peacetime, have always worn civilian clothes when off duty.

One rapid but fairly sure guide to the social atmosphere of a country is the parade-step of its army. A military parade is really a kind of ritual dance, something like a ballet, expressing a certain philosophy of life. The goose-step, for instance, is one of the most horrible sights in the world, far more terrifying than a dive-bomber. It is simply an affirmation of naked power; contained in it, quite consciously and intentionally, is the vision of a boot crashing down on a face. Its ugliness is part of its essence, for what it is saying is 'Yes, I *am* ugly, and you daren't laugh at me', like the bully who makes faces at his victim. Why is the goose-step not used in England? There are, heaven knows, plenty of army officers who would be only too glad to introduce some such thing. It is not used because the people in the street would laugh. Beyond a certain point, military display is only possible in countries where the common people dare not laugh at the army. The Italians adopted the goose-step at about the time when Italy passed definitely under German control, and, as one would expect, they do it less well than the Germans. The Vichy government, if it survives, is bound to introduce a stiffer parade-ground discipline into what is left of the French army. In the British army the drill is rigid and complicated, full of memories of the eighteenth century, but without definite swagger; the march is merely a formalized walk. It belongs to a society which is ruled by the sword, no doubt, but a sword which must never be taken out of the scabbard.

And yet the gentleness of English civilization is mixed up with barbarities and anachronisms. Our criminal law is as out of date as the muskets in the Tower. Over against the Nazi Storm Trooper you have got to set that typically English figure, the hanging judge, some gouty old bully with his mind rooted in the nineteenth century, handing out savage sentences. In England people are still hanged by the neck and flogged with the cat-o'-nine-tails. Both of these punishments are obscene as well as cruel, but there has never been any genuinely popular outcry against them. People accept them (and Dartmoor, and Borstal) almost as they accept the weather. They are part of 'the law', which is assumed to be unalterable.

Here one comes upon an all-important English trait: the respect for constitutionalism and legality, the belief in 'the law' as something above the State and above the individual, something which is cruel and stupid, of course, but at any rate *incorruptible*.

It is not that anyone imagines the law to be just. Everyone knows that there is one law for the rich and another for the poor. But no one accepts the implications of this, everyone takes it for granted that the law, such as it is, will be respected, and feels a sense of outrage when it is not. Remarks like 'They can't run me in; I haven't done anything wrong', or 'They can't do that; it's against the law', are part of the atmosphere of England. The professed enemies of society have this feeling as strongly as anyone else. One sees it in prison-books like Wilfred Macartney's *Walls Have Mouths* or Jim Phelan's *Jail Journey*, in the solemn idiocies that take place at the trials of conscientious objectors, in letters to the papers from eminent Marxist professors, pointing out that this or that is a 'miscarriage of British justice'. Everyone believes in his heart that the law can be, ought to be, and on the whole, will be impartially administered. The totalitarian idea that there is no such thing as law, there is only power, has never taken root. Even the intelligentsia have only accepted it in theory.

An illusion can become a half-truth, a mask can alter the expression of a face. The familiar arguments to the effect that democracy is 'just the same as' or 'just as bad as' totalitarianism never take account of this fact. All such arguments boil down to saying that half a loaf is the same as no bread. In England such concepts as justice, liberty and objective truth are still believed in. They may be illusions, but they are very powerful illusions. The belief in them influences conduct, national life is different because of them. In proof of which, look about you. Where are the rubber truncheons, where is the castor oil? The sword is still in the scabbard, and while it stays there corruption cannot go beyond a certain point. The English electoral system, for instance, is an all-but open fraud. In a dozen obvious ways it is gerrymandered in the interest of the moneyed class. But until some deep change has occurred in the public mind, it cannot become *completely* corrupt. You do not arrive at the polling booth to find men with revolvers telling you which way to vote, nor are the votes miscounted, nor is there any direct bribery. Even hypocrisy is a powerful safeguard. The hanging judge, that evil old man in scarlet robe and horsehair wig, whom nothing short of dynamite will ever teach what century he is living in, but who will at any rate interpret the law according to the books and will in no circumstances take a money bribe, is one of the symbolic figures of England. He is a symbol of the strange mixture of reality and illusion, democracy and privilege, humbug and decency, the subtle network of compromises, by which the nation keeps itself in its familiar shape.

III

I have spoken all the while of 'the nation', 'England', 'Britain', as though 45 million souls could somehow be treated as a unit. But is not England notoriously two nations, the rich and the poor? Dare one pretend that there is anything in common between people with £100,000 a year and people with £1 a week? And even Welsh and Scottish readers are likely to have been offended because I have used the word 'England' oftener than 'Britain', as though the whole population dwelt in London and the Home Counties and neither north nor west possessed a culture of its own.

One gets a better view of this question if one considers the minor point first. It is quite true that the so-called races of Britain feel themselves to be very different from one another. A Scotsman, for instance, does not thank you if you call him an Englishman. You can see the hesitation we feel on this point by the fact that we call our islands by no less than six different names, England, Britain, Great Britain, the British Isles, the United Kingdom and, in very exalted moments, Albion. Even the differences between north and south England loom large in our own eyes. But somehow these differences fade away the moment that any two Britons are confronted by a European. It is very rare to meet a foreigner, other than an American, who can distinguish between English and Scots or even English and Irish. To a Frenchman, the Breton and the Auvergnat seem very different beings, and the accent of Marseilles is a stock joke in Paris. Yet we speak of 'France' and 'the French', recognizing France as an entity, a single civilization, which in fact it is. So also with ourselves. Looked at from the outside, even the Cockney and the Yorkshireman have a strong family resemblance.

And even the distinction between rich and poor dwindles somewhat when one regards the nation from the outside. There is no question about the inequality of wealth in England. It is grosser than in any European country, and you have only to look down the nearest street to see it. Economically, England is certainly two nations, if not three or four. But at the same time the vast majority of the people *feel* themselves to be a single nation and are conscious of resembling one another more than they resemble foreigners. Patriotism is usually stronger than class-hatred, and always stronger than any kind of internationalism. Except for a brief moment in 1920 (the 'Hands off Russia' movement) the British working class have never thought or acted internationally. For two and a half years they watched their comrades in Spain slowly strangled, and never aided them by even a single strike.* But when their own country (the country of Lord Nuffield and Mr Montagu Norman) was in danger, their attitude was very different. At the moment when it seemed likely that England might be invaded, Anthony Eden appealed over the radio for Local Defence Volunteers. He got a quarter of a million men in the first twenty-four hours, and another million in the subsequent month. One has only to compare these figures with, for

* It is true that they aided them to a certain extent with money. Still, the sums raised for the various aid-Spain funds would not equal five per cent of the turnover of the football pools during the same period.

instance, the number of conscientious objectors to see how vast is the strength of traditional loyalties compared with new ones.

In England patriotism takes different forms in different classes, but it runs like a connecting thread through nearly all of them. Only the Europeanized intelligentsia are really immune to it. As a positive emotion it is stronger in the middle class than in the upper class – the cheap public schools, for instance, are more given to patriotic demonstrations than the expensive ones – but the number of definitely treacherous rich men, the Laval-Quisling type, is probably very small. In the working class patriotism is profound, but it is unconscious. The working man's heart does not leap when he sees a Union Jack. But the famous 'insularity' and 'xenophobia' of the English is far stronger in the working class than in the bourgeoisie. In all countries the poor are more national than the rich, but the English working class are outstanding in their abhorrence of foreign habits. Even when they are obliged to live abroad for years they refuse either to accustom themselves to foreign food or to learn foreign languages. Nearly every Englishman of working-class origin considers it effeminate to pronounce a foreign word correctly. During the war of 1914–18 the English working class were in contact with foreigners to an extent that is rarely possible. The sole result was that they brought back a hatred of all Europeans, except the Germans, whose courage they admired. In four years on French soil they did not even acquire a liking for wine. The insularity of the English, their refusal to take foreigners seriously, is a folly that has to be paid for very heavily from from time to time. But it plays its part in the English *mystique*, and the intellectuals who have tried to break it down have generally done more harm than good. At bottom it is the same quality in the English character that repels the tourist and keeps out the invader.

Here one comes back to two English characteristics that I pointed out, seemingly rather at random, at the beginning of the last chapter. One is the lack of artistic ability.

This is perhaps another way of saying that the English are outside the European culture. For there is one art in which they have shown plenty of talent, namely literature. But this is also the only art that cannot cross frontiers. Literature, especially poetry, and lyric poetry most of all, is a kind of family joke, with little or no value outside its own language-group. Except for Shakespeare, the best English poets are barely known in Europe, even as names. The only poets who are widely read are Byron, who is admired for the wrong reasons, and Oscar Wilde, who is pitied as a victim of English hypocrisy. And linked up with this, though not very obviously, is the lack of philosophical faculty, the absence in nearly all Englishmen of any need for an ordered system of thought or even for the use of logic.

Up to a point, the sense of national unity is a substitute for a 'world-view'. Just because patriotism is all but universal and not even the rich are uninfluenced by it, there can come moments when the whole nation suddenly swings together and does the same thing, like a herd of cattle facing a wolf. There was such a moment unmistakably, at the time of the disaster in France. After eight months of vaguely wondering what the war was about, the people suddenly knew what they had got to do: first, to get the army away from Dunkirk, and secondly to prevent invasion. It was like the awakening of a giant. Quick! Danger! The Philistines be upon thee, Samson! And then the swift unanimous action – and then, alas, the prompt relapse into sleep. In a divided nation that would have been exactly the moment for a big peace movement to arise. But does this mean that the instinct of the English will always tell them to do the right thing? Not at all; merely that it will tell them to do the same thing. In the 1931 General Election, for instance, we all did the wrong thing in perfect unison. We were as single-minded as the Gadarene swine. But I honestly doubt whether we can say that we were shoved down the slope against our will.

It follows that British democracy is less of a fraud than

it sometimes appears. A foreign observer sees only the huge
inequality of wealth, the unfair electoral system, the
governing-class control over the press, the radio and
education, and concludes that democracy is simply a
polite name for dictatorship. But this ignores the considerable agreement that does unfortunately exist between the
leaders and the led. However much one may hate to admit
it, it is almost certain that between 1931 and 1940 the
National Government represented the will of the mass of
the people. It tolerated slums, unemployment and a
cowardly foreign policy. Yes, but so did public opinion. It
was a stagnant period, and its natural leaders were medio-
crities.

In spite of the campaigns of a few thousand left-wingers,
it is fairly certain that the bulk of the English people were
behind Chamberlain's foreign policy. More, it is fairly certain that the same struggle was going on in Chamberlain's
mind as in the minds of ordinary people. His opponents
professed to see in him a dark and wily schemer, plotting
to sell England to Hitler, but it is far likelier that he was
merely a stupid old man doing his best according to his
very dim lights. It is difficult otherwise to explain the
contradictions of his policy, his failure to grasp any of the
courses that were open to him. Like the mass of the people,
he did not want to pay the price either of peace or of war.
And public opinion was behind him all the while, in policies
that were completely incompatible with one another. It
was behind him when he went to Munich, when he tried
to come to an understanding with Russia, when he gave
the guarantee to Poland, when he honoured it, and when
he prosecuted the war half-heartedly. Only when the
results of his policy became apparent did it turn against
him; which is to say that it turned against its own lethargy
of the past seven years. Thereupon the people picked a
leader nearer to their mood, Churchill, who was at any
rate able to grasp that wars are not won without fighting.
Later, perhaps, they will pick another leader who can
grasp that only Socialist nations can fight effectively.

Do I mean by all this that England is a genuine democracy? No, not even a reader of the *Daily Telegraph* could quite swallow that.

England is the most class-ridden country under the sun. It is a land of snobbery and privilege, ruled largely by the old and silly. But in any calculation about it one has got to take into account its emotional unity, the tendency of nearly all its inhabitants to feel alike and act together in moments of supreme crisis. It is the only great country in Europe that is not obliged to drive hundreds of thousands of its nationals into exile or the concentration camp. At this moment, after a year of war, newspapers and pamphlets abusing the Government, praising the enemy and clamouring for surrender are being sold on the streets, almost without interference. And this is less from a respect for freedom of speech than from a simple perception that these things don't matter. It is safe to let a paper like *Peace News* be sold, because it is certain that 95 per cent of the population will never want to read it. The nation is bound together by an invisible chain. At any normal time the ruling class will rob, mismanage, sabotage, lead us into the muck; but let popular opinion really make itself heard, let them get a tug from below that they cannot avoid feeling, and it is difficult for them not to respond. The left-wing writers who denounce the whole of the ruling class as 'pro-Fascist' are grossly over-simplifying. Even among the inner clique of politicians who brought us to our present pass, it is doubtful whether there were any *conscious* traitors. The corruption that happens in England is seldom of that kind. Nearly always it is more in the nature of self-deception, of the right hand not knowing what the left hand doeth. And being unconscious, it is limited. One sees this at its most obvious in the English press. Is the English press honest or dishonest? At normal times it is deeply dishonest. All the papers that matter live off their advertisements, and the advertisers exercise an indirect censorship over news. Yet I do not suppose there is one paper in England that can be straightforwardly bribed with hard cash. In the France of the Third Republic all but a very few of the newspapers could notoriously be bought over the counter like so many pounds of cheese. Public life in England has never been *openly* scandalous. It has not reached the pitch of disintegration at which humbug can be dropped.

England is not the jewelled isle of Shakespeare's much-quoted passage, nor is it the inferno depicted by Dr Goebbels. More than either it resembles a family, a rather stuffy Victorian family, with not many black sheep in it but with all its cupboards bursting with skeletons. It has rich relations who have to be kowtowed to and poor relations who are horribly sat upon, and there is a deep conspiracy of silence about the source of the family income. It is a family in which the young are generally thwarted and most of the power is in the hands of irresponsible uncles and bedridden aunts. Still, it is a family. It has its private language and its common memories, and at the approach of an enemy it closes its ranks. A family with the wrong members in control – that, perhaps, is as near as one can come to describing England in a phrase.

IV

Probably the Battle of Waterloo *was* won on the playing-fields of Eton, but the opening battles of all subsequent wars have been lost there. One of the dominant facts in English life during the past three-quarters of a century has been the decay of ability in the ruling class.

In the years between 1920 and 1940 it was happening with the speed of a chemical reaction. Yet at the moment of writing it is still possible to speak of a ruling class. Like the knife which has had two new blades and three new handles, the upper fringe of English society is still almost what it was in the mid nineteenth century. After 1832 the old landowning aristocracy steadily lost power, but instead of disappearing or becoming a fossil they simply intermarried with the merchants, manufacturers and financiers who had replaced them, and soon turned them into accurate copies of themselves. The wealthy ship-owner or cotton-miller set up for himself an alibi as a country gentleman, while his sons learned the right mannerisms at public schools which had been designed for just that purpose. England was ruled by an aristocracy constantly recruited from parvenus. And considering what energy the self-made men possessed, and considering that they were buying their way into a class which at any rate had a tradition of public service, one might have expected that able rulers could be produced in some such way.

And yet somehow the ruling class decayed, lost its ability, its daring, finally even its ruthlessness, until a time came when stuffed shirts like Eden or Halifax could stand out as men of exceptional talent. As for Baldwin, one could not even dignify him with the name of stuffed shirt. He was simply a hole in the air. The mishandling of England's domestic problems during the nineteen-twenties had been bad enough, but British foreign policy between 1931 and 1939 is one of the wonders of the world. Why? What had happened? What was it that at every decisive moment made every British statesman do the wrong thing with so unerring an instinct?

The underlying fact was that the whole position of the moneyed class had long ceased to be justifiable. There they sat, at the centre of a vast empire and a world-wide financial network, drawing interest and profits and spending them – on what? It was fair to say that life within the British Empire was in many ways better than life outside it. Still, the Empire was undeveloped, India slept in the Middle Ages, the Dominions lay empty, with foreigners jealously barred out, and even England was full of slums and un-employment. Only half a million people, the people in the country houses, definitely benefited from the existing system. Moreover, the tendency of small businesses to merge together into large ones robbed more and more of the moneyed class of their function and turned them into mere *owners*, their work being done for them by salaried managers and technicians. For long past there had been in England an entirely functionless class, living on money that was invested they hardly knew where, the 'idle rich', the people whose photographs you can look at in the *Tatler* and the *Bystander*, always supposing that you want to. The existence of these people was by any standard unjustifiable. They were simply parasites, less useful to society than his fleas are to a dog.

By 1920 there were many people who were aware of all this. By 1930 millions were aware of it. But the British ruling class obviously could not admit to themselves that their usefulness was at an end. Had they done that they would have had to abdicate. For it was not possible for them to turn themselves into mere bandits, like the American millionaires, consciously clinging to unjust privileges and beating down opposition by bribery and tear-gas bombs. After all, they belonged to a class with a certain tradition, they had been to public schools where the duty of dying for your country, if necessary, is laid down as the first and greatest of the Commandments. They had to *feel* themselves true patriots, even while they plundered their countrymen. Clearly there was only one escape for them – into stupidity. They could keep society in its existing shape only by being *unable* to grasp that any improvement was possible. Difficult though this was, they achieved it, largely by fixing their eyes on the past and refusing to notice the changes that were going on round them.

There is much in England that this explains. It explains the decay of country life, due to the keeping-up of a sham feudalism which drives the more spirited workers off the land. It explains the immobility of the public schools, which have barely altered since the eighties of the last century. It explains the military incompetence which has again and again startled the world. Since the fifties every war in which England has engaged has started off with a series of disasters, after which the situation has been saved by people comparatively low in the social scale. The higher commanders, drawn from the aristocracy, could never prepare for modern war, because in order to do so they would have had to admit to themselves that the world was changing. They have always clung to obsolete methods and weapons, because they inevitably saw each war as a repetition of the last. Before the Boer War they prepared for the Zulu War, before 1914 for the Boer War, and before the present war for 1914. Even at this moment hundreds of thousands of men in England are being trained with the bayonet, a weapon entirely useless except for opening tins. It is worth noticing that the Navy and, latterly, the Air Force, have always been more efficient than the regular Army. But the Navy is only partially, and the Air Force hardly at all, within the ruling-class orbit.

It must be admitted that so long as things were peaceful the methods of the British ruling class served them well enough. Their own people manifestly tolerated them. However unjustly England might be organized, it was at any rate not torn by class warfare or haunted by secret police. The Empire was peaceful as no area of comparable size has ever been. Throughout its vast extent, nearly a quarter of the earth, there were fewer armed men than would be found necessary by a minor Balkan State. As people to live under, and looking at them merely from a liberal, *negative* standpoint, the British ruling class had their points. They were preferable to the truly modern men, the Nazis and Fascists. But it had long been obvious that they would be helpless against any serious attack from the outside.

They could not struggle against Nazism or Fascism, because they could not understand them. Neither could they have struggled against Communism, if Communism had been a serious force in western Europe. To understand Fascism they would have had to study the theory of Socialism, which would have forced them to realize that the economic system by which they lived was unjust, inefficient and out of date. But it was exactly this fact that they had trained themselves never to face. They dealt with Fascism as the cavalry generals of 1914 dealt with the machine gun – by ignoring it. After years of aggression and massacres, they had grasped only one fact, that Hitler and Mussolini were hostile to Communism. Therefore, it was argued, they *must* be friendly to the British dividend-drawer. Hence the truly frightening spectacle of Conservative M.Ps. wildly cheering the news that British ships, bringing food to the Spanish Republican government, had been bombed by Italian aeroplanes. Even when they had begun to grasp that Fascism was dangerous, its essentially revolutionary nature, the huge military effort it was capable of making, the sort of tactics it would use, were quite beyond their comprehension. At the time of the Spanish civil war, anyone with as much political knowledge as can be acquired from a sixpenny pamphlet on Socialism knew that if Franco won, the result would be strategically disastrous for England; and yet generals and admirals who had given their lives to the study of war were unable to grasp this fact. This vein of political ignorance runs right through English official life, through Cabinet ministers, ambassadors, consuls, judges, magistrates, policemen. The policeman who arrests the 'Red' does not understand the theories the 'Red' is preaching; if he did, his own position as bodyguard of the moneyed class might seem less pleasant to him. There is reason to think that even military espionage is hopelessly hampered by ignorance of the new economic doctrines and the ramifications of the underground parties.

The British ruling class were not altogether wrong in thinking that Fascism was on their side. It is a fact that any rich man, unless he is a Jew, has less to fear from Fascism than from either Communism or democratic Socialism. One ought never to forget this, for nearly the whole of German and Italian propaganda is designed to cover it up. The natural instinct of men like Simon, Hoare, Chamberlain, etc., was to come to an agreement with Hitler. But – and here the peculiar feature of English life that I have spoken of, the deep sense of national solidarity, comes in – they could only do so by breaking up the Empire and selling their own people into semi-slavery. A truly corrupt class would have done this without hesitation, as in France. But things had not gone that distance in

England. Politicians who would make cringing speeches about 'the duty of loyalty to our conquerors' are hardly to be found in English public life. Tossed to and fro between their incomes and their principles, it was impossible that men like Chamberlain should do anything but make the worst of both worlds.

One thing that has always shown that the English ruling class are *morally* fairly sound, is that in time of war they are ready enough to get themselves killed. Several dukes, earls and what-not were killed in the recent campaign in Flanders. That could not happen if these people were the cynical scoundrels that they are sometimes declared to be. It is important not to misunderstand their motives, or one cannot predict their actions. What is to be expected of them is not treachery or physical cowardice, but stupidity, unconscious sabotage, an infallible instinct for doing the wrong thing. They are not wicked, or not altogether wicked; they are merely unteachable. Only when their money and power are gone will the younger among them begin to grasp what century they are living in.

V

The stagnation of the Empire in the between-war years affected everyone in England, but it had an especially direct effect upon two important sub-sections of the middle class. One was the military and imperialist middle class, generally nicknamed the Blimps, and the other the left-wing intelligentsia. These two seemingly hostile types, symbolic opposites – the half-pay colonel with his bull neck and diminutive brain, like a dinosaur, the highbrow with his domed forehead and stalk-like neck – are mentally linked together and constantly interact upon one another; in any case they are born to a considerable extent into the same families.

Thirty years ago the Blimp class was already losing its vitality. The middle-class families celebrated by Kipling, the prolific lowbrow families whose sons officered the Army and Navy and swarmed over all the waste places of the earth from the Yukon to the Irrawaddy, were dwindling before 1914. The thing that had killed them was the telegraph. In a narrowing world, more and more governed from Whitehall, there was every year less room for individual initiative. Men like Clive, Nelson, Nicholson, Gordon would find no place for themselves in the modern British Empire. By 1920 nearly every inch of the colonial empire was in the grip of Whitehall. Well-meaning, over-civilized men, in dark suits and black felt hats, with neatly-rolled umbrellas crooked over the left forearm, were imposing their constipated view of life on Malaya and Nigeria, Mombasa and Mandalay. The one-time empire-builders were reduced to the status of clerks, buried deeper and deeper under mounds of paper and red tape. In the early twenties one could see, all over the Empire, the older officials, who had known more spacious days, writhing impotently under the changes that were happening. From that time onwards it has been next door to impossible to induce young men of spirit to take any part in imperial administration. And what was true of the official world was true also of the commercial. The great monopoly companies swallowed up hosts of petty traders. Instead of going out to trade adventurously in the Indies, one went to an office stool in Bombay or Singapore. And life in Bombay or Singapore was actually duller and safer than life in London. Imperialist sentiment remained strong in the middle class, chiefly owing to family tradition, but the job of administering the Empire had ceased to appeal. Few able men went east of Suez if there was any way of avoiding it.

But the general weakening of imperialism, and to some extent of the whole British morale, that took place during the nineteen-thirties, was partly the work of the left-wing intelligentsia, itself a kind of growth that had sprouted from the stagnation of the Empire.

It should be noted that there is now no intelligentsia that is not in some sense 'Left'. Perhaps the last right-wing intellectual was T. E. Lawrence. Since about 1930 everyone describable as an 'intellectual' has lived in a state of chronic discontent with the existing order. Necessarily so, because society as it was constituted had no room for him. In an Empire that was simply stagnant, neither being developed nor falling to pieces, and in an England ruled by people whose chief asset was their stupidity, to be 'clever' was to be suspect. If you had the kind of brain that could understand the poems of T. S. Eliot or the theories of Karl Marx, the higher-ups would see to it that you were kept out of any important job. The intellectuals could find a function for themselves only in the literary reviews and the left-wing political parties.

The mentality of the English left-wing intelligentsia can be studied in half a dozen weekly and monthly papers. The immediately striking thing about all these papers is their generally negative, querulous attitude, their complete lack at all times of any constructive suggestion. There is little in them except the irresponsible carping of people who have never been and never expect to be in a position of power. Another marked characteristic is the emotional shallowness of people who live in a world of ideas and have little contact with physical reality. Many intellectuals of the Left were flabbily pacifist up to 1935, shrieked for war against Germany in the years 1935–9, and then promptly cooled off when the war started. It is broadly though not precisely true that the people who were most 'Anti-Fascist' during the Spanish civil war are most defeatist now. And underlying this is the really important fact about so many of the English intelligentsia – their severance from the common culture of the country.

In intention, at any rate, the English intelligentsia are Europeanized. They take their cookery from Paris and their opinions from Moscow. In the general patriotism of the country they form a sort of island of dissident thought. England is perhaps the only great country whose intellectuals are ashamed of their own nationality. In left-wing circles it is always felt that there is something slightly disgraceful in being an Englishman and that it is a duty to snigger at every English institution, from horse-racing to suet puddings. It is a strange fact, but it is unquestionably true, that almost any English intellectual would feel more ashamed of standing to attention during 'God save the King' than of stealing from a poor-box. All through the critical years many left-wingers were chipping away at English morale, trying to spread an outlook that was sometimes squashily pacifist, sometimes violently pro-Russian, but always anti-British. It is questionable how much effect this had, but it certainly had some. If the English people suffered for several years a real weakening of morale, so that the Fascist nations judged that they were 'decadent' and that it was safe to plunge into war, the intellectual sabotage from the Left was partly responsible. Both the *New Statesman* and the *News Chronicle* cried out against the Munich settlement, but even they had done something to make it possible. Ten years of systematic Blimp-baiting affected even the Blimps themselves and made it harder than it had been before to get intelligent young men to enter the armed forces. Given the stagnation of the Empire the military middle class must have decayed in any case, but the spread of a shallow Leftism hastened the process.

It is clear that the special position of the English intellectuals during the past ten years, as purely *negative* creatures, mere anti-Blimps, was a by-product of ruling-class stupidity. Society could not use them, and they had not got it in them to see that devotion to one's country implies 'for better, for worse'. Both Blimps and highbrows took for granted, as though it were a law of nature, the divorce between patriotism and intelligence. If you were a patriot you read *Blackwood's Magazine* and publicly thanked God that you were 'not brainy'. If you were an intellectual you sniggered at the Union Jack and regarded physical courage as barbarous. It is obvious that this preposterous convention cannot continue. The Bloomsbury highbrow, with his mechanical snigger, is as out of date as the cavalry colonel. A modern nation cannot afford either of them. Patriotism and intelligence will have to come together again. It is the fact that we are fighting a war, and a very peculiar kind of war, that may make this possible.

VI

One of the most important developments in England during the past twenty years has been the upward and downward extension of the middle class. It has happened on such a scale as to make the old classification of society into capitalists, proletarians and petit-bourgeois (small property-owners) almost obsolete.

England is a country in which property and financial power are concentrated in very few hands. Few people in modern England *own* anything at all, except clothes, furniture and possibly a house. The peasantry have long since disappeared, the independent shopkeeper is being destroyed, the small business-man is diminishing in numbers. But at the same time modern industry is so complicated that it cannot get along without great numbers of managers, salesmen, engineers, chemists and technicians of all kinds, drawing fairly large salaries. And these in turn call into being a professional class of doctors, lawyers, teachers, artists, etc., etc. The tendency of advanced capitalism has therefore been to enlarge the middle class and not to wipe it out, as it once seemed likely to do.

But much more important than this is the spread of middle-class ideas and habits among the working-class. The British working class are now better off in almost all ways than they were thirty years ago. This is partly due to the efforts of the trade unions, but partly to the mere advance of physical science. It is not always realized that within rather narrow limits the standard of life of a country can rise without a corresponding rise in real wages. Up to a point civilization can lift itself up by its boot-tags. However unjustly society is organized, certain technical advances are bound to benefit the whole community, because certain kinds of goods are necessarily held in common. A millionaire cannot, for example, light the streets for himself while darkening them for other people. Nearly all citizens of civilized countries now enjoy the use of good roads, germ-free water, police protection, free libraries and probably free education of a kind. Public education in England has been meanly starved of money, but it has nevertheless improved, largely owing to the devoted efforts of the teachers, and the habit of reading has become enormously more widespread. To an increasing extent the rich and the poor read the same books, and they also see the same films and listen to the same radio programmes. And the differences in their way of life have been diminished by the mass production of cheap clothes and improvements in housing. So far as outward appearance goes, the clothes of rich and poor, especially in the case of women, differ far less than they did thirty or even fifteen years ago. As to housing, England still has slums which are a blot on civilization, but much building has been done during the past ten years, largely by the local authorities. The modern council house, with its bathroom and electric light, is smaller than the stockbroker's villa, but it is recognizably the same kind of house, which the farm labourer's cottage is not. A person who has grown up in a council housing estate is likely to be – indeed, visibly *is* – more middle class in outlook than a person who has grown up in a slum.

The effect of all this is a general softening of manners. It is enhanced by the fact that modern industrial methods tend always to demand less muscular effort and therefore to leave people with more energy when their day's work is done. Many workers in the light industries are less truly manual labourers than is a doctor or a grocer. In tastes, habits, manners and outlook the working class and the middle class are drawing together. The unjust distinctions remain, but the real differences diminish. The old-style 'proletarian' – collarless, unshaven and with muscles warped by heavy labour – still exists, but he is constantly decreasing in numbers; he only predominates in the heavy-industry areas of the north of England.

After 1918 there began to appear something that had
never existed in England before: people of indeterminate
social class. In 1910 every human being in these islands
could be 'placed' in an instant by his clothes, manners and
accent. That is no longer the case. Above all, it is not the
case in the new townships that have developed as a result
of cheap motor cars and the southward shift of industry.
The place to look for the germs of the future England is in
the light-industry areas and along the arterial roads. In
Slough, Dagenham, Barnet, Letchworth, Hayes – everywhere, indeed, on the outskirts of great towns – the old
pattern is gradually changing into something new. In those
vast new wildernesses of glass and brick the sharp distinctions of the older kind of town, with its slums and mansions,
or of the country, with its manor houses and squalid cot-
tages, no longer exist. There are wide gradations of income
but it is the same kind of life that is being lived at different
levels, in labour-saving flats or council houses, along the
concrete roads and in the naked democracy of the swim-
ming-pools. It is a rather restless, cultureless life, centring
round tinned food, *Picture Post*, the radio and the internal
combustion engine. It is a civilization in which children
grow up with an intimate knowledge of magnetoes and in
complete ignorance of the Bible. To that civilization belong
the people who are most at home in and most definitely *of*
the modern world, the technicians and the higher-paid
skilled workers, the airmen and their mechanics, the radio
experts, film producers, popular journalists and industrial
chemists. They are the indeterminate stratum at which the
older class distinctions are beginning to break down.

This war, unless we are defeated, will wipe out most of
the existing class privileges. There are every day fewer
people who wish them to continue. Nor need we fear that
as the pattern changes life in England will lose its peculiar
flavour. The new red cities of Greater London are crude
enough, but these things are only the rash that accompanies
a change. In whatever shape England emerges from the
war, it will be deeply tinged with the characteristics that I

have spoken of earlier. The intellectuals who hope to see it Russianized or Germanized will be disappointed. The gentleness, the hypocrisy, the thoughtlessness, the reverence for law and the hatred of uniforms will remain, along with the suet puddings and the misty skies. It needs some very great disaster, such as prolonged subjugation by a foreign enemy, to destroy a national culture. The Stock Exchange will be pulled down, the horse plough will give way to the tractor, the country houses will be turned into children's holiday camps, the Eton and Harrow match will be forgotten, but England will still be England, an everlasting animal stretching into the future and the past, and like all living things, having the power to change out of recognition and yet remain the same.

1941

SHOOTING AN ELEPHANT

In Moulmein, in Lower Burma, I was hated by large numbers of people – the only time in my life that I have been important enough for this to happen to me. I was sub-divisional police officer of the town, and in an aimless, petty kind of way anti-European feeling was very bitter. No one had the guts to raise a riot, but if a European woman went through the bazaars alone somebody would probably spit betel juice over her dress. As a police officer I was an obvious target and was baited whenever it seemed safe to do so. When a nimble Burman tripped me up on the football field and the referee (another Burman) looked the other way, the crowd yelled with hideous laughter. This happened more than once. In the end the sneering yellow faces of young men that met me everywhere, the insults hooted after me when I was at a safe distance, got badly on my nerves. The young Buddhist priests were the worst of all. There were several thousands of them in the town and none of them seemed to have anything to do except stand on street corners and jeer at Europeans.

All this was perplexing and upsetting. For at that time I had already made up my mind that imperialism was an evil thing and the sooner I chucked up my job and got out of it the better. Theoretically – and secretly, of course – I was all for the Burmese and all against their oppressors, the British. As for the job I was doing, I hated it more bitterly than I can perhaps make clear. In a job like that you see the dirty work of Empire at close quarters. The wretched prisoners huddling in the stinking cages of the lock-ups, the grey, cowed faces of the long-term convicts, the scarred buttocks of the men who had been flogged with bamboos – all these oppressed me with an intolerable sense

91

of guilt. But I could get nothing into perspective. I was young and ill-educated and I had had to think out my problems in the utter silence that is imposed on every Englishman in the East. I did not even know that the British Empire is dying, still less did I know that it is a great deal better than the younger empires that are going to supplant it. All I knew was that I was stuck between my hatred of the empire I served and my rage against the evil-spirited little beasts who tried to make my job impossible. With one part of my mind I thought of the British Raj as an unbreakable tyranny, as something clamped down, in *saecula saeculorum*, upon the will of prostrate peoples; with another part I thought that the greatest joy in the world would be to drive a bayonet into a Buddhist priest's guts. Feelings like these are the normal by-products of imperialism; ask any Anglo-Indian official, if you can catch him off duty.

One day something happened which in a roundabout way was enlightening. It was a tiny incident in itself, but it gave me a better glimpse than I had had before of the real nature of imperialism – the real motives for which despotic governments act. Early one morning the sub-inspector at a police station the other end of the town rang me up on the phone and said that an elephant was ravaging the bazaar. Would I please come and do something about it? I did not know what I could do, but I wanted to see what was happening and I got on to a pony and started out. I took my rifle, an old .44 Winchester and much too small to kill an elephant, but I thought the noise might be useful *in terrorem*. Various Burmans stopped me on the way and told me about the elephant's doings. It was not, of course, a wild elephant, but a tame one which had gone 'must'. It had been chained up, as tame elephants always are when their attack of 'must' is due, but on the previous night it had broken its chain and escaped. Its mahout, the only person who could manage it when it was in that state, had set out in pursuit, but had taken the wrong direction and was now twelve hours' journey away, and in the morning the elephant had suddenly reappeared in the town.

The Burmese population had no weapons and were quite helpless against it. It had already destroyed somebody's bamboo hut, killed a cow and raided some fruit-stalls and devoured the stock; also it had met the municipal rubbish van, and, when the driver jumped out and took to his heels, had turned the van over and inflicted violences upon it.

The Burmese sub-inspector and some Indian constables were waiting for me in the quarter where the elephant had been seen. It was a very poor quarter, a labyrinth of squalid bamboo huts, thatched with palm-leaf, winding all over a steep hillside. I remember that it was a cloudy, stuffy morning at the beginning of the rains. We began questioning the people as to where the elephant had gone, and, as usual, failed to get any definite information. That is invariably the case in the East; a story always sounds clear enough at a distance, but the nearer you get to the scene of events the vaguer it becomes. Some of the people said that the elephant had gone in one direction, some said that he had gone in another, some professed not even to have heard of any elephant. I had almost made up my mind that the whole story was a pack of lies, when we heard yells a little distance away. There was a loud, scandalized cry of 'Go away, child! Go away this instant!' and an old woman with a switch in her hand came round the corner of a hut, violently shooing away a crowd of naked children. Some more women followed, clicking their tongues and exclaiming; evidently there was something that the children ought not to have seen. I rounded the hut and saw a man's dead body sprawling in the mud. He was an Indian, a black Dravidian coolie, almost naked, and he could not have been dead many minutes. The people said that the elephant had come suddenly upon him round the corner of the hut, caught him with its trunk, put its foot on his back and ground him into the earth. This was the rainy season and the ground was soft, and his face had scored a trench a foot deep and a couple of yards long. He was lying on his belly with arms crucified and head sharply twisted to one side. His face was coated with mud, the eyes wide open, the teeth bared and grinning with an expression of unendurable agony. (Never tell me, by the way, that the dead look peaceful. Most of the corpses I have seen looked devilish.) The friction of the great beast's foot had stripped the skin from his back as neatly as one skins a rabbit. As soon as I saw the dead man I sent an orderly to a friend's house nearby to borrow an elephant rifle. I had already sent back the pony, not wanting it to go mad with fright and throw me if it smelt the elephant.

The orderly came back in a few minutes with a rifle and five cartridges, and meanwhile some Burmans had arrived and told us that the elephant was in the paddy fields below, only a few hundred yards away. As I started forward practically the whole population of the quarter flocked out of the houses and followed me. They had seen the rifle and were all shouting excitedly that I was going to shoot the elephant. They had not shown much interest in the elephant when he was merely ravaging their homes, but it was different now that he was going to be shot. It was a bit of fun to them, as it would be to an English crowd; besides they wanted the meat. It made me vaguely uneasy. I had no intention of shooting the elephant – I had merely sent for the rifle to defend myself if necessary – and it is always unnerving to have a crowd following you. I marched down the hill, looking and feeling a fool, with the rifle over my shoulder and an ever-growing army of people jostling at my heels. At the bottom, when you got away from the huts, there was a metalled road and beyond that a miry waste of paddy fields a thousand yards across, not yet ploughed but soggy from the first rains and dotted with coarse grass. The elephant was standing eight yards from the road, his left side towards us. He took not the slightest notice of the crowd's approach. He was tearing up bunches of grass, beating them against his knees to clean them and stuffing them into his mouth.

I had halted on the road. As soon as I saw the elephant I knew with perfect certainty that I ought not to shoot him. It is a serious matter to shoot a working elephant – it is comparable to destroying a huge and costly piece of machinery – and obviously one ought not to do it if it can possibly be avoided. And at that distance, peacefully eating, the elephant looked no more dangerous than a cow. I thought then and I think now that his attack of 'must' was already passing off; in which case he would merely wander harmlessly about until the mahout came back and caught him. Moreover, I did not in the least want to shoot him. I decided that I would watch him for a little while to make sure that he did not turn savage again, and then go home.

But at that moment I glanced round at the crowd that had followed me. It was an immense crowd, two thousand at the least and growing every minute. It blocked the road for a long distance on either side. I looked at the sea of yellow faces above the garish clothes – faces all happy and excited over this bit of fun, all certain that the elephant was going to be shot. They were watching me as they would watch a conjurer about to perform a trick. They did not like me, but with the magical rifle in my hands I was momentarily worth watching. And suddenly I realized that I should have to shoot the elephant after all. The people expected it of me and I had got to do it; I could feel their two thousand wills pressing me forward, irresistibly. And it was at this moment, as I stood there with the rifle in my hands, that I first grasped the hollowness, the futility of the white man's dominion in the East. Here was I, the white man with his gun, standing in front of the unarmed native crowd – seemingly the leading actor of the piece; but in reality I was only an absurd puppet pushed to and fro by the will of those yellow faces behind. I perceived in this moment that when the white man turns tyrant it is his own freedom that he destroys. He becomes a sort of hollow, posing dummy, the conventionalized figure of a sahib. For it is the condition of his rule that he shall spend his life in trying to impress the 'natives', and so in every crisis he has got to do what the 'natives' expect of him. He wears a mask, and his face grows to fit it. I had got to shoot the elephant. I had committed myself to doing it when I sent for the rifle.

A sahib has got to act like a sahib; he has got to appear resolute, to know his own mind and do definite things. To come all that way, rifle in hand, with two thousand people marching at my heels, and then to trail feebly away, having done nothing – no, that was impossible. The crowd would laugh at me. And my whole life, every white man's life in the East, was one long struggle not to be laughed at.

But I did not want to shoot the elephant. I watched him beating his bunch of grass against his knees, with that pre-occupied grandmotherly air that elephants have. It seemed to me that it would be murder to shoot him. At that age I was not squeamish about killing animals, but I had never shot an elephant and never wanted to. (Somehow it always seems worse to kill a *large* animal.) Besides, there was the beast's owner to be considered. Alive, the elephant was worth at least a hundred pounds; dead, he would only be worth the value of his tusks, five pounds, possibly. But I had got to act quickly. I turned to some experienced-looking Burmans who had been there when we arrived, and asked them how the elephant had been behaving. They all said the same thing: he took no notice of you if you left him alone, but he might charge if you went too close to him.

It was perfectly clear to me what I ought to do. I ought to walk up to within, say, twenty-five yards of the elephant and test his behaviour. If he charged I could shoot, if he took no notice of me it would be safe to leave him until the mahout came back. But also I knew that I was going to do no such thing. I was a poor shot with a rifle and the ground was soft mud into which one would sink at every step. If the elephant charged and I missed him, I should have about as much chance as a toad under a steam-roller. But even then I was not thinking particularly of my own skin, only of the watchful yellow faces behind. For at that moment, with the crowd watching me, I was not afraid in the ordinary sense, as I would have been if I had been alone. A white man mustn't be frightened in front of 'natives'; and so, in general, he isn't frightened. The sole thought in my mind was that if anything went wrong those two thousand Burmans would see me pursued, caught, trampled on and reduced to a grinning corpse like that Indian up the hill. And if that happened it was quite probable that some of them would laugh. That would never do. There was only one alternative. I shoved the cartridges into the magazine and lay down on the road to get a better aim.

The crowd grew very still, and a deep, low, happy sigh, as of people who see the theatre curtain go up at last, breathed from innumerable throats. They were going to have their bit of fun after all. The rifle was a beautiful German thing with cross-hair sights. I did not then know that in shooting an elephant one should shoot to cut an imaginary bar running from ear-hole to ear-hole. I ought, therefore, as the elephant was sideways on, to have aimed straight at his ear-hole; actually I aimed several inches in front of this, thinking the brain would be further forward.

When I pulled the trigger I did not hear the bang or feel the kick – one never does when a shot goes home – but I heard the devilish roar of glee that went up from the crowd. In that instant, in too short a time, one would have thought, even for the bullet to get there, a mysterious, terrible change had come over the elephant. He neither stirred nor fell, but every line of his body had altered. He looked suddenly stricken, shrunken, immensely old, as though the frightful impact of the bullet had paralysed him without knocking him down. At last, after what seemed a long time – it might have been five seconds, I dare say – he sagged flabbily to his knees. His mouth slobbered. An enormous senility seemed to have settled upon him. One could have imagined him thousands of years old. I fired again into the same spot. At the second shot he did not collapse but climbed with desperate slowness to his feet and stood weakly upright, with legs sagging and head drooping. I fired a third time. That was the shot that did for him. You could see the agony of it jolt his whole body and knock the last remnant of strength from his legs. But in falling he seemed for a moment to rise, for as his hind legs collapsed beneath him he seemed to tower upwards like a huge rock toppling, his trunk reaching skywards like a tree. He trumpeted, for the first and only time. And then down he came, his belly towards me, with a crash that seemed to shake the ground even where I lay.

I got up. The Burmans were already racing past me across the mud. It was obvious that the elephant would never rise again, but he was not dead. He was breathing very rhythmically with long rattling gasps, his great mound of a side painfully rising and falling. His mouth was wide open – I could see far down into caverns of pale pink throat. I waited a long time for him to die, but his breathing did not weaken. Finally I fired my two remaining shots into the spot where I thought his heart must be. The thick blood welled out of him like red velvet, but still he did not die. His body did not even jerk when the shots hit him, the tortured breathing continued without a pause. He was dying, very slowly and in great agony, but in some world remote from me where not even a bullet could damage him further. I felt that I had got to put an end to that dreadful noise. It seemed dreadful to see the great beast lying there, powerless to move and yet powerless to die, and not even to be able to finish him. I sent back for my small rifle and poured shot after shot into his heart and down his throat. They seemed to make no impression. The tortured gasps continued as steadily as the ticking of a clock.

In the end I could not stand it any longer and went away. I heard later that it took him half an hour to die. Burmans were bringing dahs and baskets even before I left, and I was told they had stripped his body almost to the bones by the afternoon.

Afterwards, of course, there were endless discussions about the shooting of the elephant. The owner was furious, but he was only an Indian and could do nothing. Besides, legally I had done the right thing, for a mad elephant has to be killed, like a mad dog, if its owner fails to control it. Among the Europeans opinion was divided. The older men said I was right, the younger men said it was a damn shame to shoot an elephant for killing a coolie, because an

elephant was worth more than any damn Coringhee coolie.
And afterwards I was very glad that the coolie had been
killed; it put me legally in the right and it gave me a sufficient pretext for shooting the elephant. I often wondered
whether any of the others grasped that I had done it solely
to avoid looking a fool.

1936

LEAR, TOLSTOY AND THE FOOL

TOLSTOY'S pamphlets are the least-known part of his work, and his attack on Shakespeare* is not even an easy document to get hold of, at any rate in an English translation. Perhaps, therefore, it will be useful if I give a summary of the pamphlet before trying to discuss it.

Tolstoy begins by saying that throughout life Shakespeare has aroused in him 'an irresistible repulsion and tedium'. Conscious that the opinion of the civilized world is against him, he has made one attempt after another on Shakespeare's works, reading and re-reading them in Russian, English and German; but 'I invariably underwent the same feelings; repulsion, weariness and bewilderment'. Now, at the age of seventy-five, he has once again re-read the entire works of Shakespeare, including the historical plays, and

I have felt with an even greater force, the same feelings – this time, however, not of bewilderment, but of firm, indubitable conviction that the unquestionable glory of a great genius which Shakespeare enjoys, and which compels writers of our time to imitate him and readers and spectators to discover in him non-existent merits – thereby distorting their aesthetic and ethical understanding – is a great evil, as is every untruth.

Shakespeare, Tolstoy adds, is not merely no genius, but is not even 'an average author', and in order to demonstrate this fact he will examine *King Lear*, which, as he is able to show by quotations from Hazlitt, Brandes and others, has been extravagantly praised and can be taken as an example of Shakespeare's best work.

* *Shakespeare and the Drama.* Written about 1903 as an introduction to another pamphlet, *Shakespeare and the Working Classes*, by Ernest Crosby.

Tolstoy then makes a sort of exposition of the plot of *King Lear*, finding it at every step to be stupid, verbose, unnatural, unintelligible, bombastic, vulgar, tedious and full of incredible events, 'wild ravings', 'mirthless jokes', anachronisms, irrelevancies, obscenities, worn-out stage conventions and other faults both moral and aesthetic. *Lear* is, in any case, a plagiarism of an earlier and much better play, *King Leir*, by an unknown author, which Shakespeare stole and then ruined. It is worth quoting a specimen paragraph to illustrate the manner in which Tolstoy goes to work. Act III, Scene 2 (in which Lear, Kent and the Fool are together in the storm) is summarized thus:

Lear walks about the heath and says words which are meant to express his despair: he desires that the winds should blow so hard that they (the winds) should crack their cheeks and that the rain should flood everything, that lightning should singe his white head, and the thunder flatten the world and destroy all germs 'that make ungrateful man'! The fool keeps uttering still more senseless words. Enter Kent: Lear says that for some reason during this storm all criminals shall be found out and convicted. Kent, still unrecognized by Lear, endeavours to persuade him to take refuge in a hovel. At this point the fool utters a prophecy in no wise related to the situation and they all depart.

Tolstoy's final verdict on *Lear* is that no unhypnotized observer, if such an observer existed, could read it to the end with any feeling except 'aversion and weariness'. And exactly the same is true of 'all the other extolled dramas of Shakespeare, not to mention the senseless dramatized tales, *Pericles, Twelfth Night, The Tempest, Cymbeline, Troilus and Cressida.*'

Having dealt with *Lear* Tolstoy draws up a more general indictment against Shakespeare. He finds that Shakespeare has a certain technical skill which is partly traceable to his having been an actor, but otherwise no merits whatever. He has no power of delineating character or of making words and actions spring naturally out of situations, his language is uniformly exaggerated and ridiculous, he constantly thrusts his own random thoughts into the mouth of any character who happens to be handy, he displays a 'complete absence of aesthetic feeling', and his words 'have nothing whatever in common with art and poetry'.

'Shakespeare might have been whatever you like,' Tolstoy concludes, 'but he was not an artist.' Moreover, his opinions are not original or interesting, and his tendency is 'of the lowest and most immoral'. Curiously enough, Tolstoy does not base this last judgement on Shakespeare's own utterances, but on the statements of two critics, Gervinus and Brandes. According to Gervinus (or at any rate Tolstoy's reading of Gervinus) 'Shakespeare taught... that one *may be too good*', while according to Brandes: 'Shakespeare's fundamental principle ... is that *the end justifies the means*.' Tolstoy adds on his own account that Shakespeare was a jingo patriot of the worst type, but apart from this he considers that Gervinus and Brandes have given a true and adequate description of Shakespeare's view of life.

Tolstoy then recapitulates in a few paragraphs the theory of art which he had expressed at greater length elsewhere. Put still more shortly, it amounts to a demand for dignity of subject matter, sincerity, and good craftsmanship. A great work of art must deal with some subject which is 'important to the life of mankind', it must express something which the author genuinely feels, and it must use such technical methods as will produce the desired effect. As Shakespeare is debased in outlook, slipshod in execution and incapable of being sincere even for a moment, he obviously stands condemned.

But here there arises a difficult question. If Shakespeare is all that Tolstoy has shown him to be, how did he ever come to be so generally admired? Evidently the answer can only lie in a sort of mass hypnosis, or 'epidemic suggestion'. The whole civilized world has somehow been deluded into thinking Shakespeare a good writer, and even the plainest demonstration to the contrary makes no impression, because one is not dealing with a reasoned opinion but with something akin to religious faith. Throughout history, says Tolstoy, there has been an endless series of these 'epidemic suggestions' – for example, the Crusades, the search for the Philosopher's Stone, the craze for tulip growing which once swept over Holland, and so on and so forth. As a contemporary instance he cites, rather significantly, the Dreyfus case, over which the whole world grew violently excited for no sufficient reason. There are also sudden short-lived crazes for new political and philosophical theories, or for this or that writer, artist or scientist – for example, Darwin who (in 1903) is 'beginning to be forgotten'. And in some cases a quite worthless popular idol may remain in favour for centuries, for 'it also happens that such crazes, having arisen in consequence of special reasons accidentally favouring their establishment correspond in such a degree to the views of life spread in society, and especially in literary circles, that they are maintained for a long time'. Shakespeare's plays have continued to be admired over a long period because 'they corresponded to the irreligious and immoral frame of mind of the upper classes of his time and ours'.

As to the manner in which Shakespeare's fame *started*, Tolstoy explains it as having been 'got up' by German professors towards the end of the eighteenth century. His reputation 'originated in Germany, and thence was transferred to England'. The Germans chose to elevate Shakespeare because, at a time when there was no German drama worth speaking about and French classical literature was beginning to seem frigid and artificial, they were captivated by Shakespeare's 'clever development of scenes' and also found in him a good expression of their own attitude towards life. Goethe pronounced Shakespeare a great poet, whereupon all the other critics flocked after him like a troop of parrots, and the general infatuation has lasted ever since. The result has been a further debasement of the drama – Tolstoy is careful to include his own plays when condemning the contemporary stage – and a further corruption of the prevailing moral outlook. It follows that 'the false glorification of Shakespeare' is an important evil which Tolstoy feels it his duty to combat.

This, then, is the substance of Tolstoy's pamphlet. One's first feeling is that in describing Shakespeare as a bad writer he is saying something demonstrably untrue. But this is not the case. In reality there is no kind of evidence or argument by which one can show that Shakespeare, or any other writer, is 'good'. Nor is there any way of definitely proving that – for instance – Warwick Deeping is 'bad'. Ultimately there is no test of literary merit except survival, which is itself an index to majority opinion. Artistic theories such as Tolstoy's are quite worthless, because they not only start out with arbitrary assumptions, but depend on vague terms ('sincere', 'important' and so forth) which can be interpreted in any way one chooses. Properly speaking one cannot *answer* Tolstoy's attack. The interesting question is: why did he make it? But it should be noticed in passing that he uses many weak or dishonest arguments. Some of these are worth pointing out, not because they invalidate his main charge but because they are, so to speak, evidence of malice.

To begin with, his examination of King Lear is not 'impartial', as he twice claims. On the contrary, it is a prolonged exercise in misrepresentation. It is obvious that when you are summarizing *King Lear* for the benefit of someone who has not read it, you are not really being impartial if you introduce an important speech (Lear's speech when Cordelia is dead in his arms) in this manner: 'Again begin Lear's awful ravings, at which one feels ashamed, as at unsuccessful jokes.' And in a long series of instances Tolstoy slightly alters or colours the passages he is criticizing, always in such a way as to make the plot appear a little more complicated and improbable, or the language a little more exaggerated. For example, we are told that Lear 'has no necessity or motive for his abdication', although his reason for abdicating (that he is old and wishes to retire from the cares of state) has been clearly indicated in the first scene. It will be seen that even in the passage which I quoted earlier, Tolstoy has wilfully misunderstood one phrase and slightly changed the meaning of another, making nonsense of a remark which is reasonable enough in its context. None of these misreadings is very gross in itself, but their cumulative effect is to exaggerate the psychological incoherence of the play. Again, Tolstoy is not able to explain why Shakespeare's plays were still in print, and still on the stage, two hundred years after his death (*before* the 'epidemic suggestion' started, that is); and his whole account of Shakespeare's rise to fame is guesswork punctuated by outright misstatements. And again, various of his accusations contradict one another: for example, Shakespeare is a mere entertainer and 'not in earnest', but on the other hand he is constantly putting his own thoughts into the mouths of his characters. On the whole it is difficult to feel that Tolstoy's criticisms are uttered in good faith. In any case it is impossible that he should fully have believed in his main thesis – believed, that is to say, that for a century or more the entire civilized world had been taken in by a huge and palpable lie which he alone was able to see through. Certainly his dislike of Shakespeare is real enough, but the reasons for it may be different, or partly different, from what he avows; and therein lies the interest of his pamphlet.

At this point one is obliged to start guessing. However, there is one possible clue, or at least there is a question which may point the way to a clue. It is: why did Tolstoy, with thirty or more plays to choose from, pick out *King Lear* as his especial target? True, *Lear* is so well known and has been so much praised that it could justly be taken as representative of Shakespeare's best work; still, for the purpose of a hostile analysis Tolstoy would probably choose the play he disliked most. Is it not possible that he bore an especial enmity towards this particular play because he was aware, consciously or unconsciously, of the resemblance between Lear's story and his own? But it is better to approach this clue from the opposite direction – that is, by examining *Lear* itself, and the qualities in it that Tolstoy fails to mention.

One of the first things an English reader would notice in Tolstoy's pamphlet is that it hardly deals with Shakespeare as a poet. Shakespeare is treated as a dramatist, and in so far as his popularity is not spurious, it is held to be due to tricks of stagecraft which give good opportunities to clever actors. Now, so far as the English-speaking countries go, this is not true. Several of the plays which are most valued by lovers of Shakespeare (for instance, *Timon of Athens*) are seldom or never acted, while some of the most actable, such as *A Midsummer Night's Dream*, are the least admired. Those who care most for Shakespeare value him in the first place for his use of language, the 'verbal music' which even Bernard Shaw, another hostile critic, admits to be 'irresistible'. Tolstoy ignores this, and does not seem to realize that a poem may have a special value for those who speak the language in which it was written. However, even if one puts oneself in Tolstoy's place and tries to think of Shakespeare as a foreign poet it is still clear that there is something that Tolstoy has left out. Poetry, it seems, is *not* solely a matter of sound and association, and valueless outside its own language-group: otherwise how is it that some poems, including poems written in dead languages, succeed in crossing frontiers? Clearly a lyric like 'To-morrow is Saint Valentine's Day' could not be satisfactorily translated, but in Shakespeare's major work there is something describable as poetry that can be separated from the words. Tolstoy is right in saying that *Lear* is not a very good play, as a play. It is too drawn-out and has too many characters and sub-plots. One wicked daughter would have been quite enough, and Edgar is a superfluous character: indeed it would probably be a better play if Gloucester and both his sons were eliminated. Nevertheless, something, a kind of pattern, or perhaps only an atmosphere, survives the complications and the *longueurs*. *Lear* can be imagined as a puppet show, a mime, a ballet, a series of pictures. Part of its poetry, perhaps the most essential part, is inherent in the story and is dependent neither on any particular set of words, nor on flesh-and-blood presentation.

Shut your eyes and think of *King Lear*, if possible without calling to mind any of the dialogue. What do you see? Here at any rate is what I see; a majestic old man in a long black robe, with flowing white hair and beard, a figure out of Blake's drawings (but also, curiously enough, rather like Tolstoy), wandering through a storm and cursing the heavens, in company with a Fool and a lunatic. Presently the scene shifts and the old man, still cursing, still understanding nothing, is holding a dead girl in his arms while the Fool dangles on a gallows somewhere in the background. This is the bare skeleton of the play, and even here Tolstoy wants to cut out most of what is essential. He objects to the storm, as being unnecessary, to the Fool, who in his eyes is simply a tedious nuisance and an excuse for making bad jokes, and to the death of Cordelia, which, as he sees it, robs the play of its moral. According to Tolstoy, the earlier play, *King Leir*, which Shakespeare adapted

terminates more naturally and more in accordance with the moral demands of the spectator than does Shakespeare's: namely, by the King of the Gauls conquering the husbands of the elder sisters, and by Cordelia, instead of being killed, restoring Leir to his former position.

In other words the tragedy ought to have been a comedy, or perhaps a melodrama. It is doubtful whether the sense of tragedy is compatible with belief in God: at any rate, it is not compatible with disbelief in human dignity and with the kind of 'moral demand' which feels cheated when virtue fails to triumph. A tragic situation exists precisely when virtue does *not* triumph but when it is still felt that man is nobler than the forces which destroy him. It is perhaps more significant that Tolstoy sees no justification for the presence of the Fool. The Fool is integral to the play. He acts not only as a sort of chorus, making the central situation clearer by commenting on it more intelligently than the other characters, but as a foil to Lear's frenzies. His jokes, riddles and scraps of rhyme, and his endless digs at Lear's high-minded folly, ranging from mere derision to a sort of melancholy poetry ('All thy other titles thou hast given away; that thou wast born with'), are like a trickle of sanity running through the play, a reminder that somewhere or other in spite of the injustices, cruelties, intrigues, deceptions and misunderstandings that are being enacted here, life is going on much as usual. In Tolstoy's impatience with the Fool one gets a glimpse of his deeper quarrel with Shakespeare. He objects, with some justification, to the raggedness of Shakespeare's plays, the irrelevancies, the incredible plots, the exaggerated language: but what at bottom he probably most dislikes is a sort of exuberance, a tendency to take – not so much a pleasure as simply an interest in the actual process of life. It is a mistake to write Tolstoy off as a moralist attacking an artist. He never said that art, as such, is wicked or meaningless, nor did he even say that technical virtuosity is unimportant. But his main aim, in his later years, was to narrow the range of human consciousness. One's interests, one's points of attachment to the physical world and the day-to-day struggle, must be as few and not as many as possible. Literature must consist of parables, stripped of detail and almost independent of language. The parables – this is where Tolstoy differs from the average vulgar puritan – must themselves be works of art, but pleasure and curiosity must be excluded from them. Science, also, must be divorced from curiosity. The business of science, he says, is not to discover what happens but to teach men how they ought to live. So also with history and politics. Many problems (for example, the Dreyfus case) are simply not worth solving, and he is willing to leave them as loose ends. Indeed his whole theory of 'crazes' or 'epidemic suggestions', in which he lumps together such things as the Crusades and the Dutch passion of tulip growing, shows a willingness to regard many human activities as mere ant-like rushings to and fro, inexplicable and uninteresting. Clearly he could have no patience with a chaotic, detailed, discursive writer like Shakespeare. His reaction is that of an irritable old man who is being pestered by a noisy child. 'Why do you keep jumping up and down

like that? Why can't you sit still like I do?' In a way the
old man is in the right, but the trouble is that the child has a
feeling in its limbs which the old man has lost. And if the
old man knows of the existence of this feeling, the effect is
merely to increase his irritation: he would make children
senile, if he could. Tolstoy does not know, perhaps, just
what he misses in Shakespeare, but he is aware that he
misses something, and he is determined that others shall be
deprived of it as well. By nature he was imperious as well as
egotistical. Well after he was grown up he would still
occasionally strike his servant in moments of anger, and
somewhat later, according to his English biographer,
Derrick Leon, he felt 'a frequent desire upon the slenderest
provocation to slap the faces of those with whom he dis-
agreed'. One does not necessarily get rid of that kind of
temperament by undergoing religious conversion, and
indeed it is obvious that the illusion of having been reborn
may allow one's native vices to flourish more freely than
ever, though perhaps in subtler forms. Tolstoy was capable
of abjuring physical violence and of seeing what this implies,
but he was not capable of tolerance or humility, and even
if one knew nothing of his other writings, one could deduce
his tendency towards spiritual bullying from this single
pamphlet.

However, Tolstoy is not simply trying to rob others of a
pleasure he does not share. He is doing that, but his quarrel
with Shakespeare goes further. It is the quarrel between
the religious and the humanist attitudes towards life. Here
one comes back to the central theme of *King Lear*, which
Tolstoy does not mention, although he sets forth the plot in
some detail.

Lear is one of the minority of Shakespeare's plays that are
unmistakably *about* something. As Tolstoy justly complains,
much rubbish has been written about Shakespeare as a
philosopher, as a psychologist, as a 'great moral teacher',
and what-not. Shakespeare was not a systematic thinker,
his most serious thoughts are uttered irrelevantly or indirectly, and we do not know to what extent he wrote with

a 'purpose' or even how much of the work attributed to him was actually written by him. In the sonnets he never even refers to the plays as part of his achievement, though he does make what seems to be a half-ashamed allusion to his career as an actor. It is perfectly possible that he looked on at least half of his plays as mere pot-boilers and hardly bothered about purpose or probability so long as he could patch up something, usually from stolen material, which would more or less hang together on the stage. However, that is not the whole story. To begin with, as Tolstoy himself points out, Shakespeare has a habit of thrusting un-called-for general reflections into the mouths of his charac-ters. This is a serious fault in a dramatist, but it does not fit in with Tolstoy's picture of Shakespeare as a vulgar hack who has no opinions of his own and merely wishes to produce the greatest effect with the least trouble. And more than this, about a dozen of his plays, written for the most part later than 1600, do unquestionably have a meaning and even a moral. They revolve round a central subject which in some cases can be reduced to a single word. For example, *Macbeth* is about ambition, *Othello* is about jealousy, and *Timon of Athens* is about money. The subject of *Lear* is renunciation, and it is only by being wilfully blind that one can fail to understand what Shakespeare is saying.

Lear renounces his throne but expects everyone to continue treating him as a king. He does not see that if he surrenders power, other people will take advantage of his weakness: also that those who flatter him the most grossly, i.e. Regan and Goneril, are exactly the ones who will turn against him. The moment he finds that he can no longer make people obey him as he did before, he falls into a rage which Tolstoy describes as 'strange and unnatural', but which in fact is perfectly in character. In his madness and despair, he passes through two moods which again are natural enough in his circumstances, though in one of them it is probable that he is being used partly as a mouthpiece for Shakespeare's own opinions. One is the mood of disgust in which Lear repents, as it were, for having been a king,

and grasps for the first time the rottenness of formal justice
and vulgar morality. The other is a mood of impotent fury
in which he wreaks imaginary revenges upon those who have
wronged him. 'To have a thousand with red burning spits
come hissing in upon 'em!', and:

> It were a delicate stratagem to shoe
> A troop of horse with felt: I'll put't in proof;
> And when I have stol'n upon these sons-in-law,
> Then kill, kill, kill, kill, kill, kill!

Only at the end does he realize, as a sane man, that power,
revenge and victory are not worth while:

> No, no, no, no! Come, let's away to prison ...
> .... and we'll wear out
> In a wall'd prison, packs and sects of great ones
> That ebb and flow by th' moon.

But by the time he makes this discovery it is too late, for his
death and Cordelia's are already decided on. That is the
story, and, allowing for some clumsiness in the telling, it is a
very good story.

But is it not also curiously similar to the history of Tolstoy
himself? There is a general resemblance which one can
hardly avoid seeing, because the most impressive event in
Tolstoy's life, as in Lear's, was a huge and gratuitous act of
renunciation. In his old age, he renounced his estate, his
title and his copyrights, and made an attempt – a sincere
attempt, though it was not successful – to escape from his
privileged position and live the life of a peasant. But the
deeper resemblance lies in the fact that Tolstoy, like Lear,
acted on mistaken motives and failed to get the results he
had hoped for. According to Tolstoy, the aim of every
human being is happiness, and happiness can only be
attained by doing the will of God. But doing the will of God
means casting off all earthly pleasures and ambitions, and
living only for others. Ultimately, therefore, Tolstoy renounced the world under the expectation that this would
make him happier. But if there is one thing certain about

his later years, it is that he was *not* happy. On the contrary, he was driven almost to the edge of madness by the behaviour of the people about him, who persecuted him precisely *because* of his renunciation. Like Lear, Tolstoy was not humble and not a good judge of character. He was inclined at moments to revert to the attitudes of an aristocrat, in spite of his peasant's blouse, and he even had two children whom he had believed in and who ultimately turned against him – though, of course, in a less sensational manner than Regan and Goneril. His exaggerated revulsion from sexuality was also distinctly similar to Lear's. Tolstoy's remark that marriage is 'slavery, satiety, repulsion' and means putting up with the proximity of 'ugliness, dirtiness, smell, sores', is matched by Lear's well-known outburst:

> But to the girdle do the gods inherit,
> Beneath is all the fiends';
> There's hell, there's darkness, there's the sulphurous pit,
> Burning, scalding, stench, consumption, etc., etc.

And though Tolstoy could not foresee it when he wrote his essay on Shakespeare, even the ending of his life – the sudden unplanned flight across country, accompanied only by a faithful daughter, the death in a cottage in a strange village – seems to have in it a sort of phantom reminiscence of *Lear*.

Of course, one cannot assume that Tolstoy was aware of this resemblance, or would have admitted it if it had been pointed out to him. But his attitude towards the play must have been influenced by its theme. Renouncing power, giving away your lands, was a subject on which he had reason to feel deeply. Probably, therefore, he would be more angered and disturbed by the moral that Shakespeare draws than he would be in the case of some other play – *Macbeth*, for example – which did not touch so closely on his own life. But what exactly *is* the moral of *Lear*? Evidently there are two morals, one explicit, the other implied in the story.

Shakespeare starts by assuming that to make yourself powerless is to invite an attack. This does not mean that *everyone* will turn against you (Kent and the Fool stand by Lear from first to last), but in all probability *someone* will. If you throw away your weapons, some less scrupulous person will pick them up. If you turn the other cheek, you will get a harder blow on it than you got on the first one. This does not always happen, but it is to be expected, and you ought not to complain if it does happen. The second blow is, so to speak, part of the act of turning the other cheek. First of all, therefore, there is the vulgar, common-sense moral drawn by the Fool: 'Don't relinquish power, don't give away your lands.' But there is also another moral. Shakespeare never utters it in so many words, and it does not very much matter whether he was fully aware of it. It is contained in the story, which, after all, he made up, or altered to suit his purposes. It is: 'Give away your lands if you want to, but don't expect to gain happiness by doing so. Probably you won't gain happiness. If you live for others, you must live *for others*, and not as a roundabout way of getting an advantage for yourself.'

Obviously neither of these conclusions could have been pleasing to Tolstoy. The first of them expresses the ordinary, belly-to-earth selfishness from which he was genuinely trying to escape. The other conflicts with his desire to eat his cake and have it – that is, to destroy his own egoism and by so doing to gain eternal life. Of course, *Lear* is not a sermon in favour of altruism. It merely points out the results of practising self-denial for selfish reasons. Shakespeare had a considerable streak of worldliness in him, and if he had been forced to take sides in his own play, his sympathies would probably have lain with the Fool. But at least he could see the whole issue and treat it at the level of tragedy. Vice is punished, but virtue is not rewarded. The morality of Shakespeare's later tragedies is not religious in the ordinary sense, and certainly is not Christian. Only two of them, *Hamlet* and *Othello*, are supposedly occurring inside the Christian era, and even in those, apart from the antics of the ghost in *Hamlet*, there is no indication of a 'next world' where everything is to be put right. All of these tragedies start out with the humanist assumption that life, although full of sorrow, is worth living, and that Man is a noble animal – a belief which Tolstoy in his old age did not share.

Tolstoy was not a saint, but he tried very hard to make himself into a saint, and the standards he applied to literature were other-worldly ones. It is important to realize that the difference between a saint and an ordinary human being is a difference of kind and not of degree. That is, the one is not to be regarded as an imperfect form of the other. The saint, at any rate Tolstoy's kind of saint, is not trying to work an improvement in earthly life: he is trying to bring it to an end and put something different in its place. One obvious expression of this is the claim that celibacy is 'higher' than marriage. If only, Tolstoy says in effect, we would stop breeding, fighting, struggling and enjoying, if we could get rid not only of our sins but of everything else that binds us to the surface of the earth – including love, then the whole painful process would be over and the Kingdom of Heaven would arrive. But a normal human being does not want the Kingdom of Heaven: he wants life on earth to continue. This is not solely because he is 'weak', 'sinful' and anxious for a 'good time'. Most people get a fair amount of fun out of their lives, but on balance life is suffering, and only the very young or the very foolish imagine otherwise. Ultimately it is the Christian attitude which is self-interested and hedonistic, since the aim is always to get away from the painful struggle of earthly life and find eternal peace in some kind of Heaven or Nirvana. The humanist attitude is that the struggle must continue and that death is the price of life. 'Men must endure their going hence, even as their coming hither: Ripeness is all' – which is an un-Christian sentiment. Often there is a seeming truce between the humanist and the religious believer, but in fact their attitudes cannot be reconciled: one must choose between this world and the next. And the enormous majority of human beings, if they understood the issue, would choose this world. They do make that choice when they continue working, breeding and dying instead of

crippling their faculties in the hope of obtaining a new lease
of existence elsewhere.

We do not know a great deal about Shakespeare's
religious beliefs, and from the evidence of his writings it
would be difficult to prove that he had any. But at any rate
he was not a saint or a would-be saint: he was a human
being, and in some ways not a very good one. It is clear,
for instance, that he liked to stand well with the rich and
powerful, and was capable of flattering them in the most
servile way. He is also noticeably cautious, not to say
cowardly, in his manner of uttering unpopular opinions.
Almost never does he put a subversive or sceptical remark
into the mouth of a character likely to be identified with
himself. Throughout his plays the acute social critics, the
people who are not taken in by accepted fallacies, are
buffoons, villains, lunatics or persons who are shamming
insanity or are in a state of violent hysteria. *Lear* is a play in
which this tendency is particularly well marked. It contains
a great deal of veiled social criticism – a point Tolstoy
misses – but it is all uttered either by the Fool, by Edgar
when he is pretending to be mad, or by Lear during his
bouts of madness. In his sane moments Lear hardly ever
makes an intelligent remark. And yet the very fact that
Shakespeare had to use these subterfuges shows how widely
his thoughts ranged. He could not restrain himself from
commenting on almost everything, although he put on a
series of masks in order to do so. If one has once read Shake-
peare with attention, it is not easy to go a day without
quoting him, because there are not many subjects of major
importance that he does not discuss or at least mention
somewhere or other, in his unsystematic but illuminating
way. Even the irrelevancies that litter every one of his
plays – the puns and riddles, the lists of names, the scraps
of 'reportage' like the conversation of the carriers in *Henry IV*,
the bawdy jokes, the rescued fragments of forgotten ballads
– are merely the products of excessive vitality. Shakespeare
was not a philosopher or a scientist, but he did have curiosity, he loved the surface of the earth and the process of

life – which, it should be repeated, is *not* the same thing as wanting to have a good time and stay alive as long as possible. Of course, it is not because of the quality of his thought that Shakespeare has survived, and he might not even be remembered as a dramatist if he had not also been a poet. His main hold on us is through language. How deeply Shakespeare himself was fascinated by the music of words can probably be inferred from the speeches of Pistol. What Pistol says is largely meaningless, but if one considers his lines singly they are magnificent rhetorical verse. Evidently, pieces of resounding nonsense ('Let floods o'erswell, and fiends for food howl on', etc.) were constantly appearing in Shakespeare's mind of their own accord, and a half-lunatic character had to be invented to use them up.

Tolstoy's native tongue was not English, and one cannot blame him for being unmoved by Shakespeare's verse, nor even, perhaps, for refusing to believe that Shakespeare's skill with words was something out of the ordinary. But he would also have rejected the whole notion of valuing poetry for its texture – valuing it, that is to say, as a kind of music. If it could somehow have been proved to him that his whole explanation of Shakespeare's rise to fame is mistaken, that inside the English-speaking world, at any rate, Shakespeare's popularity is genuine, that his mere skill in placing one syllable beside another has given acute pleasure to generation after generation of English-speaking people – all this would not have been counted as a merit to Shakespeare, but rather the contrary. It would simply have been one more proof of the irreligious, earthbound nature of Shakespeare and his admirers. Tolstoy would have said that poetry is to be judged by its meaning, and that seductive sounds merely cause false meanings to go unnoticed. At every level it is the same issue – this world against the next: and certainly the music of words is something that belongs to this world.

A sort of doubt has always hung around the character of Tolstoy, as round the character of Gandhi. He was not a vulgar hypocrite, as some people declared him to be, and he would probably have imposed even greater sacrifices on himself than he did, if he had not been interfered with at every step by the people surrounding him, especially his wife. But on the other hand it is dangerous to take such men as Tolstoy at their disciples' valuation. There is always the possibility – the probability, indeed – that they have done no more than exchange one form of egoism for another. Tolstoy renounced wealth, fame and privilege; he abjured violence in all its forms and was ready to suffer for doing so; but it is not easy to believe that he abjured the principle of coercion, or at least the *desire* to coerce others. There are families in which the father will say to his child, 'You'll get a thick ear if you do that again', while the mother, her eyes brimming over with tears, will take the child in her arms and murmur lovingly, 'Now, darling, *is* it kind to Mummy to do that?' And who would maintain that the second method is less tyrannous than the first? The distinction that really matters is not between violence and non-violence, but between having and not having the appetite for power. There are people who are convinced of the wickedness both of armies and of police forces, but who are nevertheless much more intolerant and inquisitorial in outlook than the normal person who believes that it is necessary to use violence in certain circumstances. They will not say to somebody else, 'Do this, that and the other or you will go to prison', but they will, if they can, get inside his brain and dictate his thoughts for him in the minutest particulars. Creeds like pacifism and anarchism, which seem on the surface to imply a complete renunciation of power, rather encourage this habit of mind. For if you have embraced a creed which appears to be free from the ordinary dirtiness of politics – a creed from which you yourself cannot expect to draw any material advantage – surely that proves that you are in the right? And the more you are in the right, the more natural that everyone else should be bullied into thinking likewise.

If we are to believe what he says in his pamphlet, Tolstoy has never been able to see any merit in Shakespeare, and was always astonished to find that his fellow-writers, Turgenev, Fet and others thought differently. We may be sure that in his unregenerate days Tolstoy's conclusion would have been: 'You like Shakespeare – I don't. Let's leave it at that.' Later, when his perception that it takes all sorts to make a world had deserted him, he came to think of Shakespeare's writings as something dangerous to himself. The more pleasure people took in Shakespeare, the less they would listen to Tolstoy. Therefore nobody must be *allowed* to enjoy Shakespeare, just as nobody must be allowed to drink alcohol or smoke tobacco. True, Tolstoy would not prevent them by force. He is not demanding that the police shall impound every copy of Shakespeare's works. But he will do dirt on Shakespeare, if he can. He will try to get inside the mind of every lover of Shakespeare and kill his enjoyment by every trick he can think of, including – as I have shown in my summary of his pamphlet – arguments which are self-contradictory or even doubtfully honest.

But finally the most striking thing is how little difference it all makes. As I said earlier, one cannot *answer* Tolstoy's pamphlet, at least on its main counts. There is no argument by which one can defend a poem. It defends itself by surviving, or it is indefensible. And if this test is valid, I think the verdict in Shakespeare's case must be 'not guilty'. Like every other writer, Shakespeare will be forgotten sooner or later, but it is unlikely that a heavier indictment will ever be brought against him. Tolstoy was perhaps the most admired literary man of his age, and he was certainly not its least able pamphleteer. He turned all his powers of denunciation against Shakespeare, like all the guns of a battleship roaring simultaneously. And with what result? Forty years later Shakespeare is still there completely unaffected, and of the attempt to demolish him nothing remains except the yellowing pages of a pamphlet which hardly anyone has read, and which would be forgotten altogether if Tolstoy had not also been the author of *War and Peace* and *Anna Karenina*.

1947

POLITICS *vs* LITERATURE:

An Examination of *Gulliver's Travels*

In *Gulliver's Travels* humanity is attacked, or criticized, from at least three different angles, and the implied character of Gulliver himself necessarily changes somewhat in the process. In Part I he is the typical eighteenth-century voyager, bold, practical and unromantic, his homely outlook skilfully impressed on the reader by the biographical details at the beginning, by his age (he is a man of forty, with two children, when his adventures start), and by the inventory of the things in his pockets, especially his spectacles, which make several appearances. In Part II he has in general the same character, but at moments when the story demands it he has a tendency to develop into an imbecile who is capable of boasting of 'our noble Country, the Mistress of Arts and Arms, the Scourge of France', etc., etc., and at the same time of betraying every available scandalous fact about the country which he professes to love. In Part III he is much as he was in Part I, though, as he is consorting chiefly with courtiers and men of learning, one has the impression that he has risen in the social scale. In Part IV he conceives a horror of the human race which is not apparent, or only intermittently apparent, in the earlier books, and changes into a sort of unreligious anchorite whose one desire is to live in some desolate spot where he can devote himself to meditating on the goodness of the Houyhnhnms. However, these inconsistencies are forced upon Swift by the fact that Gulliver is there chiefly to provide a contrast. It is necessary, for instance, that he should appear sensible in Part I and at least intermittently silly in Part II, because in both books the essential manoeuvre is the same, i.e. to make the human being look ridiculous by imagining him as a creature six inches high. Whenever

Gulliver is not acting as a stooge there is a sort of continuity in his character, which comes out especially in his resourcefulness and his observation of physical detail. He is much the same kind of person, with the same prose style, when he bears off the warships of Blefuscu, when he rips open the belly of the monstrous rat, and when he sails away upon the ocean in his frail coracle made from the skins of Yahoos. Moreover, it is difficult not to feel that in his shrewder moments Gulliver is simply Swift himself, and there is at least one incident in which Swift seems to be venting his private grievance against contemporary Society. It will be remembered that when the Emperor of Lilliput's palace catches fire, Gulliver puts it out by urinating on it. Instead of being congratulated on his presence of mind, he finds that he has committed a capital offence by making water in the precincts of the palace, and

I was privately assured, that the Empress, conceiving the greatest Abhorrence of what I had done, removed to the most distant Side of the Court, firmly resolved that those buildings should never be repaired for her Use; and, in the Presence of her chief Confidents, could not forbear vowing Revenge.

According to Professor G. M. Trevelyan (*England under Queen Anne*), part of the reason for Swift's failure to get preferment was that the Queen was scandalized by the *Tale of a Tub* – a pamphlet in which Swift probably felt that he had done a great service to the English Crown, since it scarifies the Dissenters and still more the Catholics while leaving the Established Church alone. In any case no one would deny that *Gulliver's Travels* is a rancorous as well as a pessimistic book, and that especially in Parts i and iii it often descends into political partisanship of a narrow kind. Pettiness and magnanimity, republicanism and authoritarianism, love of reason and lack of curiosity, are all mixed up in it. The hatred of the human body with which Swift is especially associated is only dominant in Part iv, but somehow this new preoccupation does not come as a surprise. One feels that all these adventures, and all these changes of mood, could have happened to the same person, and the inter-connexion between Swift's political loyalties and his ultimate despair is one of the most interesting features of the book.

Politically, Swift was one of those people who are driven into a sort of perverse Toryism by the follies of the progressive party of the moment. Part 1 of *Gulliver's Travels*, ostensibly a satire on human greatness, can be seen, if one looks a little deeper, to be simply an attack on England, on the dominant Whig Party, and on the war with France, which – however bad the motives of the Allies may have been – did save Europe from being tyrannized over by a single reactionary power. Swift was not a Jacobite nor strictly speaking a Tory, and his declared aim in the war was merely a moderate peace treaty and not the outright defeat of England. Nevertheless there is a tinge of quislingism in his attitude, which comes out in the ending of Part 1 and slightly interferes with the allegory. When Gulliver flees from Lilliput (England) to Blefuscu (France) the assumption that a human being six inches high is inherently contemptible seems to be dropped. Whereas the people of Lilliput have behaved towards Gulliver with the utmost treachery and meanness, those of Blefuscu behave generously and straightforwardly, and indeed this section of the book ends on a different note from the all-round disillusionment of the earlier chapters. Evidently Swift's animus is, in the first place, against *England*. It is 'your Natives' (i.e. Gulliver's fellow-countrymen) whom the King of Brobdingnag considers to be 'the most pernicious Race of little odious vermin that Nature ever suffered to crawl upon the surface of the Earth', and the long passage at the end, denouncing colonization and foreign conquest, is plainly aimed at England, although the contrary is elaborately stated. The Dutch, England's allies and target of one of Swift's most famous pamphlets, are also more or less wantonly attacked in Part III. There is even what sounds like a personal note in the passage in which Gulliver records his satisfaction that the various countries he has discovered cannot be made colonies of the British Crown:

The *Houyhnhnms*, indeed, appear not to be so well prepared for War, a Science to which they are perfect Strangers, and especially against missive Weapons. However, supposing myself to be a Minister of State, I could never give my advice for invading them. ... Imagine twenty thousand of them breaking into the midst of an *European* army, confounding the Ranks, overturning the Carriages, battering the Warriors' Faces into Mummy, by terrible Yerks from their hinder hoofs ...

Considering that Swift does not waste words, that phrase, 'battering the warriors' faces into mummy', probably indicates a secret wish to see the invincible armies of the Duke of Marlborough treated in a like manner. There are similar touches elsewhere. Even the country mentioned in Part III, where 'the Bulk of the People consist, in a Manner, wholly of Discoverers, Witnesses, Informers, Accusers, Prosecutors, Evidences, Swearers, together with their several subservient and subaltern Instruments, all under the Colours, the Conduct, and Pay of Ministers of State', is called Langdon, which is within one letter of being an anagram of England. (As the early editions of the book contain misprints, it may perhaps have been intended as a complete anagram.) Swift's *physical* repulsion from humanity is certainly real enough, but one has the feeling that his debunking of human grandeur, his diatribes against lords, politicians, court favourites, etc., has mainly a local application and springs from the fact that he belonged to the unsuccessful party. He denounces injustice and oppression, but he gives no evidence of liking democracy. In spite of his enormously greater powers, his implied position is very similar to that of the innumerable silly-clever Conservatives of our own day – people like Sir Alan Herbert, Professor G. M. Young, Lord Elton, the Tory Reform Committee or the long line of Catholic apologists from W. H. Mallock onwards: people who specialize in cracking neat jokes at the expense of whatever is 'modern' and 'progressive', and whose opinions are often all the more extreme because they know that they cannot influence the actual drift of events. After all, such a pamphlet as *An Argument to prove that the*

Abolishing of Christianity, etc., is very like 'Timothy Shy' having a bit of clean fun with the Brains Trust, or Father Ronald Knox exposing the errors of Bertrand Russell. And the ease with which Swift has been forgiven – and forgiven, sometimes, by devout believers – for the blasphemies of *A Tale of a Tub* demonstrates clearly enough the feebleness of religious sentiments as compared with political ones.

However, the reactionary cast of Swift's mind does not show itself chiefly in his political affiliations. The important thing is his attitude towards Science, and, more broadly, towards intellectual curiosity. The famous Academy of Lagado, described in Part III of *Gulliver's Travels*, is no doubt a justified satire on most of the so-called scientists of Swift's own day. Significantly, the people at work in it are described as 'Projectors', that is, people not engaged in disinterested research but merely on the look-out for gadgets which will save labour and bring in money. But there is no sign – indeed, all through the book there are many signs to the contrary – that 'pure' science would have struck Swift as a worth-while activity. The more serious kind of scientist has already had a kick in the pants in Part II, when the 'Scholars' patronized by the King of Brobdingnag try to account for Gulliver's small stature:

After much Debate, they concluded unanimously that I was only *Relplum Scalcath*, which is interpreted literally, *Lusus Naturae*; a Determination exactly agreeable to the modern philosophy of *Europe*, whose Professors, disdaining the old Evasion of *Occult Causes*, whereby the followers of *Aristotle* endeavoured in vain to disguise their Ignorance, have invented this wonderful solution of All Difficulties, to the unspeakable Advancement of human Knowledge.

If this stood by itself one might assume that Swift is merely the enemy of *sham* science. In a number of places, however, he goes out of his way to proclaim the uselessness of all learning or speculation not directed towards some practical end:

The learning of (the Brobdingnagians) is very defective, consisting only in Morality, History, Poetry, and Mathematics, wherein they must be allowed to excel. But, the last of these is wholly applied to what may be useful in Life, to the improvement of Agriculture, and all mechanical Arts so that among us it would be little esteemed. And as to Ideas, Entities, Abstractions, and Transcendentals, I could never drive the least Conception into their Heads.

The Houyhnhnms, Swift's ideal beings, are backward even in a mechanical sense. They are unacquainted with metals, have never heard of boats, do not, properly speaking, practise agriculture (we are told that the oats which they live upon 'grow naturally'), and appear not to have invented wheels.* They have no alphabet, and evidently have not much curiosity about the physical world. They do not believe that any inhabited country exists beside their own, and though they understand the motions of the sun and moon, and the nature of eclipses, 'this is the utmost progress of their *Astronomy*'. By contrast, the philosophers of the flying island of Laputa are so continuously absorbed in mathematical speculations that before speaking to them one has to attract their attention by flapping them on the ear with a bladder. They have catalogued ten thousand fixed stars, have settled the periods of ninety-three comets, and have discovered, in advance of the astronomers of Europe, that Mars has two moons – all of which information Swift evidently regards as ridiculous, useless and uninteresting. As one might expect, he believes that the scientist's place, if he has a place, is in the laboratory, and that scientific knowledge has no bearing on political matters:

What I ... thought altogether unaccountable, was the strong Disposition I observed in them towards News and Politics, perpetually enquiring into Public Affairs, giving their judgements in Matters of State, and passionately disputing every inch of a Party Opinion. I have, indeed, observed the same Disposition among most of the Mathematicians I have known in *Europe*, though I could never discover the least Analogy between the two Sciences;

* Houyhnhnms too old to walk are described as being carried in 'sledges' or in 'a kind of vehicle, drawn like a sledge'. Presumably these had no wheels.

unless those people suppose, that, because the smallest Circle hath as many Degrees as the largest, therefore the Regulation and Management of the World require no more Abilities, than the Handling and Turning of a Globe.

Is there not something familiar in that phrase 'I could never discover the least analogy between the two sciences'? It has precisely the note of the popular Catholic apologists who profess to be astonished when a scientist utters an opinion on such questions as the existence of God or the immortality of the soul. The scientist, we are told, is an expert only in one restricted field: why should his opinions be of value in any other? The implication is that theology is just as much an exact science as, for instance, chemistry, and that the priest is also an expert whose conclusions on certain subjects must be accepted. Swift in effect makes the same claim for the politician, but he goes one better in that he will not allow the scientist – either the 'pure' scientist or the *ad hoc* investigator – to be a useful person in his own line. Even if he had not written Part III of *Gulliver's Travels*, one could infer from the rest of the book that, like Tolstoy and like Blake, he hates the very idea of studying the processes of Nature. The 'Reason' which he so admires in the Houyhnhnms does not primarily mean the power of drawing logical inferences from observed facts. Although he never defines it, it appears in most contexts to mean either common sense – i.e. acceptance of the obvious and contempt for quibbles and abstractions – or absence of passion and superstition. In general he assumes that we know all that we need to know already, and merely use our knowledge incorrectly. Medicine, for instance, is a useless science, because if we lived in a more natural way, there would be no diseases. Swift, however, is not a simple-lifer or an admirer of the Noble Savage. He is in favour of civilization and the arts of civilization. Not only does he see the value of good manners, good conversation, and even learning of a literary and historical kind, he also sees that agriculture, navigation and architecture need to be studied and could with advantages be improved. But his implied aim is a static, incurious civilization – the world of his own day, a little cleaner, a little saner, with no radical change and no poking into the unknowable. More than one would expect in anyone so free from accepted fallacies, he reveres the past, especially classical antiquity, and believes that modern man has degenerated sharply during the past hundred years.* In the island of sorcerers, where the spirits of the dead can be called up at will:

I desired that the Senate of *Rome* might appear before me in one large chamber, and a modern Representative in Counterview, in another. The first seemed to be an Assembly of Heroes and Demy-Gods, the other a Knot of Pedlars, Pick-pockets, Highwaymen and Bullies.

Although Swift uses this section of Part III to attack the truthfulness of recorded history, his critical spirit deserts him as soon as he is dealing with Greeks and Romans. He remarks, of course, upon the corruption of imperial Rome, but he has an almost unreasoning admiration for some of the leading figures of the ancient world:

I was struck with profound Veneration at the sight of *Brutus*, and could easily discover the most consummate Virtue, the greatest Intrepidity and Firmness of Mind, the truest Love of his Country, and general Benevolence for Mankind, in every Lineament of his Countenance. ... I had the honour to have much Conversation with *Brutus*, and was told, that his Ancestors *Junius*, *Socrates*, *Epaminondas*, *Cato* the younger, *Sir Thomas More*, and himself, were perpetually together: a *Sextumvirate*, to which all the Ages of the World cannot add a seventh.

It will be noticed that of these six people, only one is a Christian. This is an important point. If one adds together Swift's pessimism, his reverence for the past, his incuriosity and his horror of the human body, one arrives at an attitude common among religious reactionaries – that is, people who

---

* The physical decadence which Swift claims to have observed may have been a reality at that date. He attributes it to syphilis, which was a new disease in Europe and may have been more virulent than it is now. Distilled liquors, also, were a novelty in the seventeenth century and must have led at first to a great increase in drunkenness.

defend an unjust order of Society by claiming that this world cannot be substantially improved and only the 'next world' matters. However, Swift shows no sign of having any religious beliefs, at least in any ordinary sense of the words. He does not appear to believe seriously in life after death, and his idea of goodness is bound up with republicanism, love of liberty, courage, 'benevolence' (meaning in effect public spirit), 'reason' and other pagan qualities. This reminds one that there is another strain in Swift, not quite congruous with his disbelief in progress and his general hatred of humanity.

To begin with, he has moments when he is 'constructive' and even 'advanced'. To be occasionally inconsistent is almost a mark of vitality in Utopia books, and Swift sometimes inserts a word of praise into a passage that ought to be purely satirical. Thus, his ideas about the education of the young are fathered on to the Lilliputians, who have much the same views on this subject as the Houyhnhnms. The Lilliputians also have various social and legal institutions (for instance, there are old age pensions, and people are rewarded for keeping the law as well as punished for breaking it) which Swift would have liked to see prevailing in his own country. In the middle of this passage Swift remembers his satirical intention and adds, 'In relating these and the following Laws, I would only be understood to mean the original Institutions, and not the most scandalous Corruptions into which these people are fallen by the degenerate Nature of Man': but as Lilliput is supposed to represent England, and the laws he is speaking of have never had their parallel in England, it is clear that the impulse to make constructive suggestions has been too much for him. But Swift's greatest contribution to political thought in the narrower sense of the words, is his attack, especially in Part III, on what would now be called totalitarianism. He has an extraordinarily clear prevision of the spy-haunted 'police State', with its endless heresy-hunts and treason trials, all really designed to neutralize popular discontent by changing it into war hysteria. And one must remember that Swift is here inferring the whole from a quite small part, for the feeble governments of his own day did not give him illustrations ready-made. For example, there is the professor at the School of Political Projectors who 'shewed me a large Paper of Instructions for discovering Plots and Conspiracies', and who claimed that one can find people's secret thoughts by examining their excrement:

Because Men are never so serious, thoughtful, and intent, as when they are at Stool, which he found by frequent Experiment: for in such Conjunctures, when he used meerly as a trial to consider what was the best Way of murdering the King, his Ordure would have a tincture of Green; but quite different when he thought only of raising an Insurrection, or burning the Metropolis.

The professor and his theory are said to have been suggested to Swift by the – from our point of view – not particularly astonishing or disgusting fact that in a recent State trial some letters found in somebody's privy had been put in evidence. Later in the same chapter we seem to be positively in the middle of the Russian purges:

In the Kingdom of Tribnia, by the Natives called Langdon ... the Bulk of the People consist, in a Manner, wholly of Discoverers, Witnesses, Informers, Accusers, Prosecutors, Evidences, Swearers. ... It is first agreed, and settled among them, what suspected Persons shall be accused of a Plot: Then, effectual Care is taken to secure all their Letters and Papers, and put the Owners in Chains. These papers are delivered to a Sett of Artists, very dexterous in finding out the mysterious Meanings of Words, Syllables, and Letters. ... Where this method fails, they have two others more effectual, which the Learned among them call *Acrostics* and *Anagrams*. *First*, they can decypher all initial Letters into political Meanings: Thus: N shall signify a Plot, B a Regiment of Horse, L a Fleet at Sea: Or, *Secondly*, by transposing the Letters of the Alphabet in any suspected Paper, they can lay open the deepest Designs of a discontented Party. So, for Example if I should say in a Letter to a Friend, *Our Brother Tom has just got the Piles*, a skilful Decypherer would discover that the same Letters, which compose that Sentence, may be analysed in the following Words: *Resist – a Plot is brought Home – The Tour.** And this is the anagrammatic method.

* Tower

Other professors at the same school invent simplified languages, write books by machinery, educate their pupils by inscribing the lesson on a wafer and causing them to swallow it, or propose to abolish individuality altogether by cutting off part of the brain of one man and grafting it on to the head of another. There is something queerly familiar in the atmosphere of these chapters, because, mixed up with much fooling, there is a perception that one of the aims of totalitarianism is not merely to make sure that people will think the right thoughts, but actually to make them *less conscious*. Then, again, Swift's account of the Leader who is usually to be found ruling over a tribe of Yahoos, and of the 'favourite' who acts first as a dirty-worker and later as a scapegoat, fits remarkably well into the pattern of our own times. But are we to infer from all this that Swift was first and foremost an enemy of tyranny and a champion of the free intelligence? No: his own views, so far as one can discern them, are not markedly liberal. No doubt he hates lords, kings, bishops, generals, ladies of fashion, orders, titles and flummery generally, but he does not seem to think better of the common people than of their rulers, or to be in favour of increased social equality, or to be enthusiastic about representative institutions. The Houyhnhnms are organized upon a sort of caste system which is racial in character, the horses which do the menial work being of different colours from their masters and not interbreeding with them. The educational system which Swift admires in the Lilliputians takes hereditary class distinctions for granted, and the children of the poorest classes do not go to school, because 'their Business being only to till and cultivate the Earth ... therefore their Education is of little Consequence to the Public'. Nor does he seem to have been strongly in favour of freedom of speech and the Press, in spite of the toleration which his own writings enjoyed. The King of Brobdingnag is astonished at the multiplicity of religious and political sects in England, and considers that those who hold 'opinions prejudicial to the public' (in the context this seems to mean simply heretical opinions), though they need not be obliged to change them, ought to be obliged to conceal them: for 'as it was Tyranny in any Government to require the first, so it was weakness not to enforce the second'. There is a subtler indication of Swift's own attitude in the manner in which Gulliver leaves the land of the Houyhnhnms. Intermittently, at least, Swift was a kind of anarchist, and Part IV of *Gulliver's Travels* is a picture of an anarchistic Society, not governed by law in the ordinary sense, but by the dictates of 'Reason', which are voluntarily accepted by everyone. The General Assembly of the Houyhnhnms 'exhorts' Gulliver's master to get rid of him, and his neighbours put pressure on him to make him comply. Two reasons are given. One is that the presence of this unusual Yahoo may unsettle the rest of the tribe, and the other is that a friendly relationship between a Houyhnhnm and a Yahoo is 'not agreeable to Reason or Nature, or a Thing ever heard of before among them'. Gulliver's master is somewhat unwilling to obey, but the 'exhortation' (a Houyhnhnm, we are told, is never *compelled* to do anything, he is merely 'exhorted' or 'advised') cannot be disregarded. This illustrates very well the totalitarian tendency which is explicit in the anarchist or pacifist vision of Society. In a Society in which there is no law, and in theory no compulsion, the only arbiter of behaviour is public opinion. But public opinion, because of the tremendous urge to conformity in gregarious animals, is less tolerant than any system of law. When human beings are governed by 'thou shalt not', the individual can practise a certain amount of eccentricity: when they are supposedly governed by 'love' or 'reason', he is under continuous pressure to make him behave and think in exactly the same way as everyone else. The Houyhnhnms, we are told, were unanimous on almost all subjects. The only question they ever *discussed* was how to deal with the Yahoos. Otherwise there was no room for disagreement among them, because the truth is always either self-evident, or else it is undiscoverable and unimportant. They had apparently no word for 'opinion' in their language, and in their conversations there was no 'difference of sentiments'. They had reached, in fact, the highest stage of totalitarian organization, the stage when conformity has become so general that there is no need for a police force. Swift approves of this kind of thing because among his many gifts neither curiosity nor good-nature was included. Disagreement would always seem to him sheer perversity. 'Reason,' among the Houyhn-hnms, he says, 'is not a Point Problematical, as with us, where men can argue with Plausibility on both Sides of a Question; but strikes you with immediate Conviction; as it must needs do, where it is not mingled, obscured, or dis-coloured by Passion and Interest.' In other words, we know everything already, so why should dissident opinions be tolerated? The totalitarian Society of the Houyhnhnms, where there can be no freedom and no development, follows naturally from this.

We are right to think of Swift as a rebel and iconoclast, but except in certain secondary matters, such as his insist-ence that women should receive the same education as men, he cannot be labelled 'Left'. He is a Tory anarchist, despising authority while disbelieving in liberty, and pre-serving the aristocratic outlook while seeing clearly that the existing aristocracy is degenerate and contemptible. When Swift utters one of his characteristic diatribes against the rich and powerful, one must probably, as I said earlier, write off something for the fact that he himself belonged to the less successful party, and was personally disappointed. The 'outs', for obvious reasons, are always more radical than the 'ins'.* But the most essential thing in Swift is his

---

* At the end of the book, as typical specimens of human folly and viciousness, Swift names 'a Lawyer, a Pickpocket, a Colonel, a Fool, a Lord, a Gamester, a Politician, a Whore-master, a Physician, an Evi-dence, a Suborner, an Attorney, a Traitor, or the like'. One sees here the irresponsible violence of the powerless. The list lumps together those who break the conventional code, and those who keep it. For instance, if you automatically condemn a colonel, as such, on what grounds do you con-demn a traitor? Or again, if you want to suppress pickpockets, you must have laws, which means that you must have lawyers. But the whole closing passage, in which the hatred is so authentic, and the reason

inability to believe that life – ordinary life on the solid earth, and not some rationalized, deodorized version of it – could be made worth living. Of course, no honest person claims that happiness is *now* a normal condition among adult human beings; but perhaps it *could* be made normal, and it is upon this question that all serious political controversy really turns. Swift has much in common – more, I believe, than has been noticed – with Tolstoy, another disbeliever in the possibility of happiness. In both men you have the same anarchistic outlook covering an authoritarian cast of mind; in both a similar hostility to Science, the same impatience with opponents, the same inability to see the importance of any question not interesting to themselves; and in both cases a sort of horror of the actual process of life, though in Tolstoy's case it was arrived at later and in a different way. The sexual unhappiness of the two men was not of the same kind, but there was this in common, that in both of them a sincere loathing was mixed up with a morbid fascination. Tolstoy was a reformed rake who ended by preaching complete celibacy, while continuing to practise the opposite into extreme old age. Swift was presumably impotent, and had an exaggerated horror of human dung: he also thought about it incessantly, as is evident throughout his works. Such people are not likely to enjoy even the small amount of happiness that falls to most human beings, and, from obvious motives, are not likely to admit that earthly life is capable of much improvement. Their incuriosity, and hence their intolerance, spring from the same root.

Swift's disgust, rancour and pessimism would make sense against the background of a 'next world' to which this one is the prelude. As he does not appear to believe seriously in any such thing, it becomes necessary to construct a paradise supposedly existing on the surface of the earth, but something quite different from anything we know, with all that he disapproves of – lies, folly, change,

given for it so inadequate, is somehow unconvincing. One has the feeling that personal animosity is at work.

enthusiasm, pleasure, love and dirt – eliminated from it. As his ideal being he chooses the horse, an animal whose excrement is not offensive. The Houyhnhnms are dreary beasts – this is so generally admitted that the point is not worth labouring. Swift's genius can make them credible, but there can have been very few readers in whom they have excited any feeling beyond dislike. And this is not from wounded vanity at seeing animals preferred to men; for, of the two, the Houyhnhnms are much liker to human beings than are the Yahoos, and Gulliver's horror of the Yahoos, together with his recognition that they are the same kind of creature as himself, contains a logical absurdity. This horror comes upon him at his very first sight of them. 'I never beheld,' he says, 'in all my Travels, so disagreeable an Animal, nor one against which I naturally conceived so strong an Antipathy.' But in comparison with what are the Yahoos disgusting? Not with the Houyhnhnms, because at this time Gulliver has not seen a Houyhnhnm. It can only be in comparison with himself, i.e. with a human being. Later, however, we are to be told that the Yahoos *are* human beings, and human society becomes insupportable to Gulliver because all men are Yahoos. In that case why did he not conceive his disgust of humanity earlier? In effect we are told that the Yahoos are fantastically different from men, and yet are the same. Swift has over-reached himself in his fury, and is shouting at his fellow-creatures, 'You are filthier than you are!' However, it is impossible to feel much sympathy with the Yahoos, and it is not because they oppress the Yahoos that the Houyhnhnms are un-attractive. They are unattractive because the 'Reason' by which they are governed is really a desire for death. They are exempt from love, friendship, curiosity, fear, sorrow and – except in their feelings towards the Yahoos, who occupy rather the same place in their community as the Jews in Nazi Germany – anger and hatred. 'They have no Fondness for their Colts or Foles, but the Care they take, in educating them, proceeds entirely from the Dictates of *Reason*.' They lay store by 'Friendship' and 'Benevolence', but 'these are not confined to particular Objects, but universal to the whole Race'. They also value conversation, but in their conversations there are no differences of opinion, and 'nothing passed but what was useful, expressed in the fewest and most significant Words'. They practise strict birth control, each couple producing two offspring and thereafter abstaining from sexual intercourse. Their marriages are arranged for them by their elders, on eugenic principles, and their language contains no word for 'love', in the sexual sense. When somebody dies they carry on exactly as before, without feeling any grief. It will be seen that their aim is to be as like a corpse as is possible while retaining physical life. One or two of their characteristics, it is true, do not seem to be strictly 'reasonable' in their own usage of the word. Thus, they place a great value not only on physical hardihood but on athleticism, and they are devoted to poetry. But these exceptions may be less arbitrary than they seem. Swift probably emphasizes the physical strength of the Houyhnhnms in order to make clear that they could never be conquered by the hated human race, while a taste for poetry may figure among their qualities because poetry appeared to Swift as the antithesis of Science, from his point of view the most useless of all pursuits. In Part III he names 'Imagination, Fancy, and Invention' as desirable faculties in which the Laputan mathematicians (in spite of their love of music) were wholly lacking. One must remember that although Swift was an admirable writer of comic verse, the kind of poetry he thought valuable would probably be didactic poetry. The poetry of the Houyhnhnms, he says –

must be allowed to excel (that of) all other Mortals; wherein the Justness of their Similes, and the Minuteness, as well as exactness, of their Descriptions, are, indeed, inimitable. Their Verses abound very much in both of these; and usually contain either some exalted Notions of Friendship and Benevolence, or the Praises of those who were Victors in Races, and other bodily Exercises.

Alas, not even the genius of Swift was equal to producing a

specimen by which we could judge the poetry of the Houyhnhnms. But it sounds as though it were chilly stuff (in heroic couplets, presumably), and not seriously in conflict with the principles of 'Reason'.

Happiness is notoriously difficult to describe, and pictures of a just and well-ordered Society are seldom either attractive or convincing. Most creators of 'favourable' Utopias, however, are concerned to show what life could be like if it were lived more fully. Swift advocates a simple refusal of life, justifying this by the claim that 'Reason' consists in thwarting your instincts. The Houyhnhnms, creatures without a history, continue for generation after generation to live prudently, maintaining their population at exactly the same level, avoiding all passion, suffering from no diseases, meeting death indifferently, training up their young in the same principles – and all for what? In order that the same process may continue indefinitely. The notions that life here and now is worth living, or that it could be made worth living, or that it must be sacrificed for some future good, are all absent. The dreary world of the Houyhnhnms was about as good a Utopia as Swift could construct, granting that he neither believed in a 'next world' nor could get any pleasure out of certain normal activities. But it is not really set up as something desirable in itself, but as the justification for another attack on humanity. The aim, as usual, is to humiliate Man by reminding him that he is weak and ridiculous, and above all that he stinks; and the ultimate motive, probably, is a kind of envy, the envy of the ghost for the living, of the man who knows he cannot be happy for the others who – so he fears – may be a little happier than himself. The political expression of such an outlook must be either reactionary or nihilistic, because the person who holds it will want to prevent Society from developing in some direction in which his pessimism may be cheated. One can do this either by blowing everything to pieces, or by averting social change. Swift ultimately blew everything to pieces in the only way that was feasible before the atomic bomb – that is, he went mad – but, as I have tried to show, his political aims were on the whole reactionary ones.

From what I have written it may have seemed that I am *against* Swift, and that my object is to refute him and even to belittle him. In a political and moral sense I am against him, so far as I understand him. Yet curiously enough he is one of the writers I admire with least reserve, and *Gulliver's Travels*, in particular, is a book which it seems impossible for me to grow tired of. I read it first when I was eight – one day short of eight, to be exact, for I stole and furtively read the copy which was to be given me next day on my eighth birthday – and I have certainly not read it less than half a dozen times since. Its fascination seems inexhaustible. If I had to make a list of six books which were to be preserved when all others were destroyed, I would certainly put *Gulliver's Travels* among them. This raises the question: what is the relationship between agreement with a writer's opinions, and enjoyment of his work?

If one is capable of intellectual detachment, one can *perceive* merit in a writer whom one deeply disagrees with, but *enjoyment* is a different matter. Supposing that there is such a thing as good or bad art, then the goodness or badness must reside in the work of art itself – not independently of the observer, indeed, but independently of the mood of the observer. In one sense, therefore, it cannot be true that a poem is good on Monday and bad on Tuesday. But if one judges the poem by the appreciation it arouses, then it can certainly be true, because appreciation, or enjoyment, is a subjective condition which cannot be commanded. For a great deal of his waking life, even the most cultivated person has no aesthetic feelings whatever, and the power to have aesthetic feelings is very easily destroyed. When you are frightened, or hungry, or are suffering from toothache or sea-sickness, *King Lear* is no better from your point of view than *Peter Pan*. You may know in an intellectual sense that it is better, but that is simply a fact which you remember: you will not *feel* the merit of *King Lear* until you are normal again. And aesthetic judgement can be upset just as disastrously – more disastrously, because the cause is less readily recognized – by political or moral disagreement. If a book angers, wounds or alarms you, then you will not enjoy it, whatever its merits may be. If it seems to you a really pernicious book, likely to influence other people in some undesirable way, then you will probably construct an aesthetic theory to show that it *has* no merits. Current literary criticism consists quite largely of this kind of dodging to and fro between two sets of standards. And yet the opposite process can also happen: enjoyment can overwhelm disapproval, even though one clearly recognizes that one is enjoying something inimical. Swift, whose world-view is so peculiarly unacceptable, but who is nevertheless an extremely popular writer, is a good instance of this. Why is it that we don't mind being called Yahoos, although firmly convinced that we are *not* Yahoos?

It is not enough to make the usual answer that of course Swift was wrong, in fact he was insane, but he was 'a good writer'. It is true that the literary quality of a book is to some small extent separable from its subject-matter. Some people have a native gift for using words, as some people have a naturally 'good eye' at games. It is largely a question of timing and of instinctively knowing how much emphasis to use. As an example near at hand, look back at the passage I quoted earlier, starting 'In the Kingdom of Tribnia, by the Natives called Langdon'. It derives much of its force from the final sentence: 'And this is the anagrammatic Method.' Strictly speaking this sentence is unnecessary, for we have already seen the anagram decyphered, but the mock-solemn repetition, in which one seems to hear Swift's own voice uttering the words, drives home the idiocy of the activities described, like the final tap to a nail. But not all the power and simplicity of Swift's prose, nor the imaginative effort that has been able to make not one but a whole series of impossible worlds more credible than the majority of history books – none of this would enable us to enjoy Swift if his world-view were truly wounding or shocking. Millions of people, in many countries, must have enjoyed *Gulliver's Travels* while more or less seeing its anti-human implications: and even the child who accepts Parts I and II as a simple story gets a sense of absurdity from thinking of human beings six inches high. The explanation must be that Swift's world-view is felt to be *not* altogether false – or it would probably be more accurate to say, not false all the time. Swift is a diseased writer. He remains permanently in a depressed mood which in most people is only intermittent, rather as though someone suffering from jaundice or the after-effects of influenza should have the energy to write books. But we all know that mood, and something in us responds to the expression of it. Take, for instance, one of his most characteristic works, *The Lady's Dressing Room*: one might add the kindred poem, *Upon a Beautiful Young Nymph Going to Bed*. Which is truer, the viewpoint expressed in these poems, or the viewpoint implied in Blake's phrase, 'The naked female human form divine'? No doubt Blake is nearer the truth, and yet who can fail to feel a sort of pleasure in seeing that fraud, feminine delicacy, exploded for once? Swift falsifies his picture of the world by refusing to see anything in human life except dirt, folly and wickedness, but the part which he abstracts from the whole does exist, and it is something which we all know about while shrinking from mentioning it. Part of our minds – in any normal person it is the dominant part – believes that man is a noble animal and life is worth living: but there is also a sort of inner self which at least intermittently stands aghast at the horror of existence. In the queerest way, pleasure and disgust are linked together. The human body is beautiful: it is also repulsive and ridiculous, a fact which can be verified at any swimming pool. The sexual organs are objects of desire and also of loathing, so much so that in many languages, if not in all languages, their names are used as words of abuse. Meat is delicious, but a butcher's shop makes one feel sick: and indeed all our food springs ultimately from dung and dead bodies, the two things which of all others seem to us the most horrible. A child, when it is past the infantile stage but still looking at the world with fresh eyes, is moved by horror almost as often as by wonder – horror of snot and spittle, of the dogs' excrement on the pavement, the dying toad full of maggots, the sweaty smell of grown-ups, the hideousness of old men, with their bald heads and bulbous noses. In his endless harping on disease, dirt and deformity, Swift is not actually inventing anything, he is merely leaving something out. Human behaviour, too, especially in politics, is as he describes it, although it contains other more important factors which he refuses to admit. So far as we can see, both horror and pain are necessary to the continuance of life on this planet, and it is therefore open to pessimists like Swift to say : 'If horror and pain must always be with us, how can life be significantly improved?' His attitude is in effect the Christian attitude, minus the bribe of a 'next world' – which, however, probably has less hold upon the minds of believers than the conviction that this world is a vale of tears and the grave is a place of rest. It is, I am certain, a wrong attitude, and one which could have harmful effects upon behaviour; but something in us responds to it, as it responds to the gloomy words of the burial service and the sweetish smell of corpses in a country church.

It is often argued, at least by people who admit the importance of subject-matter, that a book cannot be 'good' if it expresses a palpably false view of life. We are told that in our own age, for instance, any book that has genuine literary merit will also be more or less 'progressive' in tendency. This ignores the fact that throughout history a similar struggle between progress and reaction has been raging, and that the best books of any one age have always been written from several different viewpoints, some of them palpably more false than others. In so far as a writer is a propagandist, the most one can ask of him is that he shall genuinely believe in what he is saying, and that it shall not be something blazingly silly. To-day, for example, one can imagine a good book being written by a Catholic, a Communist, a Fascist, a pacifist, an anarchist, perhaps by an old-style Liberal or an ordinary Conservative: one cannot imagine a good book being written by a spiritualist, a Buchmanite or a member of the Ku-Klux-Klan. The views that a writer holds must be compatible with sanity, in the medical sense, and with the power of continuous thought: beyond that what we ask of him is talent, which is probably another name for conviction. Swift did not possess ordinary wisdom, but he did possess a terrible intensity of vision, capable of picking out a single hidden truth and then magnifying it and distorting it. The durability of *Gulliver's Travels* goes to show that, if the force of belief is behind it, a world-view which only just passes the test of sanity is sufficient to produce a great work of art.

1946

POLITICS AND THE ENGLISH
LANGUAGE

Most people who bother with the matter at all would admit that the English language is in a bad way, but it is generally assumed that we cannot by conscious action do anything about it. Our civilization is decadent and our language – so the argument runs – must inevitably share in the general collapse. It follows that any struggle against the abuse of language is a sentimental archaism, like preferring candles to electric light or hansom cabs to aeroplanes. Underneath this lies the half-conscious belief that language is a natural growth and not an instrument which we shape for our own purposes.

Now, it is clear that the decline of a language must ultimately have political and economic causes: it is not due simply to the bad influence of this or that individual writer. But an effect can become a cause, reinforcing the original cause and producing the same effect in an intensified form, and so on indefinitely. A man may take to drink because he feels himself to be a failure, and then fail all the more completely because he drinks. It is rather the same thing that is happening to the English language. It becomes ugly and inaccurate because our thoughts are foolish, but the slovenliness of our language makes it easier for us to have foolish thoughts. The point is that the process is reversible. Modern English, especially written English, is full of bad habits which spread by imitation and which can be avoided if one is willing to take the necessary trouble. If one gets rid of these habits one can think more clearly, and to think clearly is a necessary first step towards political regeneration: so that the fight against bad English is not frivolous and is not the exclusive concern of professional writers. I will come back to this presently, and I hope that by that time the meaning of what I have said here will have become clearer. Meanwhile, here are five specimens of the English language as it is now habitually written.

These five passages have not been picked out because they are especially bad – I could have quoted far worse if I had chosen – but because they illustrate various of the mental vices from which we now suffer. They are a little below the average, but are fairly representative samples. I number them so that I can refer back to them when necessary:

(1) I am not, indeed, sure whether it is not true to say that the Milton who once seemed not unlike a seventeenth-century Shelley had not become, out of an experience ever more bitter in each year, more alien [*sic*] to the founder of that Jesuit sect which nothing could induce him to tolerate.

> Professor Harold Laski (Essay in *Freedom of Expression*)

(2) Above all, we cannot play ducks and drakes with a native battery of idioms which prescribes such egregious collocations of vocables as the Basic *put up with* for *tolerate* or *put at a loss* for *bewilder*.

> Professor Lancelot Hogben (*Interglossa*)

(3) On the one side we have the free personality: by definition it is not neurotic, for it has neither conflict nor dream. Its desires, such as they are, are transparent, for they are just what institutional approval keeps in the forefront of consciousness; another institutional pattern would alter their number and intensity; there is little in them that is natural, irreducible, or culturally dangerous. But *on the other side*, the social bond itself is nothing but the mutual reflection of these self-secure integrities. Recall the definition of love. Is not this the very picture of a small academic? Where is there a place in this hall of mirrors for either personality or fraternity?

> Essay on psychology in *Politics* (New York)

(4) All the 'best people' from the gentlemen's clubs, and all the frantic fascist captains, united in common hatred of Socialism and bestial horror of the rising tide of the mass revolutionary movement, have turned to acts of provocation, to foul incendiarism, to medieval legends of poisoned wells, to legalize their own destruc-

tion of proletarian organizations, and rouse the agitated petty-bourgeoisie to chauvinistic fervour on behalf of the fight against the revolutionary way out of the crisis.

Communist pamphlet

(5) If a new spirit *is* to be infused into this old country, there is one thorny and contentious reform which must be tackled, and that is the humanization and galvanization of the B.B.C. Timidity here will bespeak canker and atrophy of the soul. The heart of Britain may be sound and of strong beat, for instance, but the British lion's roar at present is like that of Bottom in Shakespeare's *Midsummer Night's Dream* – as gentle as any sucking dove. A virile new Britain cannot continue indefinitely to be traduced in the eyes or rather ears, of the world by the effete languors of Langham Place, brazenly masquerading as 'standard English'. When the Voice of Britain is heard at nine o'clock, better far and infinitely less ludicrous to hear aitches honestly dropped than the present priggish, inflated, inhibited, school-ma'amish arch braying of blameless bashful mewing maidens!

Letter in Tribune

Each of these passages has faults of its own, but, quite apart from avoidable ugliness, two qualities are common to all of them. The first is staleness of imagery: the other is lack of precision. The writer either has a meaning and cannot express it, or he inadvertently says something else, or he is almost indifferent as to whether his words mean anything or not. This mixture of vagueness and sheer incompetence is the most marked characteristic of modern English prose, and especially of any kind of political writing. As soon as certain topics are raised, the concrete melts into the abstract and no one seems able to think of turns of speech that are not hackneyed: prose consists less and less of *words* chosen for the sake of their meaning, and more and more of *phrases* tacked together like the sections of a prefabricated hen-house. I list below, with notes and examples, various of the tricks by means of which the work of prose-construction is habitually dodged:

DYING METAPHORS. A newly invented metaphor assists thought by evoking a visual image, while on the other hand a metaphor which is technically 'dead' (e.g. *iron resolution*) has in effect reverted to being an ordinary word and can generally be used without loss of vividness. But in between these two classes there is a huge dump of worn-out metaphors which have lost all evocative power and are merely used because they save people the trouble of inventing phrases for themselves. Examples are: *Ring the changes on, take up the cudgels for, toe the line, ride roughshod over, stand shoulder to shoulder with, play into the hands of, no axe to grind, grist to the mill, fishing in troubled waters, on the order of the day, Achilles' heel, swan song, hotbed.* Many of these are used without knowledge of their meaning (what is a 'rift', for instance?), and incompatible metaphors are frequently mixed, a sure sign that the writer is not interested in what he is saying. Some metaphors now current have been twisted out of their original meaning without those who use them even being aware of the fact. For example, *toe the line* is sometimes written *tow the line*. Another example is *the hammer and the anvil*, now always used with the implication that the anvil gets the worst of it. In real life it is always the anvil that breaks the hammer, never the other way about: a writer who stopped to think what he was saying would be aware of this, and would avoid perverting the original phrase.

OPERATORS or VERBAL FALSE LIMBS. These save the trouble of picking out appropriate verbs and nouns, and at the same time pad each sentence with extra syllables which give it an appearance of symmetry. Characteristic phrases are: *render inoperative, militate against, make contact with, be subjected to, give rise to, give grounds for, have the effect of, play a leading part (role) in, make itself felt, take effect, exhibit a tendency to, serve the purpose of, etc., etc.* The keynote is the elimination of simple verbs. Instead of being a single word, such as *break, stop, spoil, mend, kill*, a verb becomes a *phrase*, made up of a noun or adjective tacked on to some general-purposes verb such as *prove, serve, form, play, render*. In addition, the passive voice is wherever possible used in preference to the active, and noun constructions are used instead of gerunds (*by examination of* instead of *by examining*). The range of verbs is further cut down by means of the *-ize* and *de-* formations, and the banal statements are given an appearance of profundity by means of the *not un-* formation. Simple conjunctions and prepositions are replaced by such phrases as *with respect to, having regard to, the fact that, by dint of, in view of, in the interests of, on the hypothesis that*; and the ends of sentences are saved from anticlimax by such resounding common-places as *greatly to be desired, cannot be left out of account, a development to be expected in the near future, deserving of serious consideration, brought to a satisfactory conclusion*, and so on and so forth.

PRETENTIOUS DICTION. Words like *phenomenon, element, individual* (as noun), *objective, categorical, effective, virtual, basic, primary, promote, constitute, exhibit, exploit, utilize, eliminate, liquidate*, are used to dress up simple statement and give an air of scientific impartiality to biased judgements. Adjectives like *epoch-making, epic, historic, unforgettable, triumphant, age-old, inevitable, inexorable, veritable*, are used to dignify the sordid processes of international politics, while writing that aims at glorifying war usually takes on an archaic colour, its characteristic words being: *realm, throne, chariot, mailed fist, trident, sword, shield, buckler, banner, jackboot, clarion*. Foreign words and expressions such as *cul de sac, ancien régime, deus ex machina, mutatis mutandis, status quo, gleichschaltung, weltan-schauung*, are used to give an air of culture and elegance. Except for the useful abbreviations *i.e., e.g.*, and *etc.*, there is no real need for any of the hundreds of foreign phrases now current in English. Bad writers, and especially scientific, political and sociological writers, are nearly always haunted by the notion that Latin or Greek words are grander than Saxon ones, and unnecessary words like *expedite, ameliorate, predict, extraneous, deracinated, clandestine, subaqueous* and hundreds of others constantly gain ground from their Anglo-Saxon opposite numbers.* The jargon

* An interesting illustration of this is the way in which the English flower names which were in use till very recently are being ousted by

peculiar to Marxist writing (*hyena, hangman, cannibal, petty bourgeois, these gentry, lacquey, flunkey, mad dog, White Guard,* etc.) consists largely of words and phrases translated from Russian, German or French; but the normal way of coining a new word is to use a Latin or Greek root with the appropriate affix and, where necessary, the -ize formation. It is often easier to make up words of this kind (*deregionalize, impermissible, extramarital, non-fragmentatory* and so forth) than to think up the English words that will cover one's meaning. The result, in general, is an increase in slovenliness and vagueness.

MEANINGLESS WORDS. In certain kinds of writing, particularly in art criticism and literary criticism, it is normal to come across long passages which are almost completely lacking in meaning.* Words like *romantic, plastic values, human, dead, sentimental, natural vitality,* as used in art criticism, are strictly meaningless, in the sense that they not only do not point to any discoverable object, but are hardly ever expected to do so by the reader. When one critic writes, 'The outstanding feature of Mr X's work is its living quality', while another writes, 'The immediately striking thing about Mr X's work is its peculiar deadness', the reader accepts this as a simple difference of opinion. If words like *black* and *white* were involved, instead of the jargon words *dead* and *living*, he would see at once that language was being used in an improper way. Many political words are similarly abused. The word *Fascism* has now

Greek ones, *snapdragon* becoming *antirrhinum, forget-me-not* becoming *myosotis,* etc. It is hard to see any practical reason for this change of fashion: it is probably due to an instinctive turning-away from the more homely word and a vague feeling that the Greek word is scientific.

* Example: 'Comfort's catholicity of perception and image, strangely Whitmanesque in range, almost the exact opposite in aesthetic compulsion, continues to evoke that trembling atmospheric accumulative hinting at a cruel, an inexorably serene timelessness ... Wrey Gardiner scores by aiming at simple bull's-eyes with precision. Only they are not so simple, and through this contented sadness runs more than the surface bitter-sweet of resignation.' (*Poetry Quarterly.*)

no meaning except in so far as it signifies 'something not desirable'. The words *democracy, socialism, freedom, patriotic, realistic, justice,* have each of them several different meanings which cannot be reconciled with one another. In the case of a word like *democracy,* not only is there no agreed definition but the attempt to make one is resisted from all sides. It is almost universally felt that when we call a country democratic we are praising it: consequently the defenders of every kind of régime claim that it is a democracy, and fear that they might have to stop using the word if it were tied down to any one meaning. Words of this kind are often used in a consciously dishonest way. That is, the person who uses them has his own private definition, but allows his hearer to think he means something quite different. Statements like *Marshal Pétain was a true patriot, The Soviet Press is the freest in the world, The Catholic Church is opposed to persecution,* are almost always made with intent to deceive. Other words used in variable meanings, in most cases more or less dishonestly, are: *class, totalitarian, science, progressive, reactionary, bourgeois, equality.*

Now that I have made this catalogue of swindles and perversions, let me give another example of the kind of writing that they lead to. This time it must of its nature be an imaginary one. I am going to translate a passage of good English into modern English of the worst sort. Here is a well-known verse from *Ecclesiastes*:

I returned and saw under the sun, that the race is not to the swift, nor the battle to the strong, neither yet bread to the wise, nor yet riches to men of understanding, nor yet favour to men of skill; but time and chance happeneth to them all.

Here it is in modern English:

Objective considerations of contemporary phenomena compels the conclusion that success or failure in competitive activities exhibits no tendency to be commensurate with innate capacity, but that a considerable element of the unpredictable must invariably be taken into account.

This is a parody, but not a very gross one. Exhibit (3),

above, for instance, contains several patches of the same kind of English. It will be seen that I have not made a full translation. The beginning and ending of the sentence follow the original meaning fairly closely, but in the middle the concrete illustrations – race, battle, bread – dissolve into the vague phrase 'success or failure in competitive activities'. This had to be so, because no modern writer of the kind I am discussing – no one capable of using phrases like 'objective consideration of contemporary phenomena' – would ever tabulate his thoughts in that precise and detailed way. The whole tendency of modern prose is away from concreteness. Now analyse these two sentences a little more closely. The first contains forty-nine words but only sixty syllables, and all its words are those of everyday life. The second contains thirty-eight words of ninety syllables: eighteen of its words are from Latin roots, and one from Greek. The first sentence contains six vivid images, and only one phrase ('time and chance') that could be called vague. The second contains not a single fresh, arresting phrase, and in spite of its ninety syllables it gives only a shortened version of the meaning contained in the first. Yet without a doubt it is the second kind of sentence that is gaining ground in modern English. I do not want to exaggerate. This kind of writing is not yet universal, and outcrops of simplicity will occur here and there in the worst-written page. Still, if you or I were told to write a few lines on the uncertainty of human fortunes, we should probably come much nearer to my imaginary sentence than to the one from *Ecclesiastes*.

As I have tried to show, modern writing at its worst does not consist in picking out words for the sake of their meaning and inventing images in order to make the meaning clearer. It consists in gumming together long strips of words which have already been set in order by someone else, and making the results presentable by sheer humbug. The attraction of this way of writing is that it is easy. It is easier – even quicker, once you have the habit – to say *In my opinion it is a not unjustifiable assumption that* than to say *I think*. If you use ready-made phrases, you not only don't have to hunt about for words; you also don't have to bother with the rhythms of your sentences, since these phrases are generally so arranged as to be more or less euphonious. When you are composing in a hurry – when you are dictating to a stenographer, for instance, or making a public speech – it is natural to fall into a pretentious, Latinized style. Tags like *a consideration which we should do well to bear in mind* or *a conclusion to which all of us would readily assent* will save many a sentence from coming down with a bump. By using stale metaphors, similes and idioms, you save much mental effort, at the cost of leaving your meaning vague, not only for your reader but for yourself. This is the significance of mixed metaphors. The sole aim of a metaphor is to call up a visual image. When these images clash – as in *The Fascist octopus has sung its swan song, the jackboot is thrown into the melting pot* – it can be taken as certain that the writer is not seeing a mental image of the objects he is naming; in other words he is not really thinking. Look again at the examples I gave at the beginning of this essay. Professor Laski (1) uses five negatives in fifty-three words. One of these is superfluous, making nonsense of the whole passage, and in addition there is the slip *alien* for akin, making further nonsense, and several avoidable pieces of clumsiness which increase the general vagueness. Professor Hogben (2) plays ducks and drakes with a battery which is able to write prescriptions, and, while disapproving of the everyday phrase *put up with*, is unwilling to look *egregious* up in the dictionary and see what it means. (3), if one takes an uncharitable attitude towards it, is simply meaningless: probably one could work out its intended meaning by reading the whole of the article in which it occurs. In (4), the writer knows more or less what he wants to say, but an accumulation of stale phrases chokes him like tea leaves blocking a sink. In (5), words and meaning have almost parted company. People who write in this manner usually have a general emotional meaning – they dislike one thing and want to express solidarity with another – but they are not interested in the detail of what they are saying. A scrupulous writer, in every sentence that he writes, will ask himself at least four questions, thus: What am I trying to say? What words will express it? What image or idiom will make it clearer? Is this image fresh enough to have an effect? And he will probably ask himself two more: Could I put it more shortly? Have I said anything that is avoidably ugly? But you are not obliged to go to all this trouble. You can shirk it by simply throwing your mind open and letting the ready-made phrases come crowding in. They will construct your sentences for you – even think your thoughts for you, to a certain extent – and at need they will perform the important service of partially concealing your meaning even from yourself. It is at this point that the special connexion between politics and the debasement of language becomes clear.

In our time it is broadly true that political writing is bad writing. Where it is not true, it will generally be found that the writer is some kind of rebel, expressing his private opinions and not a 'party line'. Orthodoxy, of whatever colour, seems to demand a lifeless, imitative style. The political dialects to be found in pamphlets, leading articles, manifestos, White Papers and the speeches of under-secretaries do, of course, vary from party to party, but they are all alike in that one almost never finds in them a fresh, vivid, home-made turn of speech. When one watches some tired hack on the platform mechanically repeating the familiar phrases – *bestial atrocities, iron heel, bloodstained tyranny, free peoples of the world, stand shoulder to shoulder* – one often has a curious feeling that one is not watching a live human being but some kind of dummy: a feeling which suddenly becomes stronger at moments when the light catches the speaker's spectacles and turns them into blank discs which seem to have no eyes behind them. And this is not altogether fanciful. A speaker who uses that kind of phraseology has gone some distance towards turning himself into a machine. The appropriate noises are coming out of his larynx, but his brain is not involved as it would be if he were choosing his words for himself. If the speech he is making is one that he is accustomed to make over and over again, he may be almost unconscious of what he is saying, as one is when one utters the responses in church. And this reduced state of consciousness, if not indispensable, is at any rate favourable to political conformity.

In our time, political speech and writing are largely the defence of the indefensible. Things like the continuance of British rule in India, the Russian purges and deportations, the dropping of the atom bombs on Japan, can indeed be defended, but only by arguments which are too brutal for most people to face, and which do not square with the professed aims of political parties. Thus political language has to consist largely of euphemism, question-begging and sheer cloudy vagueness. Defenceless villages are bombarded from the air, the inhabitants driven out into the countryside, the cattle machine-gunned, the huts set on fire with incendiary bullets: this is called *pacification*. Millions of peasants are robbed of their farms and sent trudging along the roads with no more than they can carry: this is called *transfer of population* or *rectification of frontiers*. People are imprisoned for years without trial, or shot in the back of the neck or sent to die of scurvy in Arctic lumber camps: this is called *elimination of unreliable elements*. Such phraseology is needed if one wants to name things without calling up mental pictures of them. Consider for instance some comfortable English professor defending Russian totalitarianism. He cannot say outright, 'I believe in killing off your opponents when you can get good results by doing so'. Probably, therefore, he will say something like this:

'While freely conceding that the Soviet régime exhibits certain features which the humanitarian may be inclined to deplore, we must, I think, agree that a certain curtailment of the right to political opposition is an unavoidable concomitant of transitional periods, and that the rigours which the Russian people have been called upon to undergo have been amply justified in the sphere of concrete achievement.'

The inflated style is itself a kind of euphemism. A mass of Latin words falls upon the facts like soft snow, blurring the outlines and covering up all the details. The great enemy of clear language is insincerity. When there is a gap between one's real and one's declared aims, one turns as it were instinctively to long words and exhausted idioms, like a cuttlefish squirting out ink. In our age there is no such thing as 'keeping out of politics'. All issues are political issues, and politics itself is a mass of lies, evasions, folly, hatred and schizophrenia. When the general atmosphere is bad, language must suffer. I should expect to find – this is a guess which I have not sufficient knowledge to verify – that the German, Russian and Italian languages have all deteriorated in the last ten or fifteen years, as a result of dictatorship.

But if thought corrupts language, language can also corrupt thought. A bad usage can spread by tradition and imitation, even among people who should and do know better. The debased language that I have been discussing is in some ways very convenient. Phrases like *a not unjustifiable assumption, leaves much to be desired, would serve no good purpose, a consideration which we should do well to bear in mind*, are a continuous temptation, a packet of aspirins always at one's elbow. Look back through this essay, and for certain you will find that I have again and again committed the very faults I am protesting against. By this morning's post I have received a pamphlet dealing with conditions in Germany. The author tells me that he 'felt impelled' to write it. I open it at random, and here is almost the first sentence that I see: '(The Allies) have an opportunity not only of achieving a radical transformation of Germany's social and political structure in such a way as to avoid a nationalistic reaction in Germany itself, but at the same time of laying the foundations of a co-operative and unified Europe.' You see, he 'feels impelled' to write – feels, presumably, that he has something new to say – and yet his words, like cavalry horses answering the bugle, group themselves automatically into the familiar dreary pattern. This invasion of one's mind by ready-made phrases (*lay the foundations, achieve a radical transformation*) can only be prevented if one is constantly on guard against them, and every such phrase anaesthetizes a portion of one's brain.

I said earlier that the decadence of our language is probably curable. Those who deny this would argue, if they produced an argument at all, that language merely reflects existing social conditions, and that we cannot influence its development by any direct tinkering with words and constructions. So far as the general tone or spirit of a language goes, this may be true, but it is not true in detail. Silly words and expressions have often disappeared, not through any evolutionary process but owing to the conscious action of a minority. Two recent examples were *explore every avenue* and *leave no stone unturned*, which were killed by the jeers of a few journalists. There is a long list of flyblown metaphors which could similarly be got rid of if enough people would interest themselves in the job; and it should also be possible to laugh the *not un-* formation out of existence,* to reduce the amount of Latin and Greek in the average sentence, to drive out foreign phrases and strayed scientific words, and, in general, to make pretentiousness unfashionable. But all these are minor points. The defence of the English language implies more than this, and perhaps it is best to start by saying what it *does not* imply.

To begin with it has nothing to do with archaism, with the salvaging of obsolete words and turns of speech, or with the setting up of a 'standard English' which must never be departed from. On the contrary, it is especially concerned with the scrapping of every word or idiom which has outworn its usefulness. It has nothing to do with correct grammar and syntax, which are of no importance so long as one makes one's meaning clear, or with the avoidance of Americanisms, or with having what is called a 'good prose style'. On the other hand it is not concerned with fake simplicity and the attempt to make written English colloquial. Nor does it even imply in every case preferring the

---

* One can cure oneself of the *not un-* formation by memorizing this sentence: *A not unblack dog was chasing a not unsmall rabbit across a not ungreen field.*

Saxon word to the Latin one, though it does imply using the fewest and shortest words that will cover one's meaning. What is above all needed is to let the meaning choose the word, and not the other way about. In prose, the worst thing one can do with words is to surrender to them. When you think of a concrete object, you think wordlessly, and then, if you want to describe the thing you have been visualizing you probably hunt about till you find the exact words that seem to fit it. When you think of something abstract you are more inclined to use words from the start, and unless you make a conscious effort to prevent it, the existing dialect will come rushing in and do the job for you, at the expense of blurring or even changing your meaning. Probably it is better to put off using words as long as possible and get one's meaning as clear as one can through pictures or sensations. Afterwards one can choose – not simply *accept* – the phrases that will best cover the meaning, and then switch round and decide what impression one's words are likely to make on another person. This last effort of the mind cuts out all stale or mixed images, all prefabricated phrases, needless repetitions, and humbug and vagueness generally. But one can often be in doubt about the effect of a word or a phrase, and one needs rules that one can rely on when instinct fails. I think the following rules will cover most cases:

(i) Never use a metaphor, simile or other figure of speech which you are used to seeing in print.

(ii) Never use a long word where a short one will do.

(iii) If it is possible to cut out a word, always cut it out.

(iv) Never use the passive where you can use the active.

(v) Never use a foreign phrase, a scientific word or a jargon word if you can think of an everyday English equivalent.

(vi) Break any of these rules sooner than say anything outright barbarous.

These rules sound elementary, and so they are, but they demand a deep change of attitude in anyone who has grown used to writing in the style now fashionable. One could keep all of them and still write bad English, but one could not write the kind of stuff that I quoted in those five specimens at the beginning of this article.

I have not here been considering the literary use of language, but merely language as an instrument for expressing and not for concealing or preventing thought. Stuart Chase and others have come near to claiming that all abstract words are meaningless, and have used this as a pretext for advocating a kind of political quietism. Since you don't know what Fascism is, how can you struggle against Fascism? One need not swallow such absurdities as this, but one ought to recognize that the present political chaos is connected with the decay of language, and that one can probably bring about some improvement by starting at the verbal end. If you simplify your English, you are freed from the worst follies of orthodoxy. You cannot speak any of the necessary dialects, and when you make a stupid remark its stupidity will be obvious, even to yourself. Political language – and with variations this is true of all political parties, from Conservatives to Anarchists – is designed to make lies sound truthful and murder respectable, and to give an appearance of solidity to pure wind. One cannot change this all in a moment, but one can at least change one's own habits, and from time to time one can even, if one jeers loudly enough, send some worn-out and useless phrase – some *jackboot, Achilles' heel, hotbed, melting pot, acid test, veritable inferno* or other lump of verbal refuse – into the dustbin where it belongs.

1946

THE PREVENTION OF LITERATURE

ABOUT a year ago I attended a meeting of the P.E.N. Club, the occasion being the tercentenary of Milton's *Areopagitica* – a pamphlet, it may be remembered, in defence of freedom of the Press. Milton's famous phrase about the sin of 'killing' a book was printed on the leaflets advertising the meeting which had been circulated beforehand.

There were four speakers on the platform. One of them delivered a speech which did deal with the freedom of the Press, but only in relation to India; another said, hesitantly, and in very general terms, that liberty was a good thing; a third delivered an attack on the laws relating to obscenity in literature. The fourth devoted most of his speech to a defence of the Russian purges. Of the speeches from the body of the hall, some reverted to the question of obscenity and the laws that deal with it, others were simply eulogies of Soviet Russia. Moral liberty – the liberty to discuss sex questions frankly in print – seemed to be generally approved, but political liberty was not mentioned. Out of this concourse of several hundred people, perhaps half of whom were directly connected with the writing trade, there was not a single one who could point out that freedom of the Press, if it means anything at all, means the freedom to criticize and oppose. Significantly, no speaker quoted from the pamphlet which was ostensibly being commemorated. Nor was there any mention of the various books that have been 'killed' in this country and the United States during the war. In its net effect the meeting was a demonstration in favour of censorship.*

* It is fair to say that the P.E.N. Club celebrations, which lasted a week or more, did not always stick at quite the same level. I happened to strike a bad day. But an examination of the speeches (printed under

There was nothing particularly surprising in this. In our age, the idea of intellectual liberty is under attack from two directions. On the one side are its theoretical enemies, the apologists of totalitarianism, and on the other its immediate practical enemies, monopoly and bureaucracy. Any writer or journalist who wants to retain his integrity finds himself thwarted by the general drift of society rather than by active persecution. The sort of things that are working against him are the concentration of the Press in the hands of a few rich men, the grip of monopoly on radio and the films, the unwillingness of the public to spend money on books, making it necessary for nearly every writer to earn part of his living by hackwork, the encroachment of official bodies like the M.O.I. and the British Council, which help the writer to keep alive but also waste his time and dictate his opinions, and the continuous war atmosphere of the past ten years, whose distorting effects no one has been able to escape. Everything in our age conspires to turn the writer, and every other kind of artist as well, into a minor official, working on themes handed to him from above and never telling what seems to him the whole of the truth. But in struggling against this fate he gets no help from his own side: that is, there is no large body of opinion which will assure him that he is in the right. In the past, at any rate throughout the Protestant centuries, the idea of rebellion and the idea of intellectual integrity were mixed up. A heretic – political, moral, religious, or aesthetic – was one who refused to outrage his own conscience. His outlook was summed up in the words of the Revivalist hymn:

> Dare to be a Daniel,
> Dare to stand alone;
> Dare to have a purpose firm,
> Dare to make it known.

To bring this hymn up to date one would have to add a

the title *Freedom of Expression*) shows that almost nobody in our own day is able to speak out as roundly in favour of intellectual liberty as Milton could do 300 years ago – and this in spite of the fact Milton was writing in a period of civil war.

'Don't' at the beginning of each line. For it is the peculiarity of our age that the rebels against the existing order, at any rate the most numerous and characteristic of them, are also rebelling against the idea of individual integrity. 'Daring to stand alone' is ideologically criminal as well as practically dangerous. The independence of the writer and the artist is eaten away by vague economic forces, and at the same time it is undermined by those who should be its defenders. It is with the second process that I am concerned here.

Freedom of thought and of the Press are usually attacked by arguments which are not worth bothering about. Anyone who has experience of lecturing and debating knows them off backwards. Here I am not trying to deal with the familiar claim that freedom is an illusion, or with the claim that there is more freedom in totalitarian countries than in democratic ones, but with the much more tenable and dangerous proposition that freedom is *undesirable* and that intellectual honesty is a form of anti-social selfishness. Although other aspects of the question are usually in the foreground, the controversy over freedom of speech and of the Press is at bottom a controversy over the desirability, or otherwise, of telling lies. What is really at issue is the right to report contemporary events truthfully, or as truthfully as is consistent with the ignorance, bias and self-deception from which every observer necessarily suffers. In saying this I may seem to be saying that straightforward 'reportage' is the only branch of literature that matters: but I will try to show later that at every literary level, and probably in every one of the arts, the same issue arises in more or less subtilized forms. Meanwhile, it is necessary to strip away the irrelevancies in which this controversy is usually wrapped up.

The enemies of intellectual liberty always try to present their case as a plea for discipline versus individualism. The issue truth-versus-untruth is as far as possible kept in the background. Although the point of emphasis may vary, the writer who refuses to sell his opinions is always branded as a mere *egoist*. He is accused, that is, either of wanting to shut himself up in an ivory tower, or of making an exhibitionist display of his own personality, or of resisting the inevitable current of history in an attempt to cling to unjustified privileges. The Catholic and the Communist are alike in assuming that an opponent cannot be both honest and intelligent. Each of them tacitly claims that 'the truth' has already been revealed, and that the heretic, if he is not simply a fool, is secretly aware of 'the truth' and merely resists it out of selfish motives. In Communist literature the attack on intellectual liberty is usually masked by oratory about 'petty-bourgeois individualism', 'the illusions of nineteenth-century liberalism', etc., and backed up by words of abuse such as 'romantic' and 'sentimental', which, since they do not have any agreed meaning, are difficult to answer. In this way the controversy is manoeuvred away from its real issue. One can accept, and most enlightened people would accept, the Communist thesis that pure freedom will only exist in a classless society, and that one is most nearly free when one is working to bring such a society about. But slipped in with this is the quite unfounded claim that the Communist party is itself aiming at the establishment of the classless society, and that in the U.S.S.R. this aim is actually on the way to being realized. If the first claim is allowed to entail the second, there is almost no assault on common sense and common decency that cannot be justified. But meanwhile, the real point has been dodged. Freedom of the intellect means the freedom to report what one has seen, heard, and felt, and not to be obliged to fabricate imaginary facts and feelings. The familiar tirades against 'escapism', and 'individualism', 'romanticism' and so forth, are merely a forensic device, the aim of which is to make the perversion of history seem respectable.

Fifteen years ago, when one defended the freedom of the intellect, one had to defend it against Conservatives, against Catholics, and to some extent – for they were not of great importance in England – against Fascists. To-day one has to defend it against Communists and 'fellow-travellers'. One ought not to exaggerate the direct influence of the small English Communist party, but there can be no question about the poisonous effect of the Russian *mythos* on English intellectual life. Because of it known facts are suppressed and distorted to such an extent as to make it doubtful whether a true history of our times can ever be written. Let me give just one instance out of the hundreds that could be cited. When Germany collapsed, it was found that very large numbers of Soviet Russians – mostly, no doubt, from non-political motives – had changed sides and were fighting for the Germans. Also, a small but not negligible proportion of the Russian prisoners and Displaced Persons refused to go back to the U.S.S.R., and some of them, at least, were repatriated against their will. These facts, known to many journalists on the spot, went almost unmentioned in the British Press, while at the same time Russophile publicists in England continued to justify the purges and deportations of 1936–8 by claiming that the U.S.S.R. 'had no quislings'. The fog of lies and misinformation that surrounds such subjects as the Ukraine famine, the Spanish civil war, Russian policy in Poland, and so forth, is not due entirely to conscious dishonesty, but any writer or journalist who is fully sympathetic to the U.S.S.R. – sympathetic, that is, in the way the Russians themselves would want him to be – does have to acquiesce in deliberate falsification on important issues. I have before me what must be a very rare pamphlet, written by Maxim Litvinoff in 1918 and outlining the recent events in the Russian Revolution. It makes no mention of Stalin, but gives high praise to Trotsky, and also to Zinoviev, Kamenev, and others. What could be the attitude of even the most intellectually scrupulous Communist towards such a pamphlet? At best, the obscurantist attitude of saying that it is an undesirable document and better suppressed. And if for some reason it were decided to issue a garbled version of the pamphlet, denigrating Trotsky and inserting references to Stalin, no Communist who remained faithful to his party could protest. Forgeries almost as gross as this have been committed in recent years. But the significant thing is not that they happen, but that even when they are known about they provoke no reaction from the Left-wing intelligentsia as a whole. The argument that to tell the truth would be 'inopportune' or would 'play into the hands of' somebody or other is felt to be unanswerable, and few people are bothered by the prospect of the lies which they condone getting out of the newspapers and into the history books.

The organized lying practised by totalitarian states is not, as is sometimes claimed, a temporary expedient of the same nature as military deception. It is something integral to totalitarianism, something that would still continue even if concentration camps and secret police forces had ceased to be necessary. Among intelligent Communists there is an underground legend to the effect that although the Russian government is obliged *now* to deal in lying propaganda, frame-up trials, and so forth, it is secretly recording the true facts and will publish them at some future time. We can, I believe, be quite certain that this is not the case, because the mentality implied by such an action is that of a liberal historian who believes that the past cannot be altered and that a correct knowledge of history is valuable as a matter of course. From the totalitarian point of view history is something to be created rather than learned. A totalitarian state is in effect a theocracy, and its ruling caste, in order to keep its position, has to be thought of as infallible. But since, in practice, no one is infallible, it is frequently necessary to rearrange past events in order to show that this or that mistake was not made, or that this or that imaginary triumph actually happened. Then, again, every major change in policy demands a corresponding change of doctrine and a revaluation of prominent historical figures. This kind of thing happens everywhere, but is clearly likelier to lead to outright falsification in societies where only *one* opinion is permissible at any given moment. Totalitarianism demands, in fact, the continuous alteration of the past, and in the long run probably demands a disbelief in the very existence of objective truth. The friends of totalitarianism in this country usually tend to argue that since absolute truth is not attainable, a big lie is no worse than a little lie. It is pointed out that *all* historical records are biased and inaccurate, or, on the other hand, that modern physics has proved that what seems to us the real world is an illusion, so that to believe in the evidence of one's senses is simply vulgar philistinism. A totalitarian society which succeeded in perpetuating itself would probably set up a schizophrenic system of thought, in which the laws of common sense held good in everyday life and in certain exact sciences, but could be disregarded by the politician, the historian, and the sociologist. Already there are countless people who would think it scandalous to falsify a scientific textbook, but would see nothing wrong in falsifying an historical fact. It is at the point where literature and politics cross that totalitarianism exerts its greatest pressure on the intellectual. The exact sciences are not, at this date, menaced to anything like the same extent. This partly accounts for the fact that in all countries it is easier for the scientists than for the writers to line up behind their respective governments.

To keep the matter in perspective, let me repeat what I said at the beginning of this essay: that in England the *immediate* enemies of truthfulness, and hence of freedom of thought, are the Press lords, the film magnates, and the bureaucrats, but that on a long view the weakening of the desire for liberty among the intellectuals themselves is the most serious symptom of all. It may seem that all this time I have been talking about the effects of censorship, not on literature as a whole, but merely on one department of political journalism. Granted that Soviet Russia constitutes a sort of forbidden area in the British Press, granted that issues like Poland, the Spanish civil war, the Russo-German pact, and so forth, are debarred from serious discussion, and that if you possess information that conflicts with the prevailing orthodoxy you are expected either to distort it or keep quiet about it – granted all this, why should literature in the wider sense be affected? Is every writer a politician, and is every book necessarily a work of straightforward 'reportage'? Even under the tightest dictatorship, cannot the individual writer remain free inside his own mind and distil or disguise his unorthodox ideas in such a way that the authorities will be too stupid to recognize them? And in any case, if the writer himself is in agreement with the prevailing orthodoxy, why should it have a cramping effect on him? Is not literature, or any of the arts, likeliest to flourish in societies in which there are no major conflicts of opinion and no sharp distinction between the artist and his audience? Does one have to assume that every writer is a rebel, or even that a writer as such is an exceptional person?

Whenever one attempts to defend intellectual liberty against the claims of totalitarianism, one meets with these arguments in one form or another. They are based on a complete misunderstanding of what literature is, and how – one should perhaps rather say *why* – it comes into being. They assume that a writer is either a mere entertainer or else a venal hack who can switch from one line of propaganda to another as easily as an organ grinder changing tunes. But after all, how is it that books ever come to be written? Above a quite low level, literature is an attempt to influence the viewpoint of one's contemporaries by recording experience. And so far as freedom of expression is concerned, there is not much difference between a mere journalist and the most 'unpolitical' imaginative writer. The journalist is unfree, and is conscious of unfreedom, when he is forced to write lies or suppress what seems to him important news: the imaginative writer is unfree when he has to falsify his subjective feelings, which from his point of view are facts. He may distort and caricature reality in order to make his meaning clearer, but he cannot misrepresent the scenery of his own mind: he cannot say with any conviction that he likes what he dislikes, or believes what he disbelieves. If he is forced to do so, the only result is that his creative faculties dry up. Nor can he solve the problem by keeping away from controversial topics. There is no such thing as genuinely non-political literature, and least of all in an age like our own, when fears, hatreds, and loyalties of a directly political kind are near to the surface of everyone's consciousness. Even a single taboo can have an all-round crippling effect upon the mind, because there is always the danger that any thought which is freely followed up may lead to the forbidden thought. It follows that the atmosphere of totalitarianism is deadly to any kind of prose writer, though a poet, at any rate a lyric poet, might possibly find it breathable. And in any totalitarian society that survives for more than a couple of generations, it is probable that prose literature, of the kind that has existed during the past four hundred years, must actually *come to an end*.

Literature has sometimes flourished under despotic régimes, but, as has often been pointed out, the despotisms of the past were not totalitarian. Their repressive apparatus was always inefficient, their ruling classes were usually either corrupt or apathetic or half-liberal in outlook, and the prevailing religious doctrines usually worked against perfectionism and the notion of human infallibility. Even so it is broadly true that prose literature has reached its highest levels in periods of democracy and free speculation. What is new in totalitarianism is that its doctrines are not only unchallengeable but also unstable. They have to be accepted on pain of damnation, but on the other hand they are always liable to be altered at a moment's notice. Consider, for example, the various attitudes, completely incompatible with one another, which an English Communist or 'fellow-traveller' has had to adopt towards the war between Britain and Germany. For years before September, 1939, he was expected to be in a continuous stew about 'the horrors of Nazism' and to twist everything he wrote into a denunciation of Hitler: after September, 1939, for twenty months, he had to believe that Germany was more sinned against than sinning, and the word 'Nazi', at least as far as print went, had to drop right out of his vocabulary. Immediately after hearing the 8 o'clock news bulletin on the morning of 22nd June, 1941, he had to start believing once again that Nazism was the most hideous evil the world had ever seen. Now, it is easy for a politician to make such changes: for a writer the case is somewhat different. If he is to switch his allegiance at exactly the right moment, he must either tell lies about his subjective feelings, or else suppress them altogether. In either case he has destroyed his dynamo. Not only will ideas refuse to come to him, but the very words he uses will seem to stiffen under his touch. Political writing in our time consists almost entirely of prefabricated phrases bolted together like the pieces of a child's Meccano set. It is the unavoidable result of self-censorship. To write in plain, vigorous language one has to think fearlessly, and if one thinks fearlessly one cannot be politically orthodox. It might be otherwise in an 'age of faith', when the prevailing orthodoxy has been long established and is not taken too seriously. In that case it would be possible, or might be possible, for large areas of one's mind to remain unaffected by what one officially believed. Even so, it is worth noticing that prose literature almost disappeared during the only age of faith that Europe has ever enjoyed. Throughout the whole of the Middle Ages there was almost no imaginative prose literature and very little in the way of historical writing: and the intellectual leaders of society expressed their most serious thoughts in a dead language which barely altered during a thousand years.

Totalitarianism, however, does not so much promise an age of faith as an age of schizophrenia. A society becomes totalitarian when its structures become flagrantly artificial: that is, when its ruling class has lost its function but succeeds in clinging to power by force or fraud. Such a society, no matter how long it persists can never afford to become either tolerant or intellectually stable. It can never permit either the truthful recording of facts, or the emotional sincerity, that literary creation demands. But to be corrupted by totalitarianism one does not have to live in a totalitarian country. The mere prevalence of certain ideas can spread a kind of poison that makes one subject after another impossible for literary purposes. Wherever there is an enforced orthodoxy – or even two orthodoxies, as often happens – good writing stops. This was well illustrated by the Spanish civil war. To many English intellectuals the war was a deeply moving experience, but not an experience about which they could write sincerely. There were only two things that you were allowed to say, and both of them were palpable lies: as a result, the war produced acres of print but almost nothing worth reading.

It is not certain whether the effects of totalitarianism upon verse need be so deadly as its effects on prose. There is a whole series of converging reasons why it is somewhat easier for a poet than for a prose writer to feel at home in an authoritarian society. To begin with, bureaucrats and other 'practical' men usually despise the poet too deeply to be much interested in what he is saying. Secondly, what the poet is saying – that is, what his poem 'means' if translated into prose – is relatively unimportant even to himself. The thought contained in a poem is always simple, and is no more the primary purpose of the poem than the anecdote is the primary purpose of the picture. A poem is an arrangement of sounds and associations, as a painting is an arrangement of brushmarks. For short snatches, indeed, as in the refrain of a song, poetry can even dispense with meaning altogether. It is therefore fairly easy for a poet to keep away from dangerous subjects and avoid uttering heresies: and even when he does utter them, they may escape notice. But above all, good verse, unlike good prose, is not necessarily an individual product. Certain kinds of poems, such as ballads, or, on the other hand, very artificial verse forms, can be composed co-operatively by groups of people. Whether the ancient English and Scottish ballads were originally produced by individuals, or by the people at large, is disputed; but at any rate they are non-individual in the sense that they constantly change in passing from mouth to mouth. Even in print no two versions of a ballad are ever quite the same. Many primitive peoples compose verse communally. Someone begins to improvise, probably accompanying himself on a musical instrument, somebody else chips in with a line or a rhyme when the first singer breaks down, and so the process continues until there exists a whole song or ballad which has no identifiable author.

In prose, this kind of intimate collaboration is quite impossible. Serious prose, in any case, has to be composed in solitude, whereas the excitement of being part of a group is actually an aid to certain kinds of versification. Verse – and perhaps good verse of its kind, though it would not be the highest kind – might survive under even the most inquisitorial régime. Even in a society where liberty and individuality had been extinguished, there would still be need either for patriotic songs and heroic ballads celebrating victories, or for elaborate exercises in flattery: and these are the kinds of poem that can be written to order, or composed communally, without necessarily lacking artistic value. Prose is a different matter, since the prose writer cannot narrow the range of his thoughts without killing his inventiveness. But the history of totalitarian societies, or of groups of people who have adopted the totalitarian outlook, suggests that loss of liberty is inimical to *all* forms of literature. German literature almost disappeared during the Hitler régime, and the case was not much better in Italy. Russian literature, so far as one can judge by translations, has deteriorated markedly since the early days of the Revolution, though some of the verse appears to be better than the prose. Few if any Russian novels that it is possible to take seriously have been translated for about fifteen years. In western Europe and America large sections of the literary intelligentsia have either passed through the Communist party or have been warmly sympathetic to it, but this whole leftward movement has produced extraordinarily few books worth reading. Orthodox Catholicism, again, seems to have a crushing effect upon certain literary forms, especially the novel. During a period of three hundred years, how many people have been at once good novelists and good Catholics? The fact is that certain themes cannot be celebrated in words, and tyranny is one of them. No one ever wrote a good book in praise of the Inquisition. Poetry *might* survive in a totalitarian age, and certain arts or half-arts, such as architecture, might even find tyranny beneficial, but the prose writer would have no choice between silence and death. Prose literature as we know it is the product of rationalism, of the Protestant centuries, of the autonomous individual. And the destruction of intellectual liberty cripples the journalist, the sociological writer, the historian, the novelist, the critic, and the poet, in that order. In the future it is possible that a new kind of literature, not involving individual feeling or truthful observation, may arise, but no such thing is at present imaginable. It seems much likelier that if the liberal culture that we have lived in since the Renaissance actually comes to an end, the literary art will perish with it.

Of course, print will continue to be used, and it is interesting to speculate what kinds of reading matter would survive in a rigidly totalitarian society. Newspapers will presumably continue until television technique reaches a higher level, but apart from newspapers it is doubtful even now whether the great mass of people in the industrialized countries feel the need for any kind of literature. They are unwilling, at any rate, to spend anywhere near so much on reading matter as they spend on several other recreations. Probably novels and stories will be completely superseded by film and radio productions. Or perhaps some kind of low-grade sensational fiction will survive, produced by a sort of conveyor-belt process that reduces human initiative to the minimum.

It would probably not be beyond human ingenuity to write books by machinery. But a sort of mechanizing process can already be seen at work in the film and radio, in publicity and propaganda, and in the lower reaches of journalism. The Disney films, for instance, are produced by what is essentially a factory process, the work being done partly mechanically and partly by teams of artists who have to subordinate their individual style. Radio features are commonly written by tired hacks to whom the subject and the manner of treatment are dictated beforehand; even so, what they write is merely a kind of raw material to be chopped into shape by producers and censors. So also with the innumerable books and pamphlets commissioned by government departments. Even more machine-like is the production of short stories, serials and poems for the very cheap magazines. Papers such as the *Writer* abound with advertisements of literary schools, all of them offering you ready-made plots at a few shillings a time. Some, together with the plot, supply the opening and closing sentences of each chapter. Others furnish you with a sort of algebraical formula by the use of which you can construct your plots yourself. Others offer packs of cards marked with characters and situations, which have only to be shuffled and dealt in order to produce ingenious stories automatically. It is probably in some such way that the literature of a totalitarian society would be produced, if literature were still felt to be necessary. Imagination – even consciousness, so far as possible – would be eliminated from the process of writing. Books would be planned in their broad lines by bureaucrats, and would pass through so many hands that when finished they would be no more an individual product than a Ford car at the end of the assembly line. It goes without saying that anything so produced would be rubbish; but anything that was *not* rubbish would endanger the structure of the state. As for the surviving literature of the past, it would have to be suppressed or at least elaborately rewritten.

Meanwhile totalitarianism has not fully triumphed anywhere. Our own society is still, broadly speaking, liberal. To exercise your right of free speech you have to fight against economic pressure and against strong sections of public opinion, but not, as yet, against a secret police force. You can say or print almost anything so long as you are willing to do it in a hole-and-corner way. But what is sinister, as I said at the beginning of this essay, is that the conscious enemies of liberty are those to whom liberty ought to mean most. The big public do not care about the matter one way or the other. They are not in favour of persecuting the heretic, and they will not exert themselves to defend him. They are at once too sane and too stupid to acquire the totalitarian outlook. The direct, conscious attack on intellectual decency comes from the intellectuals themselves.

It is possible that the Russophile intelligentsia, if they had not succumbed to that particular myth, would have succumbed to another of much the same kind. But at any rate the Russian myth is there, and the corruption it causes stinks. When one sees highly educated men looking on indifferently at oppression and persecution, one wonders which to despise more, their cynicism or their shortsightedness. Many scientists, for example, are the uncritical admirers of the U.S.S.R. They appear to think that the destruction of liberty is of no importance so long as their own line of work is for the moment unaffected. The U.S.S.R. is a large, rapidly developing country which has acute need of scientific workers and, consequently, treats them generously. Provided that they steer clear of dangerous subjects such as psychology, scientists are privileged persons. Writers, on the other hand, are viciously persecuted. It is true that literary prostitutes like Ilya Ehrenburg or Alexei Tolstoy are paid huge sums of money, but the only thing which is of any value to the writer as such – his freedom of expression – is taken away from him. Some, at least, of the English scientists who speak so enthusiastically of the opportunities enjoyed by scientists in Russia are capable of understanding this. But their reflection appears to be: 'Writers are persecuted in Russia. So what? I am not a writer.' They do not see that any attack on intellectual liberty, and on the concept of objective truth, threatens in the long run every department of thought.

For the moment the totalitarian state tolerates the scientist because it needs him. Even in Nazi Germany, scientists, other than Jews, were relatively well treated and the German scientific community, as a whole, offered no resistance to Hitler. At this stage of history, even the most autocratic ruler is forced to take account of physical reality, partly because of the lingering-on of liberal habits of thought, partly because of the need to prepare for war. So long as physical reality cannot be altogether ignored, so long as two and two have to make four when you are, for example, drawing the blueprint of an aeroplane, the scientist has his function, and can even be allowed a measure of liberty. His awakening will come later, when the totalitarian state is firmly established. Meanwhile, if he wants to safeguard the integrity of science, it is his job to develop some kind of solidarity with his literary colleagues and not regard it as a matter of indifference when writers are silenced or driven to suicide, and newspapers systematically falsified.

But however it may be with the physical sciences, or with music, painting, and architecture, it is – as I have tried to show – certain that literature is doomed if liberty of thought perishes. Not only is it doomed in any country which retains a totalitarian structure; but any writer who adopts the totalitarian outlook, who finds excuses for persecution and the falsification of reality, thereby destroys himself as a writer. There is no way out of this. No tirades against 'individualism' and 'the ivory tower', no pious platitudes to the effect that 'true individuality is only attained through identification with the community', can get over the fact that a bought mind is a spoiled mind. Unless spontaneity enters at some point or another, literary creation is impossible, and language itself becomes ossified. At some time in the future, if the human mind becomes something totally different from what it now is, we may learn to separate literary creation from intellectual honesty. At present we know only that the imagination, like certain wild animals, will not breed in captivity. Any writer or journalist who denies that fact – and nearly all the current praise of the Soviet Union contains or implies such a denial – is, in effect, demanding his own destruction.

1945-6

BOYS' WEEKLIES

You never walk far through any poor quarter in any big town without coming upon a small newsagent's shop. The general appearance of these shops is always very much the same: a few posters for the *Daily Mail* and the *News of the World* outside, a poky little window with sweet-bottles and packets of Players, and a dark interior smelling of liquorice allsorts and festooned from floor to ceiling with vilely printed twopenny papers, most of them with lurid cover-illustrations in three colours.

Except for the daily and evening papers, the stock of these shops hardly overlaps at all with that of the big news-agents. Their main selling line is the twopenny weekly, and the number and variety of these are almost unbelievable. Every hobby and pastime – cage-birds, fretwork, carpenter-ing, bees, carrier-pigeons, home conjuring, philately, chess – has at least one paper devoted to it, and generally several. Gardening and livestock-keeping must have at least a score between them. Then there are the sporting papers, the radio papers, the children's comics, the various snippet papers such as *Tit-bits*, the large range of papers devoted to the movies and all more or less exploiting women's legs, the various trade papers, the women's story-papers (the *Oracle*, *Secrets*, *Peg's Paper*, etc. etc.), the needlework papers – these so numerous that a display of them alone will often fill an entire window – and in addition the long series of 'Yank Mags' (*Fight Stories*, *Action Stories*, *Western Short Stories*, etc.), which are imported shop-soiled from America and sold at twopence halfpenny or threepence. And the periodical proper shades off into the fourpenny novelette, the *Aldine Boxing Novels*, the *Boys' Friend Library*, the *Schoolgirls' Own Library* and many others.

Probably the contents of these shops is the best available indication of what the mass of the English people really feels and thinks. Certainly nothing half so revealing exists in documentary form. Best-seller novels, for instance, tell one a great deal, but the novel is aimed almost exclusively at people above the £4-a-week level. The movies are probably a very unsafe guide to popular taste, because the film industry is virtually a monopoly, which means that it is not obliged to study its public at all closely. The same applies to some extent to the daily papers, and most of all to the radio. But it does not apply to the weekly paper with a smallish circulation and specialized subject-matter. Papers like the *Exchange and Mart*, for instance, or *Cage-birds*, or the *Oracle*, or the *Prediction*, or the *Matrimonial Times*, only exist because there is a definite demand for them, and they reflect the minds of their readers as a great national daily with a circulation of millions cannot possibly do.

Here I am only dealing with a single series of papers, the boys' twopenny weeklies, often inaccurately described as 'penny dreadfuls'. Falling strictly within this class there are at present ten papers, the *Gem*, *Magnet*, *Modern Boy*, *Triumph* and *Champion*, all owned by the Amalgamated Press, and the *Wizard*, *Rover*, *Skipper*, *Hotspur* and *Adventure*, all owned by D. C. Thomson & Co. What the circulations of these papers are, I do not know. The editors and proprietors refuse to name any figures, and in any case the circulation of a paper carrying serial stories is bound to fluctuate widely. But there is no question that the combined public of the ten papers is a very large one. They are on sale in every town in England, and nearly every boy who reads at all goes through a phase of reading one or more of them. The *Gem* and *Magnet*, which are much the oldest of these papers, are of rather different type from the rest, and they have evidently lost some of their popularity during the past few years. A good many boys now regard them as old fashioned and 'slow'. Nevertheless I want to discuss them first, because they are more interesting psychologically than the others, and also because the mere survival of such papers into the nineteen-thirties is a rather startling phenomenon.

The *Gem* and *Magnet* are sister-papers (characters out of one paper frequently appear in the other), and were both started more than thirty years ago. At that time, together with *Chums* and the old *B.O.P.*, they were the leading papers for boys, and they remained dominant till quite recently. Each of them carries every week a fifteen- or twenty-thousand-word school story, complete in itself, but usually more or less connected with the story of the week before. The *Gem* in addition to its school story carries one or more adventure serial. Otherwise the two papers are so much alike that they can be treated as one, though the *Magnet* has always been the better known of the two, probably because it possesses a really first-class character in the fat boy, Billy Bunter.

The stories are stories of what purports to be public-school life, and the schools (Greyfriars in the *Magnet* and St Jim's in the *Gem*) are represented as ancient and fashionable foundations of the type of Eton or Winchester. All the leading characters are fourth-form boys aged fourteen or fifteen, older or younger boys only appearing in very minor parts. Like Sexton Blake and Nelson Lee, these boys continue week after week and year after year, never growing any older. Very occasionally a new boy arrives or a minor character drops out, but in at any rate the last twenty-five years the personnel has barely altered. All the principal characters in both papers – Bob Cherry, Tom Merry, Harry Wharton, Johnny Bull, Billy Bunter and the rest of them – were at Greyfriars or St Jim's long before the Great War, exactly the same age as at present, having much the same kind of adventures and talking almost exactly the same dialect. And not only the characters but the whole atmosphere of both *Gem* and *Magnet* has been preserved unchanged, partly by means of very elaborate stylization. The stories in the *Magnet* are signed 'Frank Richards' and those in the *Gem*, 'Martin Clifford', but a series lasting thirty years could hardly be the work of the same person every week.* Consequently they have to be written in a style that is easily imitated – an extraordinary, artificial, repetitive style, quite different from anything else now existing in English literature. A couple of extracts will do as illustrations. Here is one from the *Magnet*:

> Groan!
> 'Shut up, Bunter!'
> Groan!
> Shutting up was not really in Billy Bunter's line. He seldom shut up, though often requested to do so. On the present awful occasion the fat Owl of Greyfriars was less inclined than ever to shut up. And he did not shut up! He groaned, and groaned, and went on groaning.
>
> Even groaning did not fully express Bunter's feelings. His feelings, in fact, were inexpressible.
>
> There were six of them in the soup! Only one of the six uttered sounds of woe and lamentation. But that one, William George Bunter, uttered enough for the whole party and a little over.
>
> Harry Wharton & Co. stood in a wrathy and worried group. They were landed and stranded, diddled, dished and done! etc., etc., etc.

Here is one from the *Gem*:

> 'Oh cwumbs!'
> 'Oh gum!'
> 'Oooogh!'
> 'Urrggh!'
> Arthur Augustus sat up dizzily. He grabbed his handkerchief and pressed it to his damaged nose. Tom Merry sat up, gasping for breath. They looked at one another.
>
> 'Bai Jove! This is a go, deah boy!' gurgled Arthur Augustus. 'I have been thwown into quite a fluttah! Oogh! The wottahs! The wuffians! The feahful outsidahs! Wow!' etc., etc., etc.

Both of these extracts are entirely typical: you would find something like them in almost every chapter of every

* 1945. This is quite incorrect. These stories have been written throughout the whole period by 'Frank Richards' and 'Martin Clifford', who are one and the same person! See articles in *Horizon*, May 1940, and *Summer Pie*, summer 1944.

number, to-day or twenty-five years ago. The first thing that anyone would notice is the extraordinary amount of tautology (the first of these two passages contains a hundred and twenty-five words and could be compressed into about thirty), seemingly designed to spin out the story, but actually playing its part in creating the atmosphere. For the same reason various facetious expressions are repeated over and over again; 'wrathy', for instance, is a great favourite, and so is 'diddled, dished and done'. 'Oooogh!', 'Grooo!' and 'Yaroo!' (stylized cries of pain) recur constantly, and so does 'Ha! ha! ha!', always given a line to itself, so that sometimes a quarter of a column or thereabouts consists of 'Ha! ha! ha!' The slang ('Go and eat coke!', 'What the thump!', 'You frabjous ass!', etc. etc.) has never been altered, so that the boys are now using slang which is at least thirty years out of date. In addition, the various nicknames are rubbed in on every possible occasion. Every few lines we are reminded that Harry Wharton & Co. are 'the Famous Five', Bunter is always 'the fat Owl' or 'the Owl of the Remove', Vernon-Smith is always 'the Bounder of Greyfriars', Gussy (the Honourable Arthur Augustus D'Arcy) is always 'the swell of St Jim's', and so on and so forth. There is a constant, untiring effort to keep the atmosphere intact and to make sure that every new reader learns immediately who is who. The result has been to make Greyfriars and St Jim's into an extraordinary little world of their own, a world which cannot be taken seriously by anyone over fifteen, but which at any rate is not easily forgotten. By a debasement of the Dickens technique a series of stereotyped 'characters' has been built up, in several cases very successfully. Billy Bunter, for instance, must be one of the best-known figures in English fiction; for the mere number of people who know him he ranks with Sexton Blake, Tarzan, Sherlock Holmes and a handful of characters in Dickens.

Needless to say, these stories are fantastically unlike life at a real public school. They run in cycles of rather differing types, but in general they are the clean-fun, knock-about type of story, with interest centring round horseplay, practical jokes, ragging masters, fights, canings, football, cricket and food. A constantly recurring story is one in which a boy is accused of some misdeed committed by another and is too much of a sportsman to reveal the truth. The 'good' boys are 'good' in the clean-living Englishman tradition – they keep in hard training, wash behind their ears, never hit below the belt etc., etc., – and by way of contrast there is a series of 'bad' boys, Racke, Crooke, Loder and others, whose badness consists in betting, smoking cigarettes and frequenting public-houses. All these boys are constantly on the verge of expulsion, but as it would mean a change of personnel if any boy were actually expelled, no one is ever caught out in any really serious offence. Stealing, for instance, barely enters as a motif. Sex is completely taboo, especially in the form in which it actually arises at public schools. Occasionally girls enter into the stories, and very rarely there is something approaching a mild flirtation, but it is entirely in the spirit of clean fun. A boy and a girl enjoy going for bicycle rides together – that is all it ever amounts to. Kissing, for instance, would be regarded as 'soppy'. Even the bad boys are presumed to be completely sexless. When the *Gem* and *Magnet* were started, it is probable that there was a deliberate intention to get away from the guilty sex-ridden atmosphere that pervaded so much of the earlier literature for boys. In the nineties the *Boys' Own Paper*, for instance, used to have its correspondence columns full of terrifying warnings against masturbation, and books like *St Winifred's* and *Tom Brown's Schooldays* were heavy with homosexual feeling, though no doubt the authors were not fully aware of it. In the *Gem* and *Magnet* sex simply does not exist as a problem. Religion is also taboo; in the whole thirty years' issue of the two papers the word 'God' probably does not occur, except in 'God save the King'. On the other hand, there has always been a very strong 'temperance' strain. Drinking and, by association, smoking are regarded as rather disgraceful even in an adult ('shady' is the usual word), but at the same time as something irresistibly fascinating, a sort of substitute for sex. In their moral atmosphere the *Gem* and *Magnet* have a great deal in common with the Boy Scout movement, which started at about the same time.

All literature of this kind is partly plagiarism. Sexton Blake, for instance, started off quite frankly as an imitation of Sherlock Holmes, and still resembles him fairly strongly; he has hawk-like features, lives in Baker Street, smokes enormously and puts on a dressing-gown when he wants to think. The *Gem* and *Magnet* probably owe something to the old school-story writers who were flourishing when they began, Gunby Hadath, Desmond Coke and the rest, but they owe more to nineteenth-century models. In so far as Greyfriars and St Jim's are like real schools at all, they are much more like Tom Brown's Rugby than a modern public school. Neither school has an O.T.C., for instance, games are not compulsory, and the boys are even allowed to wear what clothes they like. But without doubt the main origin of these papers is *Stalky & Co*. This book has had an immense influence on boys' literature, and it is one of those books which have a sort of traditional reputation among people who have never even seen a copy of it. More than once in boys' weekly papers I have come across a reference to *Stalky & Co*. in which the word was spelt 'Storky'. Even the name of the chief comic among the Greyfriars masters, Mr Prout, is taken from *Stalky & Co*., and so is much of the slang; 'jape', 'merry', 'giddy', 'bizney' (business), 'frabjous', 'don't' for 'doesn't' – all of them out of date even when *Gem* and *Magnet* started. There are also traces of earlier origins. The name 'Greyfriars' is probably taken from Thackeray, and Gosling, the school porter in the *Magnet*, talks in an imitation of Dickens's dialect.

With all this, the supposed 'glamour' of public-school life is played for all it is worth. There is all the usual paraphernalia – lock-up, roll-call, house matches, fagging, prefects, cosy teas round the study fire, etc. etc. – and constant reference to the 'old school', the 'old grey stones' (both schools were founded in the early sixteenth century), the 'team spirit' of the 'Greyfriars men'. As for the snob-appeal, it is completely shameless. Each school has a titled boy or two whose titles are constantly thrust in the reader's face; other boys have the names of well-known aristocratic families, Talbot, Manners, Lowther. We are for ever being reminded that Gussy is the Honourable Arthur A. D'Arcy, son of Lord Eastwood, that Jack Blake is heir to 'broad acres', that Hurree Jamset Ram Singh (nicknamed Inky) is the Nabob of Bhanipur, that Vernon-Smith's father is a millionaire. Till recently the illustrations in both papers always depicted the boys in clothes imitated from those of Eton; in the last few years Greyfriars has changed over to blazers and flannel trousers, but St Jim's still sticks to the Eton jacket, and Gussy sticks to his top-hat. In the school magazine which appears every week as part of the *Magnet*, Harry Wharton writes an article discussing the pocket-money received by the 'fellows in the Remove', and reveals that some of them get as much as five pounds a week! This kind of thing is a perfectly deliberate incitement to wealth-fantasy. And here it is worth noticing a rather curious fact, and that is that the school story is a thing peculiar to England. So far as I know, there are extremely few school stories in foreign languages. The reason, obviously, is that in England education is mainly a matter of status. The most definite dividing line between the petite-bourgeoisie and the working class is that the former pay for their education, and within the bourgeoisie there is another unbridgeable gulf between the 'public' school and the 'private' school. It is quite clear that there are tens and scores of thousands of people to whom every detail of life at a 'posh' public school is wildly thrilling and romantic. They happen to be outside that mystic world of quad-rangles and house-colours, but they can yearn after it, day-dream about it, live mentally in it for hours at a stretch. The question is, Who are these people? Who reads the *Gem* and *Magnet*?

Obviously one can never be quite certain about this kind of thing. All I can say from my own observation is this.

Boys who are likely to go to public schools themselves generally read the *Gem* and *Magnet*, but they nearly always stop reading them when they are about twelve; they may continue for another year from force of habit, but by that time they have ceased to take them seriously. On the other hand, the boys at very cheap private schools, the schools that are designed for people who can't afford a public school but consider the Council schools 'common', continue reading the *Gem* and *Magnet* for several years longer. A few years ago I was a teacher at two of these schools myself. I found that not only did virtually all the boys read the *Gem* and *Magnet*, but that they were still taking them fairly seriously when they were fifteen or even sixteen. These boys were the sons of shopkeepers, office employees and small business and professional men, and obviously it is this class that the *Gem* and *Magnet* are aimed at. But they are certainly read by working-class boys as well. They are generally on sale in the poorest quarters of big towns, and I have known them to be read by boys whom one might expect to be completely immune from public-school 'glamour'. I have seen a young coal miner, for instance, a lad who had already worked a year or two underground, eagerly reading the *Gem*. Recently I offered a batch of English papers to some British legionaries of the French Foreign Legion in North Africa; they picked out the *Gem* and *Magnet* first. Both papers are much read by girls,* and the Pen Pals department of the *Gem* shows that it is read in every corner of the British Empire, by Australians, Canadians, Palestine Jews, Malays, Arabs, Straits Chinese, etc., etc. The editors evidently expect their readers to be aged round about fourteen, and the advertisements (milk chocolate, postage stamps, water pistols, blushing cured, home conjuring tricks, itching powder, the Phine Phun Ring which runs a needle into your friend's hand, etc., etc.)

* There are several corresponding girls' papers. The *Schoolgirl* is companion-paper to the *Magnet* and has stories by 'Hilda Richards'. The characters are interchangeable to some extent. Bessie Bunter, Billy Bunter's sister, figures in the *Schoolgirl*.

indicate roughly the same age; there are also the Admiralty advertisements, however, which call for youths between seventeen and twenty-two. And there is no question that these papers are also read by adults. It is quite common for people to write to the editor and say that they have read every number of the *Gem* or *Magnet* for the past thirty years. Here, for instance, is a letter from a lady in Salisbury:

I can say of your splendid yarns of Harry Wharton & Co. of Greyfriars, that they never fail to reach a high standard. Without doubt they are the finest stories of their type on the market to-day, which is saying a good deal. They seem to bring you face to face with Nature. I have taken the *Magnet* from the start, and have followed the adventures of Harry Wharton & Co. with rapt interest. I have no sons, but two daughters, and there's always a rush to be the first to read the grand old paper. My husband, too, was a staunch reader of the *Magnet* until he was suddenly taken away from us.

It is well worth getting hold of some copies of the *Gem* and *Magnet*, especially the *Gem*, simply to have a look at the correspondence columns. What is truly startling is the intense interest with which the pettiest details of life at Greyfriars and St Jim's are followed up. Here, for instance, are a few of the questions sent in by readers:

'What age is Dick Roylance?' 'How old is St Jim's?' 'Can you give me a list of the Shell and their studies?' 'How much did D'Arcy's monocle cost?' 'How is it that fellows like Crooke are in the Shell and decent fellows like yourself are only in the Fourth?' 'What are the Form captain's three chief duties?' 'Who is the chemistry master at St Jim's?' (From a girl) 'Where is St Jim's situated? *Could* you tell me how to get there, as I would love to see the building? Are you boys just "phoneys", as I think you are?'

It is clear that many of the boys and girls who write these letters are living a complete fantasy-life. Sometimes a boy will write, for instance, giving his age, height, weight, chest and bicep measurements and asking which member of the Shell or Fourth Form he most exactly resembles. The demand for a list of the studies on the Shell passage, with an exact account of who lives in each, is a very common one. The editors, of course, do everything in their power to keep up the illusion. In the *Gem* Jack Blake is supposed to write answers to correspondents, and in the *Magnet* a couple of pages is always given up to the school magazine (the *Greyfriars Herald*, edited by Harry Wharton), and there is another page in which one or other character is written up each week. The stories run in cycles, two or three characters being kept in the foreground for several weeks at a time. First there will be a series of rollicking adventure stories, featuring the Famous Five and Billy Bunter; then a run of stories turning on mistaken identity, with Wibley (the make-up wizard) in the star part; then a run of more serious stories in which Vernon-Smith is trembling on the verge of expulsion. And here one comes upon the real secret of the *Gem* and *Magnet* and the probable reason why they continue to be read in spite of their obvious out-of-dateness.

It is that the characters are so carefully graded as to give almost every type of reader a character he can identify himself with. Most boys' papers aim at doing this, hence the boy-assistant (Sexton Blake's Tinker, Nelson Lee's Nipper, etc.) who usually accompanies the explorer, detective or what-not on his adventures. But in these cases there is only one boy, and usually it is much the same type of boy. In the *Gem* and *Magnet* there is a model for very nearly everybody. There is the normal athletic, high-spirited boy (Tom Merry, Jack Blake, Frank Nugent), a slightly rowdier version of this type (Bob Cherry), a more aristocratic version (Talbot, Manners), a quieter, more serious version (Harry Wharton), and a stolid, 'bulldog' version (Johnny Bull). Then there is the reckless, dare-devil type of boy (Vernon-Smith), the definitely 'clever', studious boy (Mark Linley, Dick Penfold), and the eccentric boy who is not good at games but possesses some special talent (Skinner Wibley). And there is the scholarship-boy (Tom Redwing), an important figure in this class of story because he makes it possible for boys from very poor homes to project themselves into the public-school atmosphere. In addition there are

Australian, Irish, Welsh, Manx, Yorkshire and Lancashire boys to play upon local patriotism. But the subtlety of characterization goes deeper than this. If one studies the correspondence columns one sees that there is probably *no* character in the *Gem* and *Magnet* whom some or other reader does not identify with, except the out-and-out comics, Coker, Billy Bunter, Fisher T. Fish (the money-grabbing American boy) and, of course, the masters. Bunter, though in his origin he probably owed something to the fat boy in *Pickwick*, is a real creation. His tight trousers against which boots and canes are constantly thudding, his astuteness in search of food, his postal order which never turns up, have made him famous wherever the Union Jack waves. But he is not a subject for day-dreams. On the other hand, another seeming figure of fun, Gussy (the Honourable Arthur A. D'Arcy, 'the swell of St Jim's'), is evidently much admired. Like everything else in the *Gem* and *Magnet*, Gussy is at least thirty years out of date. He is the 'knut' of the early twentieth century or even the 'masher' of the nineties ('Bai Jove, deah boy!' and 'Weally, I shall be obliged to give you a feahful thwashin'!'), the monocled idiot who made good on the fields of Mons and Le Cateau. And his evident popularity goes to show how deep the snob-appeal of this type is. English people are extremely fond of the titled ass (cf. Lord Peter Wimsey) who always turns up trumps in the moment of emergency. Here is a letter from one of Gussy's girl admirers:

I think you're too hard on Gussy. I wonder he's still in existence, the way you treat him. He's my hero. Did you know I write lyrics? How's this – to the tune of 'Goody Goody'?

> Gonna get my gas-mask, join the A.R.P.
> 'Cos I'm wise to all those bombs you drop on me.
> Gonna dig myself a trench
> Inside the garden fence;
> Gonna seal my windows up with tin
> So the tear gas can't get in;
> Gonna park my cannon right outside the kerb
> With a note to Adolf Hitler: 'Don't disturb!'

And if I never fall in Nazi hands
That's soon enough for me
Gonna get my gas-mask, join the A.R.P.

PS. – Do you get on well with girls?

I quote this in full because (dated April 1939) it is interesting as being probably the earliest mention of Hitler in the *Gem*. In the *Gem* there is also a heroic fat boy, Fatty Wynn, as a set-off against Bunter. Vernon-Smith, 'the Bounder of the Remove', a Byronic character, always on the verge of the sack, is another great favourite. And even some of the cads probably have their following. Loder, for instance, 'the rotter of the Sixth', is a cad, but he is also a highbrow and given to saying sarcastic things about football and the team spirit. The boys of the Remove only think him all the more of a cad for this, but a certain type of boy would probably identify with him. Even Racke, Crooke & Co. are probably admired by small boys who think it diabolically wicked to smoke cigarettes. (A frequent question in the correspondence column: 'What brand of cigarettes does Racke smoke?')

Naturally the politics of the *Gem* and *Magnet* are Conservative, but in a completely pre-1914 style, with no Fascist tinge. In reality their basic political assumptions are two: nothing ever changes, and foreigners are funny. In the *Gem* of 1939 Frenchmen are still Froggies and Italians are still Dagoes. Mossoo, the French master at Greyfriars, is the usual comic-paper Frog, with pointed beard, pegtop trousers, etc. Inky, the Indian boy, though a rajah, and therefore possessing snob-appeal, is also the comic babu of the *Punch* tradition. (' "The rowfulness is not the proper caper, my esteemed Bob," said Inky. "Let dogs delight in the barkfulness and bitefulness, but the soft answer is the cracked pitcher that goes longest to a bird in the bush, as the English proverb remarks." ') Fisher T. Fish is the old-style stage Yankee (' "Waal, I guess" ', etc.) dating from a peroid of Anglo-American jealousy. Wun Lung, the Chinese boy (he has rather faded out of late, no doubt because some of the *Magnet's* readers are Straits Chinese), is the nineteenth-century pantomime Chinaman, with saucer-shaped hat, pigtail and pidgin-English. The assumption all along is not only that foreigners are comics who are put there for us to laugh at, but that they can be classified in much the same way as insects. That is why in all boys' papers, not only the *Gem* and *Magnet*, a Chinese is invariably portrayed with a pigtail. It is the thing you recognize him by, like the Frenchman's beard or the Italian's barrel-organ. In papers of this kind it occasionally happens that when the setting of a story is in a foreign country some attempt is made to describe the natives as individual human beings, but as a rule it is assumed that foreigners of any one race are all alike and will conform more or less exactly to the following patterns:

Frenchman: Excitable. Wears beard, gesticulates wildly.
Spaniard, Mexican, etc.: Sinister, treacherous.
Arab, Afghan, etc.: Sinister, treacherous.
Chinese: Sinister, treacherous. Wears pigtail.
Italian: Excitable. Grinds barrel-organ or carries stiletto.
Swede, Dane, etc.: Kind-hearted, stupid.
Negro: Comic, very faithful.

The working classes only enter into the *Gem* and *Magnet* as comics or semi-villains (race-course touts, etc.). As for class-friction, trade unionism, strikes, slumps, unemployment, Fascism and civil war – not a mention. Somewhere or other in the thirty years' issue of the two papers you might perhaps find the word 'Socialism', but you would have to look a long time for it. If the Russian Revolution is anywhere referred to, it will be indirectly, in the word 'Bolshy' (meaning a person of violent disagreeable habits). Hitler and the Nazis are just beginning to make their appearance, in the sort of reference I quoted above. The war-crisis of September 1938 made just enough impression to produce a story in which Mr Vernon-Smith, the Bounder's millionaire father, cashed in on the general panic by buying up country houses in order to sell them to 'crisis scuttlers'. But that is probably as near to noticing the European situation as the *Gem* and *Magnet* will come, until the war actually starts.* That does not mean that these papers are unpatriotic – quite the contrary! Throughout the Great War the *Gem* and *Magnet* were perhaps the most consistently and cheerfully patriotic papers in England. Almost every week the boys caught a spy or pushed a conchy into the army, and during the rationing period 'EAT LESS BREAD' was printed in large type on every page. But their patriotism has nothing whatever to do with power-politics or 'ideological' warfare. It is more akin to family loyalty, and actually it gives one a valuable clue to the attitude of ordinary people, especially the huge untouched block of the middle class and the better-off working class. These people are patriotic to the middle of their bones, but they do not feel that what happens in foreign countries is any of their business. When England is in danger they rally to its defence as a matter of course, but in between-times they are not interested. After all, England is always in the right and England always wins, so why worry? It is an attitude that has been shaken during the past twenty years, but not so deeply as is sometimes supposed. Failure to understand it is one of the reasons why Left Wing political parties are seldom able to produce an acceptable foreign policy.

The mental world of the *Gem* and *Magnet*, therefore, is something like this:

The year is 1910 – or 1940, but it is all the same. You are at Greyfriars, a rosy-cheeked boy of fourteen in posh tailor-made clothes, sitting down to tea in your study on the Remove passage after an exciting game of football which was won by an odd goal in the last half-minute. There is a cosy fire in the study, and outside the wind is whistling. The ivy clusters thickly round the old grey stones. The King is on his throne and the pound is worth a pound. Over in

* This was written some months before the outbreak of war. Up to the end of September 1939 no mention of the war has appeared in either paper.

Europe the comic foreigners are jabbering and gesticulating, but the grim grey battleships of the British Fleet are steaming up the Channel and at the outposts of Empire the monocled Englishmen are holding the niggers at bay. Lord Mauleverer has just got another fiver and we are all settling down to a tremendous tea of sausages, sardines, crumpets, potted meat, jam and doughnuts. After tea we shall sit round the study fire having a good laugh at Billy Bunter and discussing the team for next week's match against Rookwood. Everything is safe, solid and unquestionable. Everything will be the same for ever and ever. That approximately is the atmosphere.

But now turn from the *Gem* and *Magnet* to the more up-to-date papers which have appeared since the Great War. The truly significant thing is that they have more points of resemblance to the *Gem* and *Magnet* than points of difference. But it is better to consider the differences first.

There are eight of these newer papers, the *Modern Boy*, *Triumph*, *Champion*, *Wizard*, *Rover*, *Skipper*, *Hotspur* and *Adventure*. All of these have appeared since the Great War, but except for the *Modern Boy* none of them is less than five years old. Two papers which ought also to be mentioned briefly here, though they are not strictly in the same class as the rest, are the *Detective Weekly* and the *Thriller*, both owned by the Amalgamated Press. The *Detective Weekly* has taken over Sexton Blake. Both of these papers admit a certain amount of sex-interest into their stories, and though certainly read by boys, they are not aimed at them exclusively. All the others are boys' papers pure and simple, and they are sufficiently alike to be considered together. There does not seem to be any notable difference between Thomson's publications and those of the Amalgamated Press.

As soon as one looks at these papers one sees their technical superiority to the *Gem* and *Magnet*. To begin with, they have the great advantage of not being written entirely by one person. Instead of one long complete story, a number of the *Wizard* or *Hotspur* consists of half a dozen or more serials, none of which goes on for ever. Consequently there is far more variety and far less padding, and none of the tiresome stylization and facetiousness of the *Gem* and *Magnet*. Look at these two extracts, for example:

Billy Bunter groaned.

A quarter of an hour had elapsed out of the two hours that Bunter was booked for extra French.

In a quarter of an hour there were only fifteen minutes! But every one of those minutes seemed inordinately long to Bunter. They seemed to crawl by like tired snails.

Looking at the clock in Class-room No. 10 the fat Owl could hardly believe that only fifteen minutes had passed. It seemed more like fifteen hours, if not fifteen days!

Other fellows were in extra French as well as Bunter. They did not matter. Bunter did! (The *Magnet*)

After a terrible climb, hacking out handholds in the smooth ice every step of the way up, Sergeant Lionheart Logan of the Mounties was now clinging like a human fly to the face of an icy cliff, as smooth and treacherous as a giant pane of glass.

An Arctic blizzard, in all its fury, was buffeting his body, driving the blinding snow into his face, seeking to tear his fingers loose from their handholds and dash him to death on the jagged boulders which lay at the foot of the cliff a hundred feet below.

Crouching among those boulders were eleven villainous trappers who had done their best to shoot down Lionheart and his companion, Constable Jim Rogers – until the blizzard had blotted the two Mounties out of sight from below. (The *Wizard*)

The second extract gets you some distance with the story, the first takes a hundred words to tell you that Bunter is in the detention class. Moreover, by not concentrating on school stories (in point of numbers the school story slightly predominates in all these papers, except the *Thriller* and *Detective Weekly*), the *Wizard, Hotspur*, etc., have far greater opportunities for sensationalism. Merely looking at the cover illustrations of the papers which I have on the table in front of me, here are some of the things I see. On one a cowboy is clinging by his toes to the wing of an aeroplane in mid-air and shooting down another aeroplane with his revolver. On another a Chinese is swimming for his life down a sewer with a swarm of ravenous-looking rats swimming after him. On another an engineer is lighting a stick of dynamite while a steel robot feels for him with its claws. On another a man in airman's costume is fighting barehanded against a rat somewhat larger than a donkey. On another a nearly naked man of terrific muscular development has just seized a lion by the tail and flung it thirty yards over the wall of an arena, with the words, 'Take back your blooming lion!' Clearly no school story can compete with this kind of thing. From time to time the school buildings may catch fire or the French master may turn out to be the head of an international anarchist gang, but in a general way the interest must centre round cricket, school rivalries, practical jokes, etc. There is not much room for bombs, death-rays, sub-machine guns, aeroplanes, mustangs, octopuses, grizzly bears or gangsters.

Examination of a large number of these papers shows that, putting aside school stories, the favourite subjects are Wild West, Frozen North, Foreign Legion, crime (always from the detective's angle), the Great War (Air Force or Secret Service, not the infantry), the Tarzan motif in varying forms, professional football, tropical exploration, historical romance (Robin Hood, Cavaliers and Roundheads, etc.) and scientific invention. The Wild West still leads, at any rate as a setting, though the Red Indian seems to be fading out. The one theme that is really new is the scientific one. Death-rays, Martians, invisible men, robots, helicopters and interplanetary rockets figure largely: here and there there are even far-off rumours of psychotherapy and ductless glands. Whereas the *Gem* and *Magnet* derive from Dickens and Kipling, the *Wizard, Champion, Modern Boy*, etc., owe a great deal to H. G. Wells, who, rather than Jules Verne, is the father of 'Scientifiction'. Naturally it is the magical Martian aspect of science that is most exploited, but one or two papers include serious articles on scientific subjects, besides quantities of informative snippets. (Examples: 'A Kauri tree in Queensland, Australia, is over 12,000 years old'; 'Nearly 50,000 thunderstorms occur every day'; 'Helium gas costs £1 per 1000 cubic feet'; 'There are over 500 varieties of spiders in Great Britain'; 'London firemen use 14,000,000 gallons of water annually', etc., etc.) There is a marked advance in intellectual curiosity and, on the whole, in the demand made on the reader's attention. In practice the *Gem* and *Magnet* and the post-war papers are read by much the same public, but the mental age aimed at seems to have risen by a year or two years – an improvement probably corresponding to the improvement in elementary education since 1909.

The other thing that has emerged in the post-war boys' papers, though not to anything like the extent one would expect, is bully-worship and the cult of violence.

If one compares the *Gem* and *Magnet* with a genuinely modern paper, the thing that immediately strikes one is the absence of the leader-principle. There is no central dominating character; instead there are fifteen or twenty characters, all more or less on an equality, with whom readers of different types can identify. In the more modern papers this is not usually the case. Instead of identifying with a schoolboy of more or less his own age, the reader of the *Skipper*, *Hotspur*, etc., is led to identify with a G-man, with a Foreign Legionary, with some variant of Tarzan, with an air ace, a master spy, an explorer, a pugilist – at any rate with some single all-powerful character who dominates everyone about him and whose usual method of solving any problem is a sock on the jaw. This character is intended as a superman, and as physical strength is the form of power that boys can best understand, he is usually a sort of human gorilla; in the Tarzan type of story he is sometimes actually a giant, eight or ten feet high. At the same time the scenes of violence in nearly all these stories are remarkably harmless and unconvincing. There is a great difference in tone between even the most bloodthirsty English paper and the threepenny Yank Mags, *Fight Stories*, *Action Stories*, etc. (not strictly boys' papers, but largely read by boys). In the Yank Mags you get real blood-lust, really gory descriptions of the all-in, jump-on-his-testicles style fighting, written in a jargon that has been perfected by people who brood endlessly on violence. A paper like *Fight Stories*, for instance, would have very little appeal except to sadists and masochists. You can see the comparative gentleness of the English civilization by the amateurish way in which prize-fighting is always described in the boys' weeklies. There is no specialized vocabulary. Look at these four extracts, two English, two American:

When the gong sounded, both men were breathing heavily and each had great red marks on his chest. Bill's chin was bleeding, and Ben had a cut over his right eye.
Into their corners they sank, but when the gong clanged again they were up swiftly, and they went like tigers at each other. (*Rover*)

He walked in stolidly and smashed a clublike right to my face. Blood spattered and I went back on my heels, but surged in and ripped my right under the heart. Another right smashed full on Ben's already battered mouth, and, spitting out the fragments of a tooth, he crashed a flailing left to my body. (*Fight Stories*)

It was amazing to watch the Black Panther at work. His muscles rippled and slid under his dark skin. There was all the power and grace of a giant cat in his swift and terrible onslaught.
He volleyed blows with a bewildering speed for so huge a fellow. In a moment Ben was simply blocking with his gloves as well as he could. Ben was really a past-master of defence. He had many fine victories behind him. But the Negro's rights and lefts crashed through openings that hardly any other fighter could have found. (*Wizard*)

Haymakers which packed the bludgeoning weight of forest monarchs crashing down under the ax hurled into the bodies of the two heavies as they swapped punches. (*Fight Stories*)

Notice how much more knowledgeable the American extracts sound. They are written for devotees of the prizering, the others are not. Also, it ought to be emphasized that on its level the moral code of the English boys' papers is a decent one. Crime and dishonesty are never held up to admiration, there is none of the cynicism and corruption of the American gangster story. The huge sale of the Yank Mags in England shows that there is a demand for that kind of thing, but very few English writers seem able to produce it. When hatred of Hitler became a major emotion in America, it was interesting to see how promptly 'anti-Fascism' was adapted to pornographic purposes by the editors of the Yank Mags. One magazine which I have in front of me is given up to a long, complete story, 'When Hell Came to America', in which the agents of a 'blood-maddened European dictator' are trying to conquer the U.S.A. with death-rays and invisible aeroplanes. There is the frankest appeal to sadism, scenes in which the Nazis tie bombs to women's backs and fling them off heights to watch them blown to pieces in mid-air, others in which they tie naked girls together by their hair and prod them with knives to make them dance, etc., etc. The editor comments solemnly on all this, and uses it as a plea for tightening up restrictions against immigrants. On another page of the same paper: 'LIVES OF THE HOTCHA CHORUS GIRLS. Reveals all the intimate secrets and fascinating pastimes of the famous Broadway Hotcha girls. NOTHING IS OMITTED. Price 10c.' 'HOW TO LOVE. 10c.' 'FRENCH PHOTO RING. 25c.' 'NAUGHTY NUDIES TRANSFERS. From the outside of the glass you see a beautiful girl, innocently dressed. Turn it around and look through the glass and oh! what a difference! Set of 3 transfers 25c.,' etc., etc., etc. There is nothing at all like this in any English paper likely to be read by boys. But the process of Americanization is going on all the same. The American ideal, the 'he-man', the 'tough guy', the gorilla who puts everything right by socking everybody on the jaw, now figures in probably a majority of boys' papers. In one serial now running in the *Skipper* he is always portrayed ominously enough, swinging a rubber truncheon.

The development of the *Wizard*, *Hotspur*, etc., as against the earlier boys' papers, boils down to this: better technique, more scientific interest, more bloodshed, more leader-worship. But, after all, it is the *lack* of development that is the really striking thing.

To begin with, there is no political development whatever. The world of the *Skipper* and the *Champion* is still the pre-1914 world of the *Magnet* and the *Gem*. The Wild West story, for instance, with its cattle-rustlers, lynch-law and other paraphernalia belonging to the eighties, is a curiously archaic thing. It is worth noticing that in papers of this type it is always taken for granted that adventures only happen at the ends of the earth, in tropical forests, in Arctic wastes, in African deserts, on Western prairies, in Chinese opium dens – everywhere in fact, except the places where things really *do* happen. That is a belief dating from thirty or forty years ago, when the new continents were in process of being opened up. Nowadays, of course, if you really want adventure, the place to look for it is in Europe. But apart from the picturesque side of the Great War, contemporary history is carefully excluded. And except that Americans are now admired instead of being laughed at, foreigners are exactly the same figures of fun that they always were. If a Chinese character appears, he is still the sinister pigtailed opium-smuggler of Sax Rohmer; no indication that things have been happening in China since 1912 – no indication that a war is going on there, for instance. If a Spaniard appears, he is still a 'dago' or 'greaser' who rolls cigarettes and stabs people in the back; no indication that things have been happening in Spain. Hitler and the Nazis have not yet appeared, or are barely making their appearance. There will be plenty about them in a little while, but it will be from a strictly patriotic angle (Britain *versus* Germany), with the real meaning of the struggle kept out of sight as much as possible. As for the Russian Revolution, it is extremely difficult to find any reference to it in any of these papers. When Russia is mentioned at all it is usually in an information snippet (example: 'There are 29,000 centenarians in the U.S.S.R.'), and any reference to the Revolution is indirect and twenty years out of date. In one story in the *Rover*, for instance, somebody has a tame bear, and as it is a Russian bear, it is nicknamed Trotsky – obviously an echo of the 1917–23 period and not of recent controversies. The clock has stopped at 1910. Britannia rules the waves, and no one has heard of slumps, booms, unemployment, dictatorships, purges or concentration camps.

And in social outlook there is hardly any advance. The snobbishness is somewhat less open than in the *Gem* and *Magnet* – that is the most one can possibly say. To begin with, the school story, always partly dependent on snob-appeal, is by no means eliminated. Every number of a boys' paper includes at least one school story, these stories slightly outnumbering the Wild Westerns. The very elaborate fantasy-life of the *Gem* and *Magnet* is not imitated and there is more emphasis on extraneous adventure, but the social atmosphere (old grey stones) is much the same. When a new school is introduced at the beginning of a story we are often told in just those words that 'it was a very posh school'. From time to time a story appears which is ostensibly directed *against* snobbery. The scholarship-boy (cf. Tom Redwing in the *Magnet*) makes fairly frequent appearances, and what is essentially the same theme is sometimes presented in this form: there is great rivalry between two schools, one of which considers itself more 'posh' than the other, and there are fights, practical jokes, football matches, etc., always ending in the discomfiture of the snobs. If one glances very superficially at some of these stories it is possible to imagine that a democratic spirit has crept into the boys' weeklies, but when one looks more closely one sees that they merely reflect the bitter jealousies that exist within the white-collar class. Their real function is to allow the boy who goes to a cheap private school (*not* a Council school) to feel that his school is just as 'posh' in the sight of God as Winchester or Eton. The sentiment of school loyalty ('We're better than the fellows down the road'), a thing almost unknown to the real working class, is still kept up. As these stories are written by many different hands, they do, of course, vary a good deal in tone. Some are reasonably free from snobbishness, in others money and pedigree are exploited even more shamelessly than in the *Gem* and *Magnet*. In one that I came across an actual *majority* of the boys mentioned were titled.

Where working-class characters appear, it is usually either as comics (jokes about tramps, convicts, etc.), or as prize-fighters, acrobats, cowboys, professional footballers and Foreign Legionaries – in other words, as adventurers. There is no facing of the facts about working-class life, or, indeed, about *working* life of any description. Very occasionally one may come across a realistic description of, say, work in a coal-mine, but in all probability it will only be there as the background of some lurid adventure. In any case the central character is not likely to be a coal-miner. Nearly all the time the boy who reads these papers – in nine cases out of ten a boy who is going to spend his life working in a shop, in a factory or in some subordinate job in an office – is led to identify with people in positions of command, above all with people who are never troubled by shortage of money. The Lord Peter Wimsey figure, the seeming idiot who drawls and wears a monocle but is always to the fore in moments of danger, turns up over and over again. (This character is a great favourite in Secret Service stories.) And, as usual, the heroic characters all have to talk B.B.C.; they may talk Scottish or Irish or American, but no one in a star part is ever permitted to drop an aitch. Here it is worth comparing the social atmosphere of the boys' weeklies with that of the women's weeklies, the *Oracle*, the *Family Star*, *Peg's Paper*, etc.

The women's papers are aimed at an older public and are read for the most part by girls who are working for a living. Consequently they are on the surface much more realistic. It is taken for granted, for example, that nearly everyone has to live in a big town and work at a more or less dull job. Sex, so far from being taboo, is *the* subject. The short, complete stories, the special feature of these papers, are generally of the 'came the dawn' type: the heroine narrowly escapes losing her 'boy' to a designing rival, or the 'boy' loses his job and has to postpone marriage, but presently gets a better job. The changeling-fantasy (a girl brought up in a poor home is 'really' the child of rich parents) is another favourite. Where sensationalism comes in, usually in the serials, it arises out of the more domestic type of crime, such as bigamy, forgery or sometimes murder; no Martians, death-rays or international anarchist gangs. These papers are at any rate aiming at credibility, and they have a link with real life in their correspondence columns, where genuine problems are being discussed. Ruby M. Ayres's column of advice in the *Oracle*, for instance, is extremely sensible and well written. And yet the world of the *Oracle* and *Peg's Paper* is a pure fantasy-world. It is the same fantasy all the time; pretending to be richer than you are. The chief impression that one carries away from almost every story in these papers is of a frightful, overwhelming 'refinement'. Ostensibly the characters are working-class people, but their habits, the interiors of their houses, their clothes, their outlook and, above all, their speech are entirely middle class. They are all living at several pounds a week above their income. And needless to say, that is just the impression that is intended. The idea is to give the bored factory-girl or worn-out mother of five a dream-life in which she pictures herself – not actually as a duchess (that convention has gone out) but as, say, the wife of a bank-manager. Not only is a five-to-six-pound-a-week standard of life set up as the ideal, but it is tacitly assumed that that is how working-class people really *do* live. The major facts are simply not faced. It is admitted, for instance, that people sometimes lose their jobs; but then the dark clouds roll away and they get better jobs instead. No mention of un-employment as something permanent and inevitable, no mention of the dole, no mention of trade unionism. No suggestion anywhere that there can be anything wrong with the system *as a system*; there are only individual misfortunes, which are generally due to somebody's wickedness and can in any case be put right in the last chapter. Always the dark clouds roll away, the kind employer raises Alfred's wages, and there are jobs for everybody except the drunks. It is still the world of the *Wizard* and the *Gem*, except that there are orange-blossoms instead of machine-guns.

The outlook inculcated by all these papers is that of a rather exceptionally stupid member of the Navy League in the year 1910. Yes, it may be said, but what does it matter? And in any case, what else do you expect?

Of course no one in his senses would want to turn the so-called penny dreadful into a realistic novel or a Socialist tract. An adventure story must of its nature be more or less remote from real life. But, as I have tried to make clear, the unreality of the *Wizard* and the *Gem* is not so artless as it looks. These papers exist because of a specialized demand, because boys at certain ages find it necessary to read about Martians, death-rays, grizzly bears and gangsters. They get what they are looking for, but they get it wrapped up in the illusions which their future employers think suitable for them. To what extent people draw their ideas from fiction is disputable. Personally I believe that most people are influenced far more than they would care to admit by novels, serial stories, films and so forth, and that from this point of view the worst books are often the most important, because they are usually the ones that are read earliest in life. It is probable that many people who would consider themselves extremely sophisticated and 'advanced' are actually carrying through life an imaginative background which they acquired in childhood from (for instance) Sapper and Ian Hay. If that is so, the boys' twopenny weeklies are of the deepest importance. Here is the stuff that is read somewhere between the ages of twelve and eighteen by a very large proportion, perhaps an actual majority, of English boys, including many who will never read anything else except newspapers; and along with it they are absorbing a set of beliefs which would be regarded as hopelessly out of date in the Central Office of the Conservative Party. All the better because it is done indirectly, there is being pumped into them the conviction that the major problems of our time do not exist, that there is nothing wrong with *laissez-faire* capitalism, that foreigners are unimportant comics and that the British Empire is a sort of charity-concern which will last for ever. Considering who owns these papers, it is difficult to believe that this is unintentional. Of the twelve papers I have been discussing (i.e. twelve including the *Thriller* and *Detective Weekly*) seven are the property of the Amalgamated Press, which is one of the biggest press-combines in the world and controls more than a hundred different papers. The *Gem* and *Magnet*, therefore, are closely linked up with the *Daily Telegraph* and the *Financial Times*. This in itself would be enough to rouse certain suspicions, even if it were not obvious that the stories in the boys' weeklies are politically vetted. So it appears that if you feel the need of a fantasy-life in which you travel to Mars and fight lions bare-handed (and what boy doesn't?), you can only have it by delivering yourself over, mentally, to people like Lord Camrose. For there is no competition. Throughout the whole of this run of papers the differences are negligible, and on this level no others exist. This raises the question, why is there no such thing as a left-wing boys' paper?

At first glance such an idea merely makes one slightly sick. It is so horribly easy to imagine what a left-wing boys' paper would be like, if it existed. I remember in 1920 or 1921 some optimistic person handing round Communist tracts among a crowd of public-school boys. The tract I received was of the question-and-answer kind:

Q. 'Can a Boy Communist be a Boy Scout, Comrade?'
A. 'No, Comrade.'
Q. 'Why, Comrade?'
A. 'Because, Comrade, a Boy Scout must salute the Union Jack, which is the symbol of tyranny and oppression.' Etc., etc.

Now suppose that at this moment somebody started a left-wing paper deliberately aimed at boys of twelve or fourteen. I do not suggest that the whole of its contents would be exactly like the tract I have quoted above, but does anyone doubt that they would be *something* like it? Inevitably such a paper would either consist of dreary up-lift or it would be under Communist influence and given over to adulation of Soviet Russia; in either case no normal boy would ever look at it. Highbrow literature apart, the whole of the existing left-wing Press, in so far as it is at all vigorously 'left', is one long tract. The one Socialist paper in England which could live a week on its merits *as a paper* is the *Daily Herald*: and how much Socialism is there in the *Daily Herald*? At this moment, therefore, a paper with a 'left' slant and at the same time likely to have an appeal to ordinary boys in their teens is something almost beyond hoping for.

But it does not follow that it is impossible. There is no clear reason why every adventure story should necessarily be mixed up with snobbishness and gutter patriotism. For, after all, the stories in the *Hotspur* and the *Modern Boy* are not Conservative tracts; they are merely adventure stories with a Conservative bias. It is fairly easy to imagine the process being reversed. It is possible, for instance, to imagine a paper as thrilling and lively as the *Hotspur*, but with subject-matter and 'ideology' a little more up to date. It is even possible (though this raises other difficulties) to imagine a women's paper at the same literary level as the *Oracle*, dealing in approximately the same kind of story, but taking rather more account of the realities of working-class life. Such things have been done before, though not in England. In the last years of the Spanish monarchy there was a large output in Spain of left-wing novelettes, some of them evidently of anarchist origin. Unfortunately at the time when they were appearing I did not see their social significance, and I lost the collection of them that I had, but no doubt copies would still be procurable. In get-up and style of story they were very similar to the English fourpenny novelette, except that their inspiration was 'left'. If, for instance, a story described police pursuing anarchists through the mountains, it would be from the point of view of the anarchist and not of the police. An example nearer to hand is the Soviet film *Chapaiev*, which has been shown a number of times in London. Technically, by the standards of the time when it was made, *Chapaiev* is a first-rate film, but mentally, in spite of the unfamiliar Russian background, it is not so very remote from Hollywood. The one thing that lifts it out of the ordinary is the remarkable performance by the actor who takes the part of the White officer (the fat one) – a performance which looks very like an inspired piece of gagging. Otherwise the atmosphere is familiar. All the usual paraphernalia is there – heroic fight against odds, escape at the last moment, shots of galloping horses, love interest, comic relief. The film is in fact a fairly ordinary one, except that its tendency is 'left'. In a Hollywood film of the Russian Civil War the Whites would probably be angels and the Reds demons. In the Russian version the Reds are angels and the Whites demons. That is also a lie, but, taking the long view, it is a less pernicious lie than the other.

Here several difficult problems present themselves. Their general nature is obvious enough, and I do not want to discuss them. I am merely pointing to the fact that, in England, popular imaginative literature is a field that left-wing thought has never begun to enter. *All* fiction from the novels in the mushroom libraries downwards is censored in the interests of the ruling class. And boys' fiction above all, the blood-and-thunder stuff which nearly every boy devours at some time or other, is sodden in the worst illusions of 1910. The fact is only unimportant if one believes that what is read in childhood leaves no impression behind. Lord Camrose and his colleagues evidently believe nothing of the kind, and, after all, Lord Camrose ought to know.

1939

MORE ABOUT PENGUINS, PELICANS
AND PUFFINS

For further information about books available from Penguins please write to Dept EP, Penguin Books Ltd, Harmondsworth, Middlesex UB7 0DA.

In the U.S.A.: For a complete list of books available from Penguins in the United States write to Dept DG, Penguin Books, 299 Murray Hill Parkway, East Rutherford, New Jersey 07073.

In Canada: For a complete list of books available from Penguins in Canada write to Penguin Books Canada Ltd, 2801 John Street, Markham, Ontario L3R 1B4.

In Australia: For a complete list of books available from Penguins in Australia write to the Marketing Department, Penguin Books Australia Ltd, P.O. Box 257, Ringwood, Victoria 3134.

In New Zealand: For a complete list of books available from Penguins in New Zealand write to the Marketing Department, Penguin Books (N.Z.) Ltd, P.O. Box 4019, Auckland 10.

In India: For a complete list of books available from Penguins in India write to Penguin Overseas Ltd, 706 Eros Apartments, 56 Nehru Place, New Delhi 110019.

George Orwell in Penguins

NINETEEN EIGHTY-FOUR

Newspeak, Doublethink, Big Brother, the Thought Police – George Orwell's world-famous satire coined new and potent words of warning for us all.

In *1984* the world is divided into three parts, Oceania, Eastasia and Eurasia, all perpetually at war. In Oceania, the Party has created a totalitarian state that annihilates all opposition. In the forefront of the Party stands Big Brother, a figure of almost mythical power.

The story of Winston Smith's rebellion against the Party, of his hatred of Big Brother, and of the thoughtcrime which must result in his destruction was first published in 1949. Now in the eighties – our present and Orwell's brilliantly imagined future – his vision of brutalized and manipulated humanity is still gripping and still supremely relevant.

and

ANIMAL FARM

BURMESE DAYS

A CLERGYMAN'S DAUGHTER

COMING UP FOR AIR

KEEP THE ASPIDISTRA FLYING

*all six novels by George Orwell are also published
in an attractive omnibus edition*

THE PENGUIN COMPLETE NOVELS OF GEORGE ORWELL

George Orwell in Penguins

DECLINE OF THE ENGLISH MURDER AND OTHER ESSAYS

A collection of some of the less accessible essays by the author of *Animal Farm*. Including his lament for the inferior quality of modern murders and his comments on the changing face of fictional crime; his long essay on Dickens, and his shrewd critical remarks on Kipling and on the peculiar genius of Salvador Dali; eyewitness accounts of a hanging in Burma and a lazar-house in Paris; with notes on nationalism, on seaside postcards, and on his own ambition – surely realized – to make political writing into an art.

and

THE LION AND THE UNICORN
Socialism and the English Genius

BURMESE DAYS

COMING UP FOR AIR

THE ROAD TO WIGAN PIER

HOMAGE TO CATALONIA

DOWN AND OUT IN PARIS AND LONDON

THE COLLECTED ESSAYS, JOURNALISM AND LETTERS OF GEORGE ORWELL
(in four volumes)
Edited by Sonia Orwell and Ian Angus

THE PENGUIN COMPLETE LONGER NON-FICTION OF GEORGE ORWELL

also published, the celebrated biography by Bernard Crick

GEORGE ORWELL: A LIFE